A Concert for Christmas

*By Helen Hawkins*

A Concert for Christmas
A Match to Remember

a&b

# A Concert for Christmas

## Helen Hawkins

Allison & Busby Limited
11 Wardour Mews
London W1F 8AN
*allisonandbusby.com*

First published in Great Britain by Allison & Busby in 2023.
This paperback edition published by Allison & Busby in 2024.

A CIP catalogue record for this book is available from
the British Library.

10 9 8 7 6 5 4 3 2 1

ISBN 978-0-7490-3079-7

Typeset in 11/16 pt Adobe Garamond Pro by
Allison & Busby Ltd.

By choosing this product, you help take care of the world's forests.
Learn more: www.fsc.org.

Printed and bound by
CPI Group (UK) Ltd, Croydon, CR0 4YY

*For Audrey*

# Chapter One

'I'm sorry, I'm sorry, I'm sorry!' Sophie raced across the green to where her friend Kate leant against one of the Christmas market huts that had popped up last week.

'Sophie, where have you been?' Kate sounded annoyed, and Sophie didn't blame her. She was very pregnant and standing around in the November cold probably wasn't ideal.

'It wasn't my fault. I promise!' Sophie skidded to a halt and dropped her bags. 'I was picking up the flyers but the guy was locking up when I got there and he had to go and find them out the back and anyway,' – she sucked in a breath – 'here they are!'

Sophie pulled a wodge of flyers out of the carrier bag on the floor and showed them to Kate. 'What do you think?'

Kate examined them for a second and frowned. 'I don't know how to tell you this, Sophie. But the date's wrong.'

'What?' Sophie snatched back the flyers and turned them over. Sure enough, printed in large white letters across the bottom of the bright red page was *24th November*. 'Oh God.' She slumped against the hut.

'I got you a gingerbread hot chocolate, though.' Kate passed her a takeaway coffee cup. 'You get a bonus gingerbread man clinging on for dear life.' She picked hers off the side of the cup and made him dance into her mouth.

'I can't believe Albert messed it up.' Sophie put the flyers back away and pulled out another bundle to check if they were the same. They were, of course.

'This is tasty, at least.' Kate raised her takeaway cup in a 'cheers'.

Sophie sipped the warm drink. She had to agree. It was rather delicious; the taste of Christmas was yummy.

'Come on,' Kate said. 'We'll be late for rehearsal.'

Sophie linked arms with her friend as they walked across the green to the town hall in the glow of a hundred Christmas lights. The plastic pig that lived in the butcher's window wore a Christmas hat trimmed with white fur and laced with tiny lights, dwarfed only by the bright lanterns that framed the window itself. Further along, the baker had transformed his window into a Christmas village scene, complete with gingerbread men, women and children dressed in all their Christmas finery. The bakery's window was a particular favourite of Sophie's: each week the scene would change in the run-up to Christmas, until on Christmas Eve, gingerbread Father Christmas would arrive with presents for all the gingerbread children.

'This is just what I need after a Tuesday afternoon of geography followed by R.E.,' Kate said, sipping more of her hot chocolate as they walked. 'Golden time was chaos today. Goodness knows what the dinner ladies put in the pudding!'

'It's probably the wind,' Sophie said, watching the trees sway across the green. Shoppers, making the most of the longer shopping hours, scurried about, clutching their hats and scarves so that they wouldn't get blown away. 'The children are always crazy when the wind's up. I really needed this.' She snapped an arm off her gingerbread man. 'Who knew organising a simple Christmas concert could be so stressful?'

'It's going to be stressful when you're in the concert, organising the concert and trying to get thirty-one ten-year-olds to the end of Christmas term.'

Sophie groaned. 'I don't know how I get myself into these things.'

She pulled a key out of her pocket, complete with enormous homemade wooden keyring, and opened the door to the town hall, balancing everything else in her spare hand.

The hall was cold and musty, with a tall ceiling and wooden floor. She dropped her stuff at the door and started to put out the old plastic chairs in rows, ready for the choir's arrival.

'Not you,' she said, as Kate began to help. She waggled her finger. 'You sit there.'

Kate frowned but followed her friend's orders, plonking herself down on a seat in the middle of the room. She shuffled from side to side, crossing and uncrossing her legs.

'Comfy?'

'Never, these days,' Kate joked, removing her coat and rubbing her enormous belly. 'So, tell me what happened. You know that's what I really want to talk about.'

Sophie continued to set up the room and avoided Kate's questioning stare.

'I don't even know where to begin,' Sophie said, tucking some hair behind her ear before picking up the next chair and adding it to the end of a row.

'Well, why don't you start at the beginning?' Kate asked.

'That's a very good place to start,' they both chorused and laughed.

'I don't know if I really want to talk about it,' Sophie said finally, resting for a moment. It was the same old story, and she was tired of telling it.

'Yes, you do!' Kate said, popping the final bit of her gingerbread man into her mouth. 'What was he like? How did it go?' Crumbs flew everywhere as she spoke.

'It was awful.'

'Oh no! Not another one! What happened this time?'

How could Sophie even explain? She had spotted him long before he saw her, and she'd known instantly it would never work. He'd pitched up with a bunch of balloons, for goodness' sake. After an hour of sitting in a crowded, noisy pub, batting away the offending items, she'd made a feeble excuse, given him a fake number and left.

'In every possible way,' Sophie said dramatically. 'It's likely I'll be single for ever and to be honest, I think it's probably for the best – especially for the men of this town.' She was only half joking.

'Not true. You're a catch.' Kate waddled over to the bin to dispose of her coffee cup. 'You'll bump into someone one day. I mean, a bakery is hardly the most romantic place in the world, but look at me and Gav!'

'I know,' Sophie said, remembering Kate's story of how Gav had swiped the last Christmas fruitcake from under Kate's nose and she'd made a joke about how she'd have 'stollen' it back. They'd moved in together by the end of the following month.

Sophie sighed. If only it could be that easy for her.

'I'm hardly likely to meet anyone at school, though. The only person who ever visits Cranswell Primary is Reverend Williams for assemblies, and I was kind of hoping for someone a little less wrinkly.'

They both laughed.

'You go other places than school.'

Sophie raised an eyebrow.

'OK, good point. Anyway, enough moping,' Kate said, settling back into her chair. 'Chalk it up to experience and move on.'

Kate would never let her dwell on a bad dating experience for too long. Secretly, Sophie enjoyed a little mope when things didn't quite go her way. It was cathartic.

'I was wondering about the charity for the concert.' Sophie changed the subject and was relieved to do so. 'I'd really like to donate the money we raise to Mum's charity this year. What do you think?'

'Sounds like a lovely idea.'

'I'll have to add it to the list of nominations but hopefully people will realise it's important.'

'You're in charge, Sophie. You could just make the decision yourself.'

'No, I need to put it to the vote. I don't want anyone to think I've gone behind their back.'

'You care too much about what other people think.'

Sophie ignored Kate's comment. She knew she overthought things occasionally, but this was important to her. And she wanted to do it right.

'Nigel will have to wheel the piano out of the cupboard when he gets here. It's too heavy for me.' She flopped down in the chair and took her coat off, warm from lugging around the furniture. She rested her head on Kate's shoulder.

'Do you think you'll audition for the solo?' Kate asked.

Sophie laughed. 'Definitely not.' There was no way she would ever volunteer to sing a solo.

'Why not? You need a distraction from your horrible dating life,' Kate said with a cheeky smile.

Sophie sat up and protested, but fell silent at the sound of the outside door banging open and the other choir members arriving.

It was a good job she'd pulled out her thick Fair Isle jumper. Sophie had been warm setting out the room, but by the time everyone else had arrived, the temperature in the draughty old church hall had dropped. She rubbed her gloved hands together and let out two deep breaths to test whether she could see them in the air. Her coat went back on.

'Right, let's get started.' Sophie stood and used her teacher's voice to get the attention of the group. They were mostly seated, and the stragglers shuffled through the rows to sit down once she'd spoken. Sophie looked out at the choir. It was made up of every type of person imaginable – including an eclectic range of singing abilities . . . but she loved this amazing bunch of people. They'd saved her when she'd first arrived in Cranswell a year ago.

'Lovely to see you all.' She smiled nervously. It didn't matter that she did this all day, every day with the children in her class; addressing an audience always got her heart racing. 'Today we're going to start working towards the songs for the Christmas concert, just a general rehearsal this evening. Solo auditions will be next week. I believe Nigel has the list, so speak to him before the end of the evening to sign up.' There was a general mumble of interest. 'Also, we need to vote for the charity we'll be supporting this year. I know we had a couple of nominations last week.' She looked down at her notes. 'The Blue Cross centre over in Sheepham and Children in Need, which happened last Friday. I'd also like to throw my mother's charity into the mix. They support mothers who have suffered a miscarriage. Shall we vote?' she said, an ever-so-slight catch in her throat.

Recovering, Sophie listed the charities again, and the group raised their hands. Sophie's mother's charity was the runaway winner and Sophie made a note of it, as if she'd ever forget. She breathed out and smiled.

'OK. We'll wait for Nigel to finish setting up and wheel the piano out and we'll make a start. Last wees and teas before we start, folks.' It sounded flippant, but for some of the town's residents, they wouldn't be able to begin without a final opportunity to visit the bathroom.

'Sure I can't convince you to audition?' Kate asked, as Sophie sat down again.

'Ha! No.'

'Ooh!' Lulu responded in her thick American accent. She sat in front of them every week and turned around now that there appeared to be something interesting going on. Sophie liked that Lulu's hair, habitually fashioned into a 60s beehive, ordinarily hid her out of view of the musical director.

'Are you thinking of auditioning, Sophie, honey?' she asked.

13

Lulu was probably a hundred years old. Her face was laced with the ghost of plastic surgery past, and she oozed a Hollywood glamour that you didn't see in the sleepy Cotswold town of Cranswell. As always, her face was made up perfectly, with a bright red slick of lipstick not quite disguising her thin wrinkled lips. Her eyes were bright and sparkling, blue and full of life. She often talked about her vibrant youth as an MGM musical star and Sophie had whiled away many an afternoon since her move here just listening to Lulu's stories.

Sophie shook her head. 'No. It's just something that Kate' – she said her name through gritted teeth and shot her a sideways glance – 'is determined to make me do. She won't shut up about it!'

'Well, you should. I know you've got a lovely voice.'

'Well, thank you, Lulu.' Her inner songstress locked away the compliment. It meant a lot coming from Lulu van Morris.

'Are you really thinking of auditioning?' Greg asked, turning around to face them. He slid his glasses up his thin nose. He was Lulu's equally old, equally nosy comrade. But he was not, however, nearly as glamorous. He was wearing a faded navy and slightly holey cardigan, the sleeves baggy from where he'd pushed them up regularly throughout his day in the coffee shop.

'God, no!' Sophie cried, a little louder than she'd expected. A couple more singers from the row in front turned to listen.

'You should, you know,' John said.

'Lovely voice,' said Ethel.

Kate smiled, sat silently and watched on as the sopranos on the front row ambushed Sophie. Sophie pulled a face that told

Kate she'd regret it later on. Kate shrugged and shot her a smug smile.

'I think I'll be a bit too busy organising the concert itself. I can't be centre stage *and* make sure that everything runs smoothly, now, can I?' Sophie said, hoping everyone would find something different to talk about – and soon.

Lulu and Greg genuinely seemed to consider her question.

'No, I suppose not,' Lulu said, her long red fingernails clutching her fur (faux, hoped Sophie) and pulling it up around her. 'It's a damned shame, though.'

Lulu offered round a paper bag of Werther's Originals. It was hard to imagine Lulu in her youth when she went and did 'old people' things like that now and then. Sophie was relieved to see that everyone's attention had moved elsewhere.

'I hate you, Kate,' Sophie said.

'You love me really.'

Sophie rolled her eyes.

The piano sailed into the hall, unaccompanied, and didn't stop when it arrived in its usual position. A gasp went around the room, and one soprano yelped. Nigel ran in after it and dived into its path, holding his arms out to stop it from crashing into the front row.

'Sorry about that, ladies and gents.'

Hang on a minute. That wasn't Nigel's voice.

The man who had saved the lives of the front row singers smiled at the room, flushed from his altercation with the piano.

'Whoops.' He reached over and stopped his music stand (another casualty of the runaway piano) toppling over and taking out the altos sitting on the front row – all two of them.

'Sorry, sorry,' he said, holding a hand up.

This man was not Nigel, their musical director of goodness knows how many years. This man, possibly in his early forties, stood the music stand back up and brushed a hand through his dark curls. He was shorter than Nigel, now that he was standing, but broadly built like a rugby player. He rolled up the sleeves of his tan turtleneck and rested his music on the stand, which he'd retrieved from the front row with a handsome smile. In that split second, Sophie glanced at his eyes: the most beautiful hazel eyes she had ever seen. In fact, they reminded her of . . . surely not. Oh God. It couldn't be, could it? It wasn't the first time she'd seen those beautiful eyes.

In one smooth movement, Sophie lifted the music up to cover her face as she simultaneously slid lower in her seat. She played with her hair as an extra barrier against being noticed.

'Where the hell is Nigel?' Sophie whispered through gritted teeth.

'Not sure.' Kate shrugged. 'Sophie, are you OK? You look like you've seen a ghost.'

'I have. The ghost of dates past.' She pointed a finger towards their apparently new musical director.

Kate looked at him, then back at Sophie, who adjusted her music again to hide her face from the MD's view. Kate, for once, appeared to be speechless, but was clearly enjoying the moment, judging by her smile.

'Right. Let's make a start,' said the man. The choir shuffled and quietened until there was silence. He had an instant command of the room.

Sophie felt a pang of envy at his cool exterior.

'Good evening, everyone. My name is Liam. Nigel asked me to step in tonight – he's had to rush up north to stay with his elderly mother. I think I'll be with you until the concert itself, which is exciting. I'm sure we all wish Mrs Calder well, though.'

Sophie watched, open-mouthed, as the choir seemed to collectively welcome Liam into the fold without question, nodding that they too wished Nigel's elderly mother all the best.

There was too much to process. What was Nigel playing at? And why had he left this Liam to tell everyone his whereabouts? Sophie grimaced at the thought of everyone else wondering why she hadn't known this was happening. How was she supposed to organise a charity concert if nobody communicated anything to her? She pulled her phone out to see if she'd missed a call or a text from Nigel. But there was nothing – the background of Sophie and Kate with wine glasses the size of their heads usually made her smile, but instead she winced. Not to mention the fact that only a week ago, she'd been sitting across the table from Liam with a bunch of helium balloons bobbing between them. She felt a fresh wave of embarrassment warm her face.

Liam continued. 'Nigel said that you've had the music for a couple of weeks, but tonight's the night he planned to start rehearsing properly for the concert. So, shall we begin by singing them through? Take your parts if you can, but otherwise the melody is fine to get us warmed up. Shall we stand?'

As Liam raised his arms with the baton in his hand, the choir stood as a group. Sophie joined them, standing a little slower, glancing around to see that no one was questioning Liam's appearance. And that Liam hadn't spotted her. She sighed heavily. She supposed they'd have to talk eventually – they were in effect organising a concert together at this point – but a few more moments of preparation wouldn't go amiss.

The choir's first sing-through was a discordant mess. Sophie sang along, but inside she was panicking. Did Liam even know what he was doing? It was more like a carol shout than a concert of beautifully sung hymns and Christmas songs. She'd said no to organising the last concert for fear of things not going as planned, and she didn't want anything to go wrong on her watch. Liam hadn't bothered teaching them any of the parts or the harmonies. He'd not even gone through the notes in the melody. He'd simply assumed that everyone in the room would know each of the song choices. She had to admit, they were fairly well-known hymns and carols, but even so, she was concerned at Liam's apparent lack of musical understanding.

Relieved when it was break time, Sophie hurried up to collect two teas in polystyrene cups for her and Kate, ducking and diving through the crowd to avoid Liam. Greg provided the breaktime beverages, utilising his skills and retired equipment from the coffee shop.

'There you go, Sophie, love. Just as you like it.' He passed the two cups through the hatch from the kitchen, a slight tremble in his hand causing one cup to spill a little. 'Don't you worry about that,' he said, reaching for a cloth and wiping the surface.

'Thanks, Greg.' Sophie turned and stopped abruptly when she found her face buried in the muscular torso of the new musical director.

'Woah!' Liam said, stepping back. His hands came up in defence. 'Careful. Are you OK?'

Sophie cleared her throat. 'Sorry.'

'Sophie, isn't it?'

'Yes, that's me,' she said eventually, taking a couple of steps towards Kate and the comfort of their seats. 'And you're Liam.'

'I'm Liam,' he repeated with a nervous smile.

Ah, so he remembered their horrible date too. He was just choosing to ignore it. Sophie would obviously follow his lead.

'Sorry I barged you. I'm just taking this over to my friend.' She indicated Kate, who, at their glances in her direction, gave a little wave.

'Nigel told me you're running the show,' Liam said before she could run away. He ran his hand through those curls again.

'He didn't tell me you were.' It sounded unkind, but she'd been surprised by his arrival.

'He told me to apologise. It was all a bit sudden, really.'

'Is everything OK?' She felt bad now. It was genuinely odd that Nigel would disappear like that. He'd been musical director for the choir for years now, certainly longer than Sophie had been living in the town.

'His mum took ill overnight and his dad told him he needed to get up there quickly. I don't think it's looking very good.' He swayed on his heels, hands in his pockets like he couldn't keep still. Was this conversation as awkward for him as it was for her?

Sophie tried to focus on what he was saying and not relive their awful date, or concentrate on his endearing, lopsided smile. With nothing else to say, she took a sip of her tea. It scalded her instantly. She felt compelled to fill the silence.

'Well, Nigel's right. I am organising the concert this year, so if you need me to talk over anything or go through the songs or whatever, just let me know, I guess.'

Why couldn't she form sentences?

'I think I'll be OK,' he said. He flashed that smile again and stepped over to the hatch where Greg was waiting to pass him a tea.

Across the hall, Kate was miming for Sophie to hurry up. She looked back at Liam to see him busy charming Lulu, and sat back down.

'That didn't look like a fun conversation,' Kate said, taking her tea from Sophie and drinking it instantly. 'Well, not for you, anyway. I enjoyed it immensely.'

Sophie stared into her drink, both hands cupped around it for warmth. 'Liam is the guy I went on a date with last week, not that either of us acknowledged it just then.'

Kate pulled a face. 'God,' she said, sipping her tea again.

'I know. Very awkward.'

'He didn't seem too awkward just then,' Kate said.

'No, Kate, awkward for me!' Sophie pushed out her bottom lip like a teenager. She was only half mocking.

Kate laughed. 'Why was it so hideous? You never said.'

Sophie sipped her tea again and looked around like she was about to share MI5 secrets. Happy that she wasn't in earshot of anyone likely to gossip, she turned to Kate.

'So, he turned up to the pub with this enormous bouquet of balloons, which, as you know, I am genuinely terrified of. So, it was a bit of a terrible start. He was late too, which annoyed me.'

'Of course it did.' Kate nodded in agreement, knowing her friend well.

'Anyway, the pub was packed, and I had this stupid great big bouquet of balloons with me. We managed to find a corner table, and I was hopeful that it would be quiet enough for us to talk – maybe I could forgive the balloons if there was good conversation, you know? But it was a tiny table, and he's . . . well, you can see,' she said, looking over to where Liam now stood, cornered by Lulu. 'He's huge.'

Kate raised an eyebrow.

'Don't be rude,' Sophie said, blushing. 'I mean you can see he's big-built, muscly. So, we sat down at this tiny table on little stools. His knees came up to his ears. We must have looked so ridiculous – him scrunched up so that he could fit into the furniture, and me with a bouquet of red helium balloons.' Shiny metallic ones, of course, Sophie remembered with a shudder. She rubbed a hand over her face as the embarrassment crept back into her consciousness.

Kate's face had frozen into a grimace.

'So, it was awkward then,' she said, stating the obvious.

Sophie nodded. 'It gets worse.'

'Surely it can't get any worse.'

'After the glass of red wine I'd obviously drunk before I got there . . .'

'Obviously,' Kate said, agreeing with the strategy.

'I thought he was quite good looking.' Sophie closed her eyes, cringing.

'Ah, so you liked him.' Kate smiled knowingly.

'At that point, I thought I might like him, yes. For a moment I sort of dared to hope that it might go well and that he'd like me too. But then the conversation got going, or rather it didn't.'

21

'Oh no.' Kate put her hands over her face in exasperation and peeped out between her fingers like she was watching a horror film.

'Oh yes.' Sophie nodded. 'Between twenty rogue helium balloons, the world's smallest table and stools, and conversation that a librarian would have tolerated, I'm sorry to admit that, when Mum called, I used it as an excuse to leave – and you know I normally avoid answering the phone to her if I can.'

'Oh, Sophie, I'm sorry. It sounds like a bit of a nightmare.'

'It could be worse,' she said sarcastically. 'He could have just turned up to MD the Christmas concert that I'm organising! Or I could have palmed him off with a fake number . . .' Sophie felt her face colour with a fresh blush.

Kate snorted into her tea, and a couple of people looked up from their conversations. 'So, when he needs to call you about the concert, he's going to think he has your number, but actually, he has a false one that you gave him at the end of your date?'

'Oh God!' Sophie groaned, curling up in her chair and resting her head on her knees. 'Yes!'

'It'll be fine,' Kate said, patting Sophie on the leg. 'You just said he's ignoring the fact your date ever happened. If he's not making it a thing, then you shouldn't either.'

'But I make everything a thing,' Sophie complained from under her cocoon.

'Good point.'

# Chapter Two

'Right, so we'll finish there,' Liam said, placing his baton carefully down on the music stand and putting his hands into his back pockets.

They'd finally added in the harmonies for two of the songs after the coffee break, and Sophie was relieved that they were beginning to sound all right. She dared to hope that in six weeks' time, they might be concert-ready.

'Before you go, I wonder whether any of the sopranos might consider staying for a moment and learning the alto line. I was concerned listening then that we sound a bit thin in the middle.' Liam paused and looked around for a moment. 'Any takers?'

Rocking back and forth on his heels, he waited, but no one volunteered.

Eventually Lulu raised her hand. 'I can sing anything.' She stood, even though no one had asked her to. Sophie half expected her to bow and wait for her rapturous applause.

'Great, thanks, Lulu,' he said, clasping his hands as if he was praying that other volunteers may follow.

Sophie felt herself slipping lower into her chair. There was absolutely no way that . . .

'Sophie? Would you be able to help us out?' Liam asked, as

everyone in the choir looked in her direction.

She knew her cheeks were a lovely shade of pink.

'I don't know . . . I don't think . . .' She fumbled about for an excuse but knew that for the sake of the concert and the choir, she'd have to agree. She looked around in the hope someone else might have volunteered, but all eyes were on her. 'All right.'

'Great. Thanks, Soph.'

It was the first time anyone had called her Soph since secondary school, and she flinched for a moment at its unfamiliarity.

'Two should be fine, but if anyone else changes their mind' – he indicated the front two rows of the choir – 'we've got plenty of sopranos, so it wouldn't hurt to switch a few of you.'

Kate readied herself to leave. 'Who am I going to follow now when we're singing?'

'I couldn't let Lulu be the only volunteer. Besides, it's in my best interests for this concert to go well.'

Kate tutted. 'I'm actually going to have to learn my notes now.'

'Kate, we're sopranos. We sing the melody!'

'Good point. Well, looks like you're staying.' She said it with a mischievous wiggle of the eyebrows.

'Yes, it does, doesn't it?' Sophie felt the anxiety settle in the pit of her stomach.

'I guess I'll see you at school tomorrow for all the gossip.' She bent down to retrieve her bag from the ground.

Sophie picked it up for her so that she didn't end up in a heap on the floor. 'Here.' She passed it to Kate. 'I will see you tomorrow, but there will be no gossip. Didn't you hear my story?' She grimaced.

'I just meant the gossip about how the alto rehearsal

goes, *Soph*.' Kate smiled at her and turned to leave the hall, waving her hand in the air as she went.

Sophie growled under her breath and tidied the room, moving the chairs back into piles at the side of the hall. Stalling, she worked her way over to the piano, where Liam and Lulu were waiting. Lulu was singing scales.

Sophie reminded herself she was only here because having another alto was important to make the music sound good. And the music needed to sound good for the concert to be a success. It certainly wasn't for any other reason, and it definitely wasn't to help the handsome new musical director.

'Come and stand next to me, honey,' Lulu said, draping an arm around Sophie's shoulders. 'How are the kiddies at school?'

'They're great – very excited about Christmas.' She enjoyed the snuggle next to Lulu's extremely fluffy jumper. The hairs floated about as Lulu moved and tickled Sophie's nose.

'Right, I won't keep you long, ladies,' Liam said, rolling up his sleeves and sitting on the piano stool.

Sophie's gaze flickered to his tanned forearms, then met Liam's eyes as she forced herself to look down at the music. She was confused that even without the red wine, Liam did something odd to her insides – infuriating as he was.

'I just thought if we bash through the notes, you could maybe sing them next rehearsal and we can just see how it sounds. I know it's tricky unlearning something to relearn it, but stop me at any point and we can make sure you've got it. Does that sound OK?'

'That's fine,' Sophie said, keen to get on so she could remove herself from the situation. She felt socially awkward at the best of times, but this was something else entirely.

'I'm sure we'll sound fabulous,' said Lulu, sharing a wink and a grin with Sophie.

Liam hid a smile and cleared his throat, shifting back into professional mode. 'All right. Here goes. I'll just do four bars at a time and you can sing it together afterwards.'

Liam played, his agile fingers deftly moving through the complex melody. Sophie stared at them while he played, willing her brain to remember the tune. He finished and looked up expectantly at Sophie and Lulu, then lifted his hand to signal that he was about to play it again.

Lulu sang with full gusto straight away, her beautiful voice filling the hall. It might have only been four bars, but she performed it as though she was singing 'Jerusalem' at the Last Night of the Proms.

Her arms folded, Sophie sang too, but much quieter; not that she'd have been any match for Lulu.

'Sounding wonderful, ladies,' Liam said. 'Let's try this next bit.' He played again as they continued through the entire song. 'Shall we sing it through?' Liam asked when they'd finished. 'I'll play the soprano part too, so you can hear how it all fits together.'

'I must just pop to the bathroom. Won't be a moment.' Lulu said it as though she'd sweep out with a flourish, but her ancient body meant that her movement across the hall was more of a shuffle.

'Soph, I was thinking about the charity for the concert,' Liam said after they'd watched Lulu go in silence.

'Oh, yes?'

'I heard everyone voted earlier for your mum's charity, but, well, Nigel's mum is pretty ill. It doesn't look good. I thought maybe we could look into charities that support dementia care and split some of the fundraising between the two.'

'It's already been decided, sorry.' She shrugged.

'I think it would be a nice gesture for Nigel,' Liam said, leaning his hands on his knees.

She didn't know why, but she felt threatened by him, like he might swoop in and steal the concert from her. 'It's a lovely idea, really it is. I just think it's all kind of sorted now.' The thought of going back to the choir and explaining a change didn't appeal. There would be questions and comments and those conversations had a habit of turning into a parish council meeting with everyone forgetting that they were actually there to sing.

'Are you sure? I haven't seen any flyers yet, so there would still be time to print the charities on there.'

The bloody flyers. It wasn't her fault that Albert had messed them up at the printers. She took a deep breath. 'I'll think about it.'

Liam turned back to the piano and played through the song again while Sophie stood there, pretending to learn the notes without actually singing anything.

'Shall we sing this through while we wait for Lulu to return?'

Sophie nodded. Singing solo in front of people was her worst nightmare, but confrontation topped that and she was pleased to change the subject. At least while she was singing, they wouldn't be arguing or feel inclined to make small talk. Singing was safe.

'Great. I'll give you a bar in.'

He began to play.

Sophie's palms were slick with sweat and she held the music

up in front of her face. She hated the affliction of crippling fear that rose within her every time she had to sing alone. Part of a choir and she excelled, rejoicing in every moment. Single her out, and Sophie crumbled. In her head, she could sell out the Royal Albert Hall. But, also in her head, she accompanied her performances with adrenaline-filled dance routines. Everyone has a dream that stays a dream, and for Sophie, that was performing on stage alone. She took a breath and began to sing.

Applause came from behind her as she finished, and Sophie turned to see Lulu shuffling back across the hall.

'That was fabulous!' She rested her walking stick against the piano. 'I knew you could sing, but you really have got a beautiful voice.'

Sophie's eyes flickered briefly to Liam. His arms were folded, and he nodded his head in agreement, the beginning of a smile playing at the corner of his lips.

'You should definitely think about auditioning for the solo next week. You'd be marvellous,' Lulu said.

'Well, let's not get ahead of ourselves,' Sophie said. 'There's a lot of work to do with organising the concert and sorting out the charity stuff.'

She looked over pointedly at Liam, who was shuffling his piano music and pretending not to listen. He rested his hands on the piano keys once more.

'Let's carry on, shall we?'

# Chapter Three

Sophie walked the short distance home. Her flat was on the other side of the green and down a narrow lane, the brook running parallel. She thought about Kate and Lulu's suggestion. A solo was the dream. Maybe if the acoustics in the town hall resembled those in her shower, she might have a chance. But even if Sophie had a chance of getting the solo – which she didn't – she knew that on the night she'd struggle to find her voice. The lights, the music, the people, her anxiety – they'd conspire to make her look like a fool. Besides, she'd be far too busy organising the concert. She wouldn't have time to worry about anything else in the run-up to Christmas.

In the comfort of her flat, Sophie poured herself a glass of wine and put on her pyjamas. She loved that last hour of the day when she got to snuggle up on the sofa under a blanket and relax in front of the television. She may not go out dancing any more, or have exciting social plans every week, but for Sophie, this was how she liked it. It really was.

Sophie's flat was one of a small block that sat overlooking the green. In the evening, especially on a weekday in the run-up to Christmas, the townspeople would still be out in force, scurrying around to take advantage of the late-night shopping and meeting friends. Sophie liked that she could kneel on her sofa and look out of the window, watching the people scuttle by. And if she leant out the window a little further, she could just about see far enough to get a glimpse of the town's Christmas tree.

Only last week, the entire town had come together to watch the Christmas lights being switched on and now, as Sophie settled onto the sofa, she gazed out of the window and looked upon, by all accounts, the biggest Christmas tree they'd ever had in Cranswell. It was decorated with hundreds of tiny white lights and oversized rainbow-coloured baubles. At the very top, a great golden star stood tall, albeit at a slightly disconcerting angle, and cast its own brilliant light show down onto the grass. Albert and the rotary club really had surpassed themselves this year. At least poor old Albert had got something right. She pushed the niggle about the flyers to one side in her mind.

A screaming child caught her attention, and she looked in the little girl's direction only to see that she was actually giggling as her father chased her across the green, her stringed mittens poking out the bottom of her duffle coat and flapping in the breeze. When he caught her, he flung her into the air as other siblings raced across the green to join them. A couple wandering hand in hand and wearing matching bobble hats looked on with smiles.

Sophie turned back to her desperately empty flat. With a sigh, she picked herself up from the sofa and refilled her wine glass. Sophie's flat was tiny, but cosy. She loved it. It was just the right amount of space for someone to bumble around in on their own, even if she ended up bumbling around by herself more and more these days. Sipping her wine, she settled down on the sofa and flicked through the channels. Now that the town Christmas tree was up, there was nothing to stop her indulging in her first Christmas film of the season.

Just as she was deciding between *It's a Wonderful Life* and *Miracle on 34th Street* (the original black and white versions of both, of course), a steel drum rendition of 'Silent Night' rang out from her phone. Her ringtone was always seasonal and she and Kate had discovered at a Christmas gift fair that steel drums and Christmas music made for a brilliant mix. She couldn't help but smile. A smile that dropped when she realised who was calling.

She let it ring off, but a minute later the steel drums were back. She put it under a cushion and settled down as the titles for *It's a Wonderful Life* began to roll. But after another minute or two, the cushion vibrated as the persistent caller refused to give up. Sophie picked up the cushion, braced herself and answered the phone.

'Why weren't you picking up?' asked her mother. 'Is everything OK?'

'Sorry, I was in the middle of something,' Sophie lied.

'Didn't you see it was me calling?' she asked.

*Well, yes*, thought Sophie. That's why she'd not picked up. 'Sorry, Mum.' She willed the conversation to move on and for her mother to get to the point, of which there was always one.

'How are you?'

'Good, th—'

'Things are crazy here.'

June was a fan of the monosyllabic answer when it came to conversations with Sophie. Sophie assumed it was to give her more time to talk about herself. She downed her glass of wine and poured herself another while her mother talked.

'It's always hectic in the run-up to Christmas, you know. People want to give at Christmas, which is lovely, but it makes life very busy for me.'

Sophie nodded her understanding and realised that her mother couldn't see her. Not that it made any difference. She'd barely paused for breath since she'd begun talking anyway.

'And people ask you for the fundraising packs so last minute, as if I haven't got my own Christmas shopping and organising to do. Goodness!'

Sophie opened her mouth to say that the choir had agreed to help raise money for her mother's charity through the Christmas concert, but then she closed it again. She wasn't entirely sure that during this particular rant, June would be pleased. She'd probably just see the extra work it would entail rather than the funds it could generate.

'How's that friend of yours?' June asked, 'umming' as she tried to recall her name. 'You know, the pregnant one.'

'Kate?' Sophie threw her head back to retrieve the dregs of her second glass of wine. They'd been small measures, she told herself.

'Yes. How's she getting on? She must be nearly ready to burst by now!'

Sophie twisted the bracelet on her wrist and shifted in her seat. 'Not quite yet.'

'Does she know what she's having?'

'Not sure.'

'I know it's hard for you, love.' June hesitated before

carrying on, her tone softening. 'I just wanted to give you the chance to talk, you know, if you needed to.' Her mother waited in a rare silence at the other end of the phone.

'I don't.'

'Well . . .' Her mother let the word hang in the air. No doubt a last-ditch attempt to give Sophie the opportunity to talk. She didn't. 'I should probably go. Lots of fundraising packs to send. We're always so busy in the run-up to Christmas.'

'You said. Are you still coming to the new flat for Christmas?'

'We were planning to, but everything's got a little mad with the charity – it always does. Everything's so chaotic at this end. Anyway, I'll let you know for definite in a week or so. You're still welcome to come here, of course.'

Sophie knew that was her mother's code for 'probably not'. She wished June would just say what she meant and have done with it, instead of pretending that they would finally come to see her flat over the festive period. Now that she was a thirty-four-year-old woman, surely it worked both ways? Why couldn't they come to her for a change? Especially now that she was beginning to settle and finally had her own place.

'Well, it was nice to talk to you, Mum.'

'You too, love.'

'Bye.'

'Bye-bye.' June yelled something inaudible, probably directed at Sophie's long-suffering father, before she hung up.

June's phone calls always felt like an ambush. There was no regularity or routine to them, and she'd pop up at the most inconvenient of times. Sophie rubbed a hand over her face, her eyes suddenly tired. Sometimes she wished she had a better relationship with them both; she hardly ever got the chance to speak to her father these days.

Slightly tipsy and frowning after the phone call, Sophie decided to put up the Christmas tree. It had been sitting in a box in the spare room since she'd moved in, and it was only a few days until December. Besides, it was the perfect way to cheer herself up.

She pulled the tree out of the box and spent some time smoothing and evening out the branches. The lights were next. She draped them, tiny white sparkling lights, all over the tree. Then, carefully, she unwrapped and placed each precious ornament evenly all over it. Each one was a memory – a visit to London with her very first boyfriend; a gift from her old school friend the Christmas when things had got really bad. Fleetingly, she wondered what this experience might be like if she found someone to share it with. They'd probably have a shared ornament that they'd bought together on their first date or on their first holiday away. Maybe they'd buy one each year for their children . . .

*Stop it. Let's not get carried away.* Sophie reminded herself that compared to last Christmas when she and her mother had argued – again – this one, in her own wonderful flat, would be far better, even if her parents didn't come to stay. In fact, it was more likely to be a good one if they didn't turn up after all.

# Chapter Four

It was duty day. The worst of all the days. Each week, all the staff at Cranswell Primary School had two allotted days, during which they would be on duty. It didn't matter if it was raining or snowing or searing heat, on duty days you spent all of your lunchtime and break time out on the playground, supervising the children as they played. Supposedly, visibility meant that the children would refrain from committing any misdemeanours. In Sophie's experience, they became more mischievous to get your attention – much more fun.

And so, for what felt like the millionth Wednesday lunchtime of the year, Sophie found herself wrapped up and shivering out in the playground as the little ones ran around her legs, screaming at her to join in with their game of Stuck in the Mud.

Taking the mickey, Kate waved through the staffroom window and exaggerated enjoying the smell of her coffee before sipping it, rubbing her huge tummy and licking her lips. Sophie looked around to make sure no children were looking and stuck her middle finger up. Kate blew her a kiss. Sophie laughed, shook her head and turned away.

It was freezing cold that day. The clouds had merged, a blanket of snow in the sky ready to drop at any moment. The heavy cloud cover eclipsed the light and it felt more like dusk than lunchtime. Sophie shivered, regretting her choice of skirt and tights. The hideous hi-vis jacket the school forced her to wear added little warmth. She pasted a hard smile on her face and folded her arms tightly to hold in the heat.

The weather was already odd enough that the children had arrived at school a little offbeat. Any time there was something different about a day, the children were like werewolves and, above all things, the weather had the biggest impact. Sophie pulled a sticker out of her hair, thinking back to the chaos of the morning; she hoped a mischievous child hadn't ambushed her while she wasn't looking.

Even now, the children ran and tumbled and skipped about the playground like insects. Despite walking in a straight line, Sophie had to hop to the side or lift her arms to let excitable children pass. Then, their unpredictability morphed into a pattern. They were all running towards the edge of the field – some more determined and excitable than others, but they were all headed in the same direction without a doubt.

Sophie walked over, a little more purpose in her step. As she'd guessed, there was a commotion coming from across the playground. As she neared, children from all over the field and playground ran over to see what was happening. Chants of 'fight, fight, fight' cut through the breeze. Sophie broke into a run and, when she reached the crowd, moved those who had gathered out of the way.

'Excuse me!' Sophie shouted. The children parted. They wanted to be seen to do the right thing, but didn't want to move too far, secretly coveting a glimpse of the drama as it unfolded.

Nearing the epicentre, Sophie caught a flash of two girls who were on the floor. Sophie switched into problem-solving mode, her mind racing as she worked out what to do and in what order. At her shouts, the girls stopped, sensing the dying noise and the presence of a teacher. They stood up sheepishly.

'You two, with me,' Sophie said, pointing at the two girls who had been scrapping on the floor. 'Let's go inside.'

Sophie walked the girls across the playground, one with her head up, a smug smile pasted across her face, the other head down, shuffling. The rest of the school dissolved back into their games and conversations. She marched the two girls into the classroom and sat them down on opposite sides of the room. Kate and Tom, the teaching assistant, came in.

'We saw what happened from the window, Miss Lawson. Can we help?' Tom asked.

'Can you take Lily?' Sophie nodded over to the girl who sat at the table, steely eyed. Lily was no stranger to a playground brawl and Sophie didn't have the energy to reprimand her again so soon after the last time. 'I'll look after Cassie.' The second girl sat on the other side of the room and had blood on her face. Sophie hadn't worked out where it was coming from, but needed to look after that before she could do anything else.

'No problem,' Tom said. 'Come on, Lily.' He held his arm out to suggest Lily should come with him. She dutifully followed him down the corridor, but not without pulling a mean face in Cassie's direction before she left.

'Are you OK with Cassie, Miss Lawson? Do you need me to do anything?' Kate asked.

'It's OK, thank you. I'm just going to do some first aid on Cassie. I'll catch up with you later, Mrs Donovan.'

Kate left as Sophie went over to the big cupboard in the corner of the room and collected the first aid kit from its hook.

'Let me look at you, Cassie.' Sophie sat opposite her and moved her long blonde hair to one side. She took a ball of cotton wool and some water and wiped it over Cassie's cheek. She'd received a nasty cut that was weeping blood. The girl sat up a little so that Sophie could reach her, but she didn't make eye contact. Her eyes were hard, and she stared down at the table.

'Do you want to tell me what happened?' Sophie asked as she went about her work.

'Not really.' Cassie shook her head and then grimaced at the sting of the antibacterial wipe as Sophie applied it.

Surprised at her response, Sophie said, 'It's OK. You're not in trouble. We just need to know what happened.' It wasn't strictly true; Cassie probably was in a bit of trouble. But the other girl, Lily, was known for being a bit of a rascal and Sophie knew that, despite her having joined the school late, Cassie wasn't normally like that. Although, now she came to think of it, she had been a little more troublesome over the past few weeks.

'Lily stole my pen.' Her voice was monotone, and she continued to avoid making eye contact.

'Thank you for telling me. Why didn't you tell me about it sooner instead of confronting Lily outside like that?'

'She always takes my things.' Cassie shrugged, and her face remained unemotional. She had a slightly downturned mouth, which made her look sullen.

Sophie kept quiet. She hoped Cassie would continue and

tell her more about what had happened. She felt a little sorry for her, but without Cassie opening up it would be hard for her to support her and fight her corner.

Cassie sighed and shifted in her seat, letting out a long breath. 'She was waving it around saying it was for babies.' A tear formed in the corner of one of Cassie's eyes. She wiped it away quickly with the sleeve of her jumper, and her hair fell back in front of her face.

'That's not very nice, is it?' Sophie said. She brushed Cassie's hair away again and took another antibacterial wipe to her face.

Cassie shook her head. 'No. It is a bit of a silly pen,' she added, relenting. 'It's all pink and sparkly and has Lupin Turtle on top.' Cassie paused to wipe her nose with her sleeve. She let out a big snort and shuddered, holding back her tears.

'I still love Lupin Turtle, even though I'm a grown-up,' Sophie said conspiratorially. She went over to the bin to dispose of the used wipes and settled back down into her seat opposite Cassie. 'Why did you fight with Lily, Cassie?' Sophie sensed she had broken down a wall and wanted to exploit it while she had the chance.

'Mum gave me that pen.'

Sophie felt the barrier return almost instantly. 'I see.'

'Before she . . . left.'

'Ah.' Sophie couldn't find the words, and she let the silence stretch for a moment longer. 'So, it's precious to you, then?'

Cassie nodded and rolled her eyes. Quite rightly. What a stupid thing to say.

'But you know, fighting isn't the way to solve all of your

problems,' Sophie said. She hated this part. The part where she had to explain that fighting was wrong and that she should have spoken to an adult about what had happened. Let's face it, Lily had been horrible to her and if they'd been grown-ups, Sophie would have wanted to punch her in the face too.

'But Lily started it,' Cassie said, sitting up in her seat. 'I always get the blame for everything,' she added, slumping back down so that she faced away from Sophie.

Sophie's jaw set for a moment and then she softened, remembering how hard it was to be a child these days. 'I know, sweetheart. Sometimes it's hard to do the right thing when you're angry.' She pulled a plaster out of its wrapper and put it over the cut on Cassie's face. 'There you go.'

'Thanks.' Her arms remained folded, and she turned again in her chair.

'You know I'm going to have to call your grandma, don't you?'

'Really? Do you have to?' She dropped her head, eyes closed.

'Yes. I do. She'll want to know what's happened to you today.'

'You mean you want to tell her so she can tell me off,' Cassie said, lifting her head to glare at Sophie.

'It's not like that, Cassie.' Sophie kept her voice calm, but Cassie's surliness was causing her blood pressure to rise.

Cassie made no reply, only folding her arms even tighter. If that was possible.

'Why don't you spend the rest of lunchtime over in the book corner? You can calm down and stay out of the cold. And you'll be all ready for your lesson this afternoon then,' Sophie said, changing tactic. She'd smother her with kindness if that's what it took to get her to open up.

Cassie nodded and sloped over to the book corner, settling down on the beanbag to read.

When she was sure Cassie had settled, Sophie left her in the classroom and headed over to the office to call Cassie's grandma.

'Everything OK?' Kate asked, following Sophie down the corridor to the office.

'Yes, I think so. It seems this whole thing was over a pen.'

'Lily said the same. Do you want me to phone her parents and you do Cassie?' Kate asked.

'Would you mind? That would save me time after school. I've got so much work to do.' *And I've got a stubborn, angry girl in there to deal with*, she thought.

'Of course, that's fine. Lily's mum and I have a *long* relationship,' Kate said with a roll of the eyes. 'We're on first-name terms,' she added.

Sophie laughed.

'I'll phone Mrs Hawthorn now,' Sophie said.

Kate did a thumbs up and left.

The phone rang and it went to answerphone. The generic recorded voice directed her to leave a message and hang up.

'Hi, this is a message for Mrs Hawthorn. It's Miss Lawson calling from Cranswell Primary. I'm sorry to say that there's been a bit of an unpleasant incident today. Nothing to worry about, but we'll need you to come in at the end of the day to have a quick meeting and sign the accident form. Cassie's fine, by the way,' she added as an afterthought, annoyed that she'd

41

not thought to begin the message with the reassurance.

Sophie looked at her watch. Three and a half minutes until afternoon lessons began. That sounded about right. In fact, three and a half minutes was positively ages. Ten years of teaching had taught Sophie exactly how to make a cup of tea and get it down her in less than that amount of time. She hurried around the corner into the staffroom. Kate was there, also attempting to get a warm drink in before lessons began.

'I thought you'd be in here in a moment,' Kate said, standing over by the kettle. 'It's brewing already for you.'

'Thanks.' Sophie reached out for the cup and dumped the tea bag in the bin. A dash of milk and an inch of cold water from the tap and it would be ready to drink straight away.

'Another crazy day,' Kate said. She leant against the countertop, looking uncomfortable.

'And it's only just the end of lunchtime.' Sophie sighed. 'We've got the nativity rehearsal to get through this afternoon before we can call it a day.' She ran a hand through her hair and rubbed her eyes in an attempt to banish the post-lunch lull. If there was anything she needed to feel energetic for, it was a nativity rehearsal.

'Yep. And we really must get Ethan to realise it's a muslin cloth he offers to wrap baby Jesus in, not a Muslim cloth.'

They laughed. They'd been trying for a fortnight to get six-year-old Ethan to say the right thing, but Sophie doubted that he'd ever get it right. And on the day of the nativity, it was completely out of her hands.

Sophie looked out the window at the children who were being called in by the whistle.

'Off we go,' Kate said. She pushed herself up from the counter and picked up her belongings from one of the dilapidated mustard-coloured chairs.

'Hey, Kate . . .'

'Hmm?' She turned, a pile of exercise books in her arms.

'You know Cassie Hawthorn? Do you know what happened with her parents? She said something about her mum leaving. Grandma picks her up, though, doesn't she? I couldn't find anything in her file when I had a quick glance just then.'

Kate shook her head. 'I'm not sure. As far as I'm aware, they've been a single-parent family since she joined the school in September. Maybe divorce brought them to the area and her mum's made herself scarce. Grandma picks her up because her dad's busy. The grandfather owns the farm out past the new housing development. Dad's helping out there, I guess.'

'Oh,' Sophie said. 'Maybe that's it then. I wish parents would tell me these things so I can brace myself for when their children bring it up. Her file just lists grandma's contact number and dad's work, which isn't very helpful and doesn't really tell me anything.'

'We should go,' Kate said, looking at her watch. 'Ready for nativity fun?'

'Always,' said Sophie, downing her tea and heading to her classroom, but not feeling entirely satisfied that she'd got the answers she wanted.

# Chapter Five

The last lesson of the day went by far too quickly and Sophie emerged from it covered in tinsel and singing 'Little Donkey' over and over again. She hummed it mindlessly as she turned the corner into reception. There was a man waiting on one of the chairs. He was wearing large work boots, caked from top to toe in mud. She wondered whether Cassie's father had turned up for once. His head was low as he scrolled through his phone, but he sat up and ran a hand through his curls when he heard Sophie coming.

'Mr Hawthorn?' Sophie extended her hand and looked up to his face, meeting his familiar hazel eyes. She went to withdraw her hand and took a step back. 'Liam,' she said, her voice thin.

'Miss Lawson,' he said, without missing a beat, moving to shake her hand despite her recoil.

His hand dwarfed hers and it felt rough on her skin – workingman's hands.

The silence stretched before them as Sophie grew acutely aware that she was shaking his hand for far longer than necessary. His arms were strong, muscular where he'd rolled up the sleeves of his jumper. In the harsh electric strip light as opposed to a dingy bar or a dimly lit town hall, Liam's hazel eyes smouldered and his dark hair was even more glorious than she remembered.

She attempted to refocus her attention on the task at hand.

'Lovely,' she said, inexplicably breathless before finding her senses, 'of you to come in so quickly,' she added, recovering, she hoped, seamlessly.

'No problem.'

He didn't seem to flinch at the coincidence. Didn't he care that this was the third time they'd met within a week? Or that not one of the meetings was in any way pleasant?

'What's been happening?' he asked, straight to the point.

Sophie was warm, her face and neck flushing at something she couldn't explain – was it the mildly uncomfortable nature of the conversation she was about to have with a parent? The shock at the coincidence of Liam Hawthorn being the father of a child in her class? Or that each time she'd seen him in the last week, she'd been mesmerised by his eyes and the scent of sandalwood and jasmine that he carried with him wherever he went? She brushed a hand through her hair, pulled her cardigan sleeves down over her hands and invited him into the classroom.

Sophie sat down on one of the children's chairs and gestured for Liam to do the same opposite. She had a flashback to his knees being up around his ears on the tiny stool in the pub during that first dreaded date, those hideous balloons bobbing about between them. She shivered and shook her head, banishing the memory.

'So, Mr Hawthorn.' She paused a moment, considering what to say and cursing herself for not thinking it through earlier in more detail – when Liam Hawthorn wasn't sitting right in front of her, waiting. 'The reason I needed to speak to you is because . . .' She swallowed and jumped in. 'Today at lunchtime, Cassie got into a fight with another child.'

Liam regarded her and waited, rather than reacting. Sophie, perhaps predictably, filled the silence. She couldn't bear the awkwardness of it all.

'She said it was something to do with her Lupin Turtle pen?' Sophie phrased it like a question, hoping he would join in with the conversation.

'I've already spoken to Cassie,' he said, ignoring her question. He sat back in his chair with his arms folded across his chest. 'She told me about the other girl, Lily. It sounds like she started it all. And that this isn't the first time she's been in trouble at school.'

Ah, so he was going to play it like that, was he? Sophie sat up in her chair and leant on the table. 'I do believe that Lily was to blame. It seems like she took Cassie's property, which led to the argument that started it all.'

'I'm just a bit confused why I'm here, Miss Lawson. Cassie has done nothing wrong, but it sounds like you want to talk about her involvement.'

'Well' – Sophie considered her words for a moment – 'I do. Whatever the circumstances leading up to it, Cassie was in a fight today. She was injured and I want to reassure you about that aspect of things, but we also need to address the way both girls handled the situation.'

Liam's eyes were cold. They'd not had the best start to their acquaintance over the past week, but Sophie hadn't seen him quite like this before. She opened her mouth to continue, hoping to calm the situation. But Liam got there first.

'How is it this Lily girl has been in so many fights, yet she's still allowed to tear into my daughter?' He spoke evenly, not a crack in his voice, but it was laced with parental anger. Sophie was an expert at recognising the signs.

She swallowed anxiously. 'Mr Hawthorn, I understand that you're feeling frustrated. It's unfortunate that we even need to be talking about this.'

He tutted and rolled his eyes.

Sophie hesitated, nervous about how to continue and irritated by Liam's petulant reaction. 'Lily will have to deal with the consequences of her poor behaviour choices, I can promise you that,' she said. 'But when I witnessed the fight and stopped it in the playground at lunchtime, both girls were attacking each other equally. They were both fighting.'

'Look, Miss Lawson.' Liam sat forward in his seat; Sophie leant back into her chair. 'I struggle to see how a school that prides itself so on keeping children safe can allow these things to happen. I suggest you talk to this Lily girl's parents and get them to sort her out. Cassie hasn't done anything wrong here.'

She struggled to look him in the eye. How was it Liam Hawthorn managed to take away her decade of experience and leave her feeling like a trainee having a difficult parental conversation for the first time? If she thought he'd annoyed her previously, he was really upping his game now. She steeled herself and continued.

'Mr Hawthorn, my colleague is having the same conversation with Lily's parents as we speak.'

'They don't need the *same* conversation,' he said, emphasising the word *same*. 'They need to be told that their child is a menace!'

His resolve remained steely. He didn't shout, but his words threw Sophie's professional façade. This conversation was going nowhere and Sophie was starting to panic. How was she going to bring this back around?

'Mr Hawthorn, I really don't think . . .' She closed her eyes and took a deep breath. 'Look, I know Cassie was angry about what happened between her and Lily today and in time she will probably feel upset too. I feel for her, I really do. But we simply cannot have children fighting in the playground.' She sounded more assertive than she had planned to. She sounded more assertive than she thought she could be.

'What do you mean, angry? In time she'll feel upset?' His eyes narrowed.

'I'm afraid Cassie wasn't particularly remorseful when I spoke to her at lunchtime. In fact, she was quite dismissive about the whole thing,' Sophie said, looking at her lap when she finished, afraid to meet Liam's eyes. She knew it had to be said, but there was a part of her genuinely worried about Liam's reaction.

'That's probably something to do with how it seems you have handled this whole situation. Look—'

'Mr Hawthorn. That's slightly unfair,' Sophie interrupted, sensing that this was escalating into one of those conversations where she handled herself perfectly well in the classroom and then cried in the office afterwards. She just hoped it didn't morph into one of those conversations where she couldn't handle the confrontation at all, and cried on the spot. It was close. She could feel hot angry tears brewing under the surface.

'Miss Lawson. If you can't control the children in this school, then I really do feel that Cassie will have to go elsewhere.'

'I don't think we're going to resolve anything here this afternoon, Mr Hawthorn.' Sophie wanted nothing more than to end the conversation and get Liam out of her classroom. 'So, I'll look forward to seeing you again at parents' evening next week. Perhaps we can talk more then, when you're not feeling quite so angry about the situation.'

It was a poor attempt at defusing what had quickly become an uncomfortable conversation, perhaps more uncomfortable than their original date – if that were possible.

'Of course I'm angry about the situation. My little girl has a cut on her face and is being punished like a bully. I refuse to have her treated like this.' He stood up and left the room in three big steps. 'Good afternoon.'

Sophie stood as he left, one of her legs shaking slightly. She was opening and closing her mouth like a goldfish, annoyed that she'd not had anything sensible to say in response and worrying that in no way had the situation been resolved – merely postponed.

Several times on the drive back to the farm, Liam looked over to Cassie but she spent the entire journey staring out the window, her hair flopping forward over her face and her fists clenched in her lap. He considered saying something to her and then decided against it, instead gripping the steering wheel tighter.

Glancing at her for the hundredth time, he noticed the bruising on her cheek coming out and the plaster that Sophie had put on it earlier.

'Are you hurting?' he asked gently.

Cassie shook her head and fixed her eyes firmly on the fields as they went past in a blur.

Liam pulled into the courtyard outside the farmhouse and climbed down out of the Land Rover. Before he could make his way round and open the door to help, Cassie had jumped out the other side and was already making her way over to the front door.

'Hiya, love.' His mother stood at the door, ready to welcome them home. Her smiling expression changed when she saw Cassie walking towards her. She stormed straight past her grandmother, kicked off her shoes and stomped towards the stairs.

For a moment, Liam's thoughts went to his wife. She had always been so neat and tidy. Taking her shoes off at the door in the middle of an argument was exactly what Emily would have done. He swallowed away the thickness in his throat.

'Cassie. Don't walk away from me. We need to talk.' He walked past his mother and squeezed the top of her arm before following Cassie through to the living room. 'Cassie.'

She stopped but didn't turn. 'What?'

'Cassie, we need to talk about what happened today. You were in a fight.'

'So?' Her shoulders rose in a shrug.

'So, it's not like you. I want to know what's up.'

'Nothing. Can I go now?' She folded her arms.

Liam's jaw ached from the tension. He didn't have the energy for another fight, not after he'd handled the meeting with Sophie Lawson so appallingly. He sighed loudly. 'Fine.'

Without another word, Cassie went upstairs to her room. At least she hadn't stomped her way up. Still, it annoyed Liam that he'd not got Cassie to open up and tell him what was wrong. Story of his life.

'Cup of tea?' His mother hovered in the doorway.

Liam exhaled and closed his eyes before turning to smile at her. 'Yes, please.'

'Come on, love.' Barbara put an arm around her son's shoulders and guided him into the kitchen. She pushed him down into a chair.

'Why is she always like this?' Liam asked. He plonked his head down on the dining table and held his hands to the back of his head.

'Be fair, love. This is just a phase. I know it's been challenging, moving back, but she hasn't always been like this.' She brushed her son's curls back, encouraging him to sit up, and placed a hot cup of tea down on the table in front of him.

'Thanks.' He picked up the mug and sipped it straight away. 'The problem is,' he said, putting his mug down again, 'is that I suddenly seem to be parenting a teenager, but she's only ten. Nobody prepared me for this.'

'I don't think anyone is prepared for any stage of parenthood, not really.' She took off her apron, hung it on the back of the kitchen door, and sat down opposite him with her own drink. She brushed back a wisp of greying hair and tucked it into her messy bun.

'Emily would have known what to do,' Liam said. His voice cracked and his chest tightened.

He didn't like to bring Emily up with his mother. He knew it hurt her to see him grieving so. Still, parenting hurdles had been so much easier when she'd been around.

'Oh, love, you'll know what to do too,' Barbara said, reaching across the table to take her son's hand. 'You might not know what to do right now and it'll be difficult while Cassie is acting so closed off, but you will resolve this and all the other behaviour that's been going on, eventually. I promise you. And it won't be the last issue you have to get over either. Her teenage years are just around the corner, you know.'

Liam groaned.

'You weren't so easy to parent either.'

He smiled at that. His childhood had been a wonderful one, thanks to his mum, but he could definitely remember getting up to all sorts of mischief when he was younger.

'Has she said anything to you?' Liam asked. It was the same question he asked Barbara daily as he tried to work out his ten-year-old-come-teenage daughter.

'Sorry, love.' Barbara shook her head and stood up, clearing their mugs away. 'Why don't you go and relax for a bit? I'm just finishing dinner. It'll be ready in half an hour or so.'

'Thanks, Mum.' He came round the table and hugged her tightly. 'I'll just pop down and put the chickens in for the night,' he said, adding hopefully, 'if Cassie wants to find me.'

On the other side of town, Sophie was just leaving school. It was late, and the sun had set a long while ago. The stars were twinkling in the dark sky. It was one of the things she loved most about living in the countryside.

She realised she was stomping across the car park. She was still reeling from her meeting with Liam. It had been their third coincidental meeting in a week, and all of them had been unpleasant. Sophie was starting to wonder what it was she was doing wrong. All she'd wanted to do that afternoon was to sort out the situation with Cassie and Lily so that Cassie could move on and work through whatever was making her sad at the moment. The more Sophie thought about it, the more she realised Cassie was behaving strangely, and she just wanted to help. Even now, as she reflected on what had happened, she couldn't believe Liam had snapped like that.

She realised she was frowning, and her head was beginning to ache. As she ferreted in her bag for her keys, muttering under her breath, her entire bag lit up and the festive steel drums rang out from within. She picked up her phone and swiped to answer without thinking.

'Hi, love.' June's nasal voice was made tinnier by the dodgy signal.

'Hang on.' Sophie fished the keys out of her bag and climbed into her freezing car. Her breath was visible, and the windows steamed up instantly. 'Hi, Mum.'

'Hi, love. How are you?'

'I'm—'

'Everything's OK here.'

'Good.' Sophie decided not to go into detail about her own rubbish day, even if she did get a chance to, which was unlikely.

'Busy, as always. I got your text about using the charity for your concert,' she said. And then after a moment, 'That's a lovely gesture.'

'Well, you know,' Sophie said, fiddling with the edge of her coat. 'It's close to my heart.'

'It's always nice to get extra support, even if it is in our busy periods.'

Sophie wished she'd not bothered answering the phone. She berated herself for not having looked at who was calling. 'Sorry, I thought you'd be pleased.'

She had hoped that June would be thrilled with a sizable donation coming her way at the end of the year. Her thoughts slipped to Liam's suggestion for a moment. Maybe they should reconsider the charity choice and think about Nigel's mum instead. She'd definitely be more grateful. No. She was being pedantic. She'd made her decision. She'd stick with it. June would be happy with the money in the end, she was sure.

'No, no,' June said, dismissing Sophie's apology. 'It will all come good. You know how I like to be busy.'

'Speaking of which, I should go, really,' Sophie said, seizing her opportunity. 'I've not made it back from work yet and I'm hungry and cold in my car. Can I phone you when I get home?' She shivered and sat on her spare hand to keep it warm.

'It's eight thirty. Why are you still at work?'

For a moment, Sophie thought her mother sounded almost concerned.

'You'll never find a new boyfriend if you spend all your time at that silly school.'

And there it was.

Sophie's gaze flickered to the roof of the car and her jaw tensed.

'Well, actually, I'm sort of OK without one.' She attempted to keep her tone light. 'Besides, I like my job.'

'Don't be silly, Sophie. Everyone wants someone.'

Silence. Sophie's deep breaths came out as storm clouds in the car. She pinched the bridge of her nose and scrunched her eyes closed.

'And you'll never find one living in a village.'

'It's a town, Mum.'

'Barely. At least here in London there are men everywhere.'

'I like living here.' She felt pathetic, once again finding the need to justify her life choices. Why did she feel like she was being told off?

'Be that as it may, it's hardly full of eligible bachelors. You're not likely to meet anyone like Jordan there.'

The name made her flinch. 'I don't want to meet anyone like Jordan.'

'You don't want to meet anyone rich, handsome, with their own hair and teeth and a successful business to boot?' June sounded sceptical, like the fact Sophie had any interests other than finding a husband was outrageous to her.

'Are you forgetting that he left me?' Sophie snapped, thumping the steering wheel. 'He left me at the worst possible moment, when things got tough and I needed him the most.'

'Things were horrible, yes.'

Sophie's eyes pricked with tears. She said nothing.

'Was it really the loss that drove him away?'

Sophie laughed. 'Drove him away? You think it was my fault?' Sophie could feel her blood pressure rising and her voice grew higher.

'Well, you did take a long time to get over it all. It was probably very difficult for him to support you. You wouldn't let me help, even though I wanted to. I'm just saying that Jordan was a good one and perhaps you shouldn't have let him go.'

'Wow.' Tears smarted at her eyes. How could her mother be so insensitive to what had happened? 'Bye, Mum.' She said it through clenched teeth and swiped to end the call, throwing her phone down on the passenger seat.

Swearing to herself, she put the key in the ignition. It took three goes for the engine to turn over, by which time, Sophie had to turn it off again to cry out her tears.

# Chapter Six

'Oops. 'Scuse me!'

The pile of tissue paper and tinsel Sophie was holding fell to the floor in slow motion as the child who'd bumped into her said nothing and rudely walked off down the corridor, hands in her pockets. Cassie again. Sophie was yet to understand why her behaviour had been so off recently.

She knelt down on the floor to gather up her resources and put them down on a chair once she'd finally made it to the staffroom. She tried to resist the urge to tidy up the pile and fold the tissue paper neatly again – in rainbow order, of course – knowing that if she did, Kate and Tom would mock her, and she had more important things to discuss.

'I'm getting really worried about Cassie,' Sophie said, pouring water from the kettle into the three mugs that sat waiting on the countertop in the staffroom.

'In what way?' asked Tom. He dropped a tea bag into each mug. Completing the trio, Kate stood ready with the milk (and probably the cold tap – it wasn't long until afternoon lessons began, after all).

'She's been really withdrawn since the fight the other day. I wonder how her dad handled things at home afterwards. Her behaviour had gone downhill a little before then too, if I'm honest. And she just barged into me and trudged off down the corridor without a word. I'm worried something's going on that she's not told us.'

'Well, now you know who her dad is, maybe that explains it,' Kate said, dropping milk into each cup.

'What do you mean?' Tom asked, stirring his drink vigorously with a teaspoon.

'Mr Hawthorn is the parent who shouted at me in a meeting. Kate thinks the reason he's so angry is because he's dealing with a difficult divorce,' Sophie explained. She took her tea and sat down on one of the worn chairs, purposefully turning her back on the untidy pile of craft resources.

'It could explain why Cassie is so unhappy at the moment, I guess,' Tom said.

'But, Kate, you said he's been a single parent since she started school in September. Divorces don't take that long, do they?' Sophie said.

'All right, Columbo.' Kate sat down opposite her, leant back in the chair and balanced her mug on her pregnant belly. 'Some children go through phases like this. It could just be hormones or something. Maybe she's just growing up, or perhaps it's to do with the move here. Sometimes children struggle to adjust to big life changes like that.'

'Mmm, maybe,' Sophie said, but she wasn't sure she agreed. Something wasn't right. Now she looked back objectively, Sophie could see that Cassie had changed in the last few weeks. It wasn't just the fight. Something else must have happened, and Sophie was determined to find out what it was.

'So, why was the meeting with her dad so horrible?' Tom

asked. He joined them, sitting down in another of the mustard chairs and landing with a bump as if he'd not expected it to be so low. His tea spilt onto his trousers and he swore.

Sophie and Kate shared a look and Kate held out a hand as if to offer Sophie the stage.

'It was pretty awful,' Sophie said, sipping her tea.

'How come?' Tom asked.

It was written all over his face that he smelt gossip and now he'd caught a whiff, Sophie knew he wasn't likely to back down until he'd heard the whole story.

'He just lost it. He said the fight was the school's fault because we don't deal with things and spent most of the time worrying about Lily and her punishment rather than his own daughter. It was horrific.' Sophie cringed at the memory and reminded herself that it wasn't her fault Liam had acted that way.

'Sorry,' Tom said. 'That sounds rubbish.'

'It could be worse,' Kate piped up from where she had listened quietly until now. 'You could have gone on a date with him before you realised he was the father of one of your Year Six children.'

Sophie shot Kate a look, and she sat back, glee all over her face, waiting to watch the next part of the conversation unfold.

'What the actual . . .'

'All right, all right,' Sophie said as she watched Tom's eyes widen with joy at this new information. 'It's nothing, really.'

'What happened?' He sat back to get comfortable for the story.

'We just went on a date last week, that's all. I obviously didn't know who he was at that point. Cassie's grandma always picks her up, so I didn't make any kind of connection. It just wasn't a great experience. We didn't really have anything in common.'

'And . . . what did he bring you as a gift?' Kate prompted.

Sophie narrowed her eyes at her.

'Yes, what did he bring you?' Tom asked, his eyes shining. He was one step away from applauding the gossip in excitement.

'He brought me a bouquet of twenty red helium balloons.' Sophie sighed.

'But you hate balloons,' Tom said, and grimaced.

Sophie nodded.

'Yeah, what is it about that? Are you actually scared of them or do you just not like them?' Kate asked.

'Ooh yes! Or did you have an awful childhood experience that made you hate them?' Tom said.

'I don't really want to talk about it.' Sophie crossed the staffroom to put her empty mug in the sink. She stood for a moment, resting her hand on the countertop. An overwhelming sense of emotion caught her off guard and she waited to make sure there weren't going to be any tears.

'Go on, you can tell us,' Tom said. 'It'll be like therapy.' They both laughed.

Silence.

Kate said, 'Sophie?' Her voice had changed to show concern, but it was too late.

'I said I don't want to talk about it.'

Sophie waded through the day in a funk. She couldn't shake the heaviness that had settled in her stomach as she replayed the stupid conversation she'd had with Kate and Tom in the staffroom. Just when she thought she was safe, another wave of embarrassment at her reaction to their jokes twisted her insides.

On top of that, she was worrying about Cassie. She watched her during the lesson as the class glued cotton wool onto their snowmen Christmas cards. The children around her giggled and chatted, but Cassie sat quietly and got on with her work. Occasionally her little tongue would poke out while she attempted to concentrate on a particularly tricky bit of her creation, but otherwise, her face remained emotionless.

'Cassie,' Sophie said, as the children skipped out of the room at the end of the day.

Cassie turned back.

'Have you got a moment?'

Without a reaction, Cassie walked back into the classroom and stood to the side of Sophie's desk.

'Do you want to sit down?' Sophie asked, offering her a plastic chair.

Cassie sighed and sat down at the table nearest to Sophie. She thought she caught Cassie rolling her eyes, but decided to ignore it.

'Did you and Lily make up after what happened the other day?' Sophie asked. It was a lame start, but she was determined to find out what was getting Cassie down. She just needed a way in, a way to get Cassie talking to her.

Cassie shook her head. 'Not really.' She looked at her hands resting in her lap. 'I didn't really bother trying, though,' she added, picking at a fingernail.

'Cassie, is everything OK?' Sophie asked.

'Fine.'

'You know you can talk to me if there's ever anything wrong.'

'You're as bad as my dad,' Cassie said rudely. 'Can't everyone just leave me alone?'

Sophie could tell she was desperate to leave, fidgeting in her chair and finding her hands particularly interesting – anything not to make eye contact with Sophie. Sophie was undeterred.

'Cassie, neither your father nor I are trying to pry or upset you. We just want to make sure you're OK.' She waited and gave Cassie some time to answer. It surprised her that, for once, she and Liam seemed to be on the same side.

'OK. Can I go now? Dad will be waiting for me.' She made to move.

Sophie sighed and sat back in her chair. It was hopeless. 'Yes, of course. Off you go.'

Cassie picked up her bag and left the room like a grumpy teenager.

Sophie was surprised that Cassie hadn't engaged with her. Having known Cassie for a while now, it seemed out of character. She was even more concerned than she had been before.

Through the window, she saw Cassie run out of the gates. Unusually, her father was there to collect her rather than her grandmother. Liam Hawthorn was all smiles and loveliness now that he wasn't shouting at Sophie. He swept his daughter up in his arms and she sort of smiled. Sophie took consolation in that. At least it seemed like everything was OK at home.

# Chapter Seven

After the fraught conversation she'd had with Kate and Tom earlier that day and her unsuccessful conversation with Cassie too, Sophie toyed with the idea of getting out of the school gates as early as possible. However, an unusual lapse in organisation because of the ongoing coordination of the Christmas concert meant that she still needed to plan her literacy lesson for Monday morning. She could have taken everything home with her, but experience told her that trying to plan at home would result in her desperately needing something from her classroom. Sophie reserved weekend work for less dangerous pursuits, like marking. With a rough plan for the lesson in her mind, she fiddled about with the PowerPoint.

She liked school when it was like this. Everyone had left; the corridors and classrooms were silent. At this time of year, it grew dark early on and the rural location of the school meant it was completely black outside; only the town way off in the distance and the stars in the sky gave off any kind of light. In her earlier years, Sophie would have got a little jumpy about what could be lurking through the window; but nowadays, she enjoyed her own company and was comforted by being alone. She liked that she couldn't see the world outside her classroom.

Her hands on her hips, Sophie appraised the current display board for literacy and knew deep down that she would need to change it before they started Monday's sequence of lessons on biographies. Tearing down the original backing paper with a satisfying rustle, she screwed it up as best she could, put it in the recycling bin and then climbed in after it to squash it down. And with it, some of the tightness in her chest from the day's events dissolved. There was something about acting like a child sometimes that was comforting. Simple pleasures lifted her mood instantly.

She collected the giant roll of backing paper from the craft cupboard and laid it down on the table, rolling it out to roughly the length of the display board. Then, on her way to collecting the scissors, she put YouTube on the computer and searched for show tunes. She didn't mind which ones came up – she loved them all. If they were sad she could wallow in the self-pity she was feeling following her conversation with Kate and Tom – and the argument with her mother. If they were all joyful and jazz hands, then she'd embrace the lift and hopefully feel a little bit better about everything. She did feel a little foolish for how she'd reacted on both occasions, after all.

Wrestling with the backing paper – holly-leaf green, of course – Sophie managed to smooth it out on the wall and staple it in place, which was always a genuine achievement, particularly if it was a one-man job. They didn't teach you the logistics of creating displays during teacher training.

While she printed and laminated useful vocabulary, her mind wandered to the meeting with Liam on Wednesday and she replayed it in her head, searching for where it had unravelled. Had she done something wrong? She thought about the way the conversation had gone. Had she said something awful? Had she suggested that Cassie was a terrible child or implied Liam was to blame for her negative behaviour? She thought her concern had come from a place of nurture and care, but now she wasn't so sure where it was all coming from. Surely she wasn't imagining Cassie's strange attitude? Time had a funny way of playing with your memories and turning them into something they weren't. She threw the idea of it being her fault out of her head straight away. Liam needed to know how his daughter was acting at school, if not to alert him to the fact that something was wrong, then to reassure him it wasn't just at home where she'd been playing up.

'I'm the Greatest Star!' came on over the speakers and as Sophie arranged her laminated resources on the wall, she began to sing along. She didn't share it often, but this was her favourite song. She often wondered whether she'd been born a decade or two too late. Sometimes she found the music would just take over her and, in her mind, she'd be on stage, a hundred lights blinding her.

She sang through to the chorus and closed her eyes for a high note, realising that she was standing on a chair that wobbled slightly beneath her. Something about singing when nobody was listening felt so freeing. This was Sophie's happy place. She stapled the display title along the top while she sang, before jumping off and throwing her arms up for the big finale.

Sophie let out a shriek and opened her eyes to see where the applause had come from. Kate filled the doorway.

'That was pretty good,' Kate said, taking a step or two inside the room.

Sophie couldn't work out if this was another example of Kate's sarcasm.

'How long have you been . . . ?' Sophie asked anxiously. She could feel a flush of colour creeping across her cheeks.

'Long enough,' Kate said with a smile.

'Oh.' Sophie busied herself again by Blu-Tacking interactive resources to the display, low enough that the children could come over and use them in their work.

'Why are you embarrassed?' Kate asked.

'Don't you know me at all?' She still didn't turn around, suddenly finding display-making to be essential work.

'That was great, Sophie. Like, really great.'

Sophie stood back to admire the display.

When she didn't reply, Kate said, 'I actually came to apologise before I left for the evening.' She lifted her bag to signal that she was on her way home. 'I'm sorry about before. Me and Tom, we both are.'

'It's fine,' Sophie said. She relented, put down her staple gun and walked over to where Kate was standing.

'Do you want to talk about what happened?' Kate asked, signalling the book corner, where they could sit and chat if Sophie wanted to.

Sophie looked at the book corner and considered having the conversation. But she wasn't ready. Not yet.

'I'm fine,' Sophie said. 'It's just been a busy week. You guys touched a nerve, and I got stroppy about it. It was my fault really. I'm OK.'

'As long as you're sure,' Kate said, giving her one last opportunity to share.

'I am.' She turned to fuss with more of her laminated resources and heard Kate go to leave.

'You know,' Kate said, turning back to her. 'You honestly should think about auditioning for the solo at choir next week.'

Sophie scrunched up her face. 'I don't think so.'

'No, really. What I just heard was awesome. You should think about it.'

'Bye, Kate.'

# Chapter Eight

'How is this week so hideous?' complained Sophie as she walked with Kate to the hall for parents' evening. 'I'm over it. Please let it be the weekend soon!'

'It's Monday,' Kate said dryly. 'And you only feel like that because you're dreading this.'

She was right. Sophie's weekend had been full of Christmas concert stuff: emailing sponsors, planning the playlist, formatting the programme. But despite how busy she'd been, she'd felt on edge about parents' evening the whole time. Last night was the worst night's sleep she'd had in a long time.

The hall was set up with desks that had been moved from adjacent classrooms. Each one had a chair for the teacher and three more for the families who would meet with them. None of the chairs were adult-sized. It was going to be an uncomfortable evening. Sophie sat down at her allotted table and plonked her head down on the desk.

'Good evening, Mr Hawthorn,' Kate said, louder than necessary to get Sophie's attention. Sophie sat up suddenly and pushed her hair back from her face, a rogue Post-it note stuck to her forehead. She fumbled to pull it off, scrunched it up and put it back down on her desk.

'Good evening, Mr Hawthorn.' She echoed Kate's words, attempting to assimilate a sense of calm. Inside, however, her heart was beating far too quickly. It was making her feel nauseous.

'Miss Lawson,' he replied, without emotion, and sat in the chair opposite her.

'Hello, Cassie,' Sophie added, as Cassie sat down next to her father. There was a moment of silence as Sophie waited for someone to speak before she realised it should be her.

'Well, let's start with you, Cassie. How do you feel about school at the moment?' She and Liam looked at Cassie. Cassie's face went from pale to bright red in an instant, or at least from what they could see of it underneath her long hair. 'It's OK. You can be honest. Are you happy?' Sophie prompted.

'It's all right, I guess,' she said after what seemed like an awfully long moment.

And realising that she wasn't going to get much more out of Cassie, Sophie started talking about the important bits before their twenty-minute slot ran out.

'Well, Mr Hawthorn, I've got lots of lovely things to say about Cassie.' Liam looked at his daughter and smiled. 'She has been working hard in all of her lessons and has been doing particularly well in her writing. She's a wonderful writer. Have you seen the Christmas story she's been working on?'

Liam shook his head. 'No, I haven't.'

Sophie pulled Cassie's book from the pile, opened it and turned it round to show her father. He pulled it across the table to have a closer look. His hand brushed lightly against Sophie's hand as he did so. She gave him a moment to read, and herself a moment to recover from the slightly odd feeling his touch had left her with.

What was going on? He was divorced, had a child, and from what she'd seen over the last week or so, seemed to be angry most of the time. And the balloons. Balloons, for crying out loud! Nothing good could come from a man who brought balloons to a date. Especially a man who had been nothing but rude to her since then.

She snapped back to the moment as Liam said, 'That's wonderful, Cassie.'

'It is, isn't it? Cassie has a really lovely grasp of language and is able to use techniques to create beautifully descriptive writing.'

Liam slid the book back across the table and almost smiled at Sophie. His eyes crinkled slightly at the edges, but the smile didn't quite reach a warmth.

'Let's talk about maths,' Sophie said, swallowing nervously. She was acutely aware of Kate sitting at the adjacent table, watching their meeting unfold. She knew she'd get the third degree after Liam left. 'I would say that maths is a little more challenging for Cassie.'

She looked to Cassie for some agreement, but her head was down and she was fiddling with the zip on her jacket.

'She does well but needs to make sure that she asks questions when she is unsure about how to work something out. She can be quite shy,' Sophie explained. She left a moment of silence, just in case Liam wanted to explain why Cassie might be a little quiet. When he didn't, Sophie continued to talk about how Cassie was doing in her other lessons.

She fumbled her way through the meeting, Liam's eyes never leaving hers. The problem was, he really was quite attractive and on more than one occasion, she lost her train of thought, only for a moment.

'So, my girl's doing good,' Liam said once Sophie had finished. He ruffled Cassie's hair.

Cassie squirmed to get out from underneath his hand. 'Dad!'

'Thank you, Miss Lawson.'

'Can we talk about behaviour?' Sophie said.

Liam's look changed from the happiness he'd felt at Cassie's report so far. His brow lowered. 'Go on,' he said.

It was invitation enough, but Sophie wasn't sure he really wanted to hear what she was going to say. She looked at Cassie and then back at Liam. This was her chance. She was really going to do this.

'Cassie has been a very well-behaved student since starting at Cranswell, but recently, I've found that she can sometimes react to certain situations in quite a . . .' Sophie searched for the appropriate word, 'negative way.'

'Really,' Liam said. He folded his arms across his chest as he sat back in his chair in an all too familiar way.

'It's not just the fight in the playground,' Sophie continued. She sensed his unease with bringing the situation up, but she could assure him she felt the same discomfort as he did. 'In class there are sometimes disagreements, sometimes over trivial things, but I'm sorry to say Cassie seems to be involved in them a little more frequently of late.' Sophie leant back from the table and waited for his reaction.

'Is this true?' To Sophie's surprise, he addressed Cassie.

Cassie wrinkled up her nose. 'No. I don't know what she's talking about.' She shrugged.

Liam turned back to Sophie. 'Can you give me some examples?'

'I can't believe you're siding with her,' Cassie said.

It was the loudest thing Sophie had ever heard her say, and as Liam and Sophie turned to react, Cassie pushed back her chair and stormed off. They watched as she left the main hall and flopped down into a chair in the corridor. Liam turned back to Sophie, his expression unreadable.

Sophie pulled her cardigan sleeves over her hands and rested them on the table. 'Cassie is doing very well academically.'

'But not socially. Is that what you're trying to say?' He ran a hand over his stubble.

'Of course not.' Sophie chewed the inside of her lip.

Silence.

'Look, Liam . . . Mr Hawthorn.' Sophie closed her eyes and took a deep breath. 'It's not unusual for children to behave differently when there's something on their mind, or if they have big life changes going on.'

Liam didn't speak.

'I just wonder whether Cassie might be dealing with something that we don't know about. We want to help.' She gave a friendly smile and willed him to respond. He didn't, his brow still lowered.

'I'm just worried about Cassie,' Sophie said.

'About *my* daughter?'

'It's my job to worry about the children.' She swallowed, her mouth suddenly dry.

'Are you trying to say there's something you think you should be worrying about? That I'm not a good enough father?'

Sophie looked away. She wanted there to be another member of staff listening in that she could use for support, but all the other teachers were engaged in their own, much more pleasant meetings. She looked back at Liam, his eyes brooding.

'That's not what I said, nor what I meant, Mr Hawthorn. Cassie's behaviour has changed recently. Children's behaviour changes for lots of different reasons. I was just trying to understand why Cassie might feel sad at the moment and find out if we can help in any way.' Foolishly, she pressed on. 'Is everything OK at home with Cassie's behaviour?'

As soon as she'd asked the question, she knew she'd made a mistake. Liam's face grew redder as she finished her question. When he responded, his voice was terrifyingly low.

'What do you mean by that?'

'Nothing. I don't mean anything by it.' She regretted having said anything at all. 'It's just that I've noticed her being a little withdrawn recently and then there was the fight, which isn't like her. I just thought there might be something going on,' she ventured. 'Something that maybe we could help with at school?'

Liam pushed his chair back and stood up. With Sophie sitting down, he towered above her. She noticed the muscles so clearly defined beneath his jumper and didn't know whether she was scared of him or drawn to him.

'There is nothing wrong with my daughter, Miss Lawson. She is fine. *We* are fine.'

'I'm sorry.' She spoke quietly and nodded piously. 'I just thought . . .'

'That's not what you get paid for, Miss Lawson. You get paid to teach.'

His words were vicious but his eyes were shining with the beginnings of tears. Sophie swallowed painfully. Her arms were crossed now, and she was up on her tiptoes under the desk so that she was one step away from being in the foetal position.

'Of course,' Sophie said, her voice trembling a little. She knew from the sensation of heat that her face had gone red. She wanted to cry at the confrontation, but swallowed down her tears.

'Good evening,' Liam said. He turned and strode across the hall, collecting Cassie from where she was sitting as he went.

It didn't matter how awful one of their meetings went, Liam Hawthorn had a way of ending it like a gentleman. That was what irritated Sophie the most. It made her feel like she'd been in the wrong somehow. All she'd wanted to do was support Cassie, and he'd shouted at her, belittled her again.

The grimace on Kate's face when she turned to talk to her only confirmed her suspicions.

'What did I do wrong?'

'That was brutal,' Kate said, rather unhelpfully.

Sophie groaned and plonked her head back down on the desk again.

But they didn't have a chance to discuss it any further because the conveyor belt of parents rolled around and the next lot were making their way over to their two desks, ready for their meetings.

'Night, love.' Liam put their copy of *Harry Potter and the Philosopher's Stone* back onto the bookshelf. It was his favourite time of the day. They had always read, the three of them together, and it was one aspect of parenting that he felt he was getting right. Perhaps it was even the only aspect he was nailing at the moment. Cassie transformed at this time of night, perhaps softened by the calm glow of the fairy lights that framed her bed – she was his little girl again. He stood and made to leave.

'Dad,' Cassie said, wriggling down under the covers. Liam turned back. 'Will you tuck me in tonight?'

His heart lifted. She hadn't asked him to tuck her in for a long time. He sat on the edge of the bed and tucked the cover around her, pausing to brush the hair back from her face and kiss her on the forehead. 'There you go.'

'Dad?' She wriggled around and rolled over, undoing his work.

'Yes, sweetheart.'

'I'm sorry about earlier.' She lifted her head and rested it in her hand. 'And I'm sorry about the fight.'

'That's all right, love.' Liam was acutely aware that a definitive parenting moment might just be about to present itself. He panicked and felt like he should say something more. 'I understand what happened the other day, and it sounds like it wasn't your fault.' He stroked her hair, wondering how much longer he'd be able to do it before his little girl was all grown up and she'd bat his hand away. 'I was sad to hear what Lily said to you, though – about Mum.'

He thought back to what Sophie had said earlier. If he was really honest with himself, he knew she was right. Something wasn't right with Cassie at the moment. He just hadn't quite got to the bottom of it yet, and it frustrated him that she'd called him out on it. He cringed to think of how he'd behaved at the parents' evening, his emotions once again getting the better of him.

'Lily is mean, that's all. She's always getting into arguments,' Cassie said, snuggling tighter and cuddling Baa Baa, who, at ten years old, looked a little worse for wear and was far more the grey sheep of the family after years of being loved. It amazed Liam how one minute she could go from the precipice of adolescence to his baby and back again so easily.

'Are you OK, though? I mean about Mum?' Liam asked. This. This was the important parenting moment he'd been anticipating. But even as he spoke, Liam knew he was blustering through it. It had been five long years since Emily had died. Cassie was so young when it happened. Perhaps now she was finally having to come to terms with it, especially since they'd moved back. His heart broke for her, and he swallowed down the lump in his throat.

'I'm fine, Dad. Let me sleep now,' she said, yawning and rolling over. 'Night night.'

Liam took the hint and left the room, turning the light off on the way. She'd not really answered his question, and that worried him more than any answer would have done. He felt sad to think she didn't want to or couldn't talk about how she was feeling. His jaw was set. He consciously relaxed it and felt some of the tension leave his body. Cassie was saying she was fine. But was she really?

Liam paused outside the bedroom door and considered going back in to finish the conversation they'd started. He decided against it and went to leave, taking two steps and then returning before forcing himself to walk down the stairs. Cassie would talk when she was ready and, in the meantime, he'd do what he could without invading her privacy or forcing her to talk to him before it was time.

He sighed, satisfied with his parenting decision, but sad that it meant he couldn't resolve the situation sooner. Something was niggling him.

Downstairs, he grabbed a beer from the fridge and slumped onto the sofa, flicking mindlessly through the TV guide and not choosing anything in particular to watch. He couldn't concentrate on what was on and his head ached from the day.

He thought about the parents' evening meeting at school and felt his face grow warm with embarrassment. Now, removed from the moment, he could see how stupid he'd been. Sophie was just trying to help, and he'd reacted horribly. He let out an audible groan and rubbed a hand over his face.

Every time their paths crossed, he seemed to do something ridiculous to upset her. He knew he'd have to apologise at rehearsal tomorrow, and the thought of admitting he was wrong made him squirm.

# Chapter Nine

'Were you late to work this morning?' Kate asked, tucking into her Tuesday night pub grub, as was tradition before rehearsals.

'It depends what you mean by "late",' Sophie said, deflecting the question. She squeezed her chair in to let someone pass. The pub was surprisingly busy for a Tuesday night.

'I mean, did you sneak into your classroom through the fire exit just as the morning bell had gone?' Kate raised an eyebrow. Clearly, she already knew the answer.

Sophie couldn't help but smile. 'You should have said. If that's what constitutes being late, then yes, I suppose you could say I was late.'

'What happened? That's not like you.'

'I had to pop to the printers again on the way to school. Steve called to say the flyers were ready but when I got there, they said "Chirstmas Concert" instead of "Christmas Concert".' She bit a chip in half angrily. 'Albert had spelt it wrong in his email and they'd just copied and pasted it, apparently.' She rolled her eyes.

'It's fitting, really,' Kate said.

'What do you mean?'

'They printed "Chirstmas", and it sounds like these flyers are pretty "cursed".' Kate laughed at her joke and reached over to her Diet Coke.

Sophie couldn't help but laugh, too. 'I can't believe they've got to print them for a third time. I looked at the mock-up on the computer before I left – that's what made me late – and this time, I'm hoping they'll do them properly.'

'Poor Albert.'

'Poor Albert? Poor me! I should have organised them myself. What an awful week.'

'It's Tuesday,' Kate said.

'I know. And it's already been hideous.'

'How come?' Kate asked, a genuine look of concern on her face. She rubbed the top of Sophie's arm supportively.

'I don't know. I'm a mess,' Sophie grumbled. 'Parents' evening was long, and it started so hideously with Cassie's dad.'

'Ah, you mean Cassie's dad who's about to lead the singing at our rehearsal?' Kate joked.

'Yes!' cried Sophie, burying her head in her arms crossed on the table. 'What am I going to do?' Her muffled voice travelled up through the gaps. Then she sat up and pushed her hair back from her face, still contorted with a lowered brow.

'It's going to be fine. Remember, you're the one who's in charge in all of these scenarios. You're the teacher. You're the concert organiser. You need to show him who's boss.'

It was a very 'Kate' response to such a situation. Sophie tried to imagine herself taking control and struggled to see it going any other way than her agreeing with everyone else in the scenario to avoid confrontation.

Sophie moved her chair in again to let someone pass. The

pub was nestled between the butcher's and the town hall, across the main street facing the green. It was cosy and felt like a village pub. The building oozed history from its Cotswold stone walls, which were covered with metal knick-knacks and miscellaneous watercolour paintings. Sophie's favourite seat was the little table in the window, tucked around the corner and out of the way, but still close enough to the huge open fire. The fire was roaring and their little pocket of the pub had grown warm with the intense heat. That, and it was packed. Their little corner of the pub wasn't really theirs any more. Sophie took off her coat and rolled up her sleeves.

'So, tell me what happened with Liam yesterday. I had to leave pretty quickly, and it seemed like you had a fair few appointments left when I finished. When I bumped into Tom at break time, he said there had been a follow-up grumble from him.'

It was true. Liam had phoned the head that morning to complain about how the school or Sophie – she didn't know which and hadn't asked – had dealt with things. It didn't surprise her. It had been a hideous parent meeting. If she'd been a parent, she would have probably complained too.

'It was awful. I knew it was going to be. Liam's one of those angry parents who don't see their child as ever having done anything wrong.'

'Always a tough one,' Kate agreed, nodding, and popped a chip in her mouth.

'He was fine when I was talking about the academic stuff but the minute I suggested Cassie might be going through something emotionally, he just changed and wouldn't hear it.'

'He's probably trying really hard, especially with whatever's going on with the mum. Maybe he's just oversensitive at the moment?' suggested Kate.

'You're not supposed to be on his side,' Sophie said, pointing a chip at Kate. 'Besides, I wish he'd realise I'm just trying to help. I'm worried about her.'

'They don't always see that, though, do they?' Kate said.

Sophie played with the last few chips on her plate and tuned in to the Bing Crosby CD that was playing softly in the background. While she listened, she weighed up whether or not to share her next thought. 'The thing is . . .'

Kate sat forward.

'The thing is, he made me feel a bit funny.' Sophie cringed as she spoke.

Kate grinned, understanding her meaning in an instant. 'So, you fancy him.' She said it like a statement rather than a question and leant forward, resting her chin in her hands.

'I don't know. Not really. My insides just did something odd,' Sophie admitted, scraping up the last of her ketchup with a chip and sitting back in the chair.

'You fancy him!' Kate shrieked, clapping like a wind-up monkey.

'Shh!' Sophie said, looking around to make sure no one was listening to their conversation. 'I don't. Not really. Besides, we decided that he's probably dealing with a messy divorce or an estranged wife or something horrible like that and he's always mean to me. Plus, remember, he's got a ten-year-old daughter. Not ideal.'

'But not impossible.'

'It's completely impossible,' Sophie said, deciding then and there that she would shake off these weird feelings when she walked into rehearsal once and for all. He was bound to do something irritating that would put her off. It seemed to be his style. 'Come on, we're going to be late for rehearsal.'

'We don't want to disappoint Mr Hawthorn now, do we?' Kate joked and got a jab in the arm from Sophie.

'I knew I shouldn't have told you,' Sophie said, reaching for her coat and wrapping it around herself, piling on her scarf and gloves, despite the short walk around the corner to the town hall. She didn't trust the hall to be much warmer than outside after last week. She helped Kate put her coat on too – her pregnant belly preventing her from doing it independently, without difficulty.

'Come on, you,' Sophie said, and they squeezed their way out of the pub.

Crossing the road, she looked up to see the stars dotted in the sky. It was beautiful and for a moment, she didn't even notice the icy breeze that had whipped up while they'd been eating. She pulled her coat around her tighter still and hurried up past the Christmas tree to the town hall.

Rehearsal hadn't started yet, and there was a hubbub of people chatting and catching up with one another. Sophie led Kate over to their seats in the middle, and they sat down.

'Yoo-hoo! Sophie, honey!'

Sophie looked up to see Lulu waving excitedly in a huge leopard-print coat, its enormous collar making it look like a leopard was actually devouring her head. Alarmed that Lulu could be sporting what was essentially a whole, real-life leopard carcass, Sophie was shocked into giving her a wave back.

'We're altos now. We gotta sit over here.' Lulu pointed to a seat that she'd saved next to her in the front row.

Sophie shot Kate a look, to which Kate returned a shrug. Sophie sloped across the room to where Lulu was waiting, not entirely relishing the thought of sitting next to Lulu and her dead animal – and right in front of their new and frustrating musical director.

'Sorry, Greg, excuse me,' she said as she squeezed past the tenors, who sat further along their row.

'Sorry, love,' Greg said, swinging his legs to one side so she could slide past. 'How did the flyers look? Albert said you were collecting them this morning.' His face was filled with anticipation.

Next to him, Albert slid a little lower in his seat and blushed.

'They looked great, Greg,' she lied. 'They just need a few tweaks and we'll start getting them out into the community.'

Albert shared a small smile of thanks, and Sophie slipped past them.

'Hello,' Lulu said when Sophie sat down. She pulled Sophie towards her, squishing her cheeks together in her hands, and added a couple of air kisses on either side of Sophie's face for good measure.

'Hi, Lulu,' Sophie said. 'How are you?'

'Fabulous, just fabulous. And very excited to be singing with you,' she added, grasping Sophie's hand in her own. The abundance of silver and gold that adorned her hands crunched against Sophie's bones, and when Lulu let go, she rubbed her fingers where Lulu's jewellery had squashed them.

'Right.' Liam's voice came from behind the piano, where he was rifling through music.

Sophie hadn't realised he was there. The hubbub waned, and everyone who hadn't yet found their seat shuffled into place. 'Let's get started, shall we? Now where are my new altos?' He caught Sophie's eye. 'Perfect.'

Sophie looked over at Kate, who was wiggling her eyebrows in mock seductiveness, and she quickly stuck her middle finger up at her. Kate laughed and snorted loudly before trying to style out her embarrassment. *Serves her right*, thought Sophie.

'So, this evening,' Liam said, finally pulling out the sheet music he'd been looking for, 'we're going to sing through the two numbers we did last week and then cover a couple more. Let's see if we can remember our harmonies.'

There was a collective groan. Sophie knew, without a doubt, that very few of them would have remembered their harmonies from a week ago. In fact, they would only really remember them in the final few days leading up to the concert itself. That was how it always was. The fear of an imminent performance was when the harmonies generally began to stick.

Liam continued, 'Then, at about nine-ish, most of you can go home and I'll run through the auditions with those that have signed up.'

Excited, Lulu squeezed Sophie's hand and let out a little squeak. She loved auditions and solos and the attention of it all. Even though Sophie wasn't auditioning herself, she felt a little knot of nerves in her stomach. It was important they got the right soloist for the concert to be a success – her concert.

'Let's have a go, shall we?' Liam said, lifting his baton. 'Let's begin with "Gaudette".'

The choir shuffled through their music to find the song, Sophie included. She was trying desperately to remember the alto line that Liam had taught them after rehearsal the week before. She didn't want to look foolish in front of him – again.

Luckily, when everyone sang, it came back to her. It was like muscle memory. Plus, it wasn't all bad that she was sitting next to a Hollywood legend – a Hollywood legend who was used to learning lines and music scores. Whenever Sophie was unsure about a note, she made sure that she tuned in to Lulu's voice and she would be OK.

Sophie breathed a sigh of relief when Liam announced that the main part of the rehearsal was over. She'd fudged her way through all the singing and avoided having to speak to Liam one to one for the entire evening.

'Thank you for this evening, folks,' Sophie said, standing to address the choir. 'We just need anyone who's signed up for a solo to stay behind and audition. Everyone else, if I can ask you to tidy up your bit of the hall and make a swift exit, I'll see you all next week. Thanks!' They applauded, as was habit at the end of a rehearsal and Sophie smiled as she looked out on their cheerful faces. They were an eclectic bunch, but she really did love them all.

'Let's have our potential soloists over here,' Liam announced.

Most of the choir were packing away their music and putting coats, scarves and hats on before they ventured out into the night.

'On my list I've got Lulu, Greg, Albert and . . .' He looked around the room and then back at the name in front of him. 'And I've got Sophie,' he said, sounding surprised to see her name on the sign-up sheet.

But perhaps not as surprised as Sophie.

'I don't understand.' Sophie froze and stopped putting her music away.

'We signed you up,' squeaked Kate, bouncing up and down as best she could at thirty-five weeks pregnant.

'We?' Sophie said through gritted teeth.

'Yes, we!' Lulu said, enveloping her in a fur-clad arm. 'We couldn't let that wonderful voice get out of auditioning.'

Lulu poked Sophie on the nose. Sophie tried not to find it patronising.

Sophie didn't know what to say.

'You're so brave, love,' John said as he passed her to leave.

'We knew you'd come through to make this concert a success,' someone else said, patting her on the back.

'We can always count on you, Sophie,' said Ethel.

'It's so lovely how determined you are to raise money for that charity of your mother's,' Greg said. 'She must be so proud of you.'

'Thanks,' Sophie said uncertainly and helped to pack away some of the extra chairs. Her fellow choristers' comments echoed in her ears and she realised that she would have to audition now whether she liked it or not.

'Go on. Liam's waiting,' Kate said, nodding her head over to where Liam was standing with Greg and Albert.

'We'd better join them,' Lulu said, scooping Sophie up to

join her in her direction of travel. 'Don't want them getting ahead of us, do we?'

'I really don't think I . . .' Sophie looked over her shoulder to mouth obscenities at Kate, but her back was already turned, and all Sophie got was a mouthful of fur trim from Lulu's coat.

Lulu patted her back as she coughed. 'Are you all right, honey? I hope it isn't your voice.'

'I'm fine,' Sophie said, thinking she was, in fact, distinctly not fine and plotting how she could get away with murdering both a pregnant friend and a Hollywood legend without becoming a suspect.

# Chapter Ten

The four of them sat down in a row of chairs that had been left out. Sophie turned her legs slightly to the side to accommodate Lulu and her oversized fashion choices.

'Why don't we sing through the audition piece together a couple of times as a practice to warm you all up properly, and then you can each sing it through as your audition after that?' Liam suggested.

Sophie's face grew warmer by the second as she desperately willed her body to relax and calm down. She unclenched her fists. It was just singing; she did it all the time. And yet, Sophie dreaded the music starting. With just four of them, there was nowhere to hide, even when they sang as a group. And then afterwards . . . Sophie couldn't even think about that yet.

The first time through, she listened and felt her way roughly through the notes. Then the second time she sang a little louder. The inevitable third time would come, though, and Liam would expect her to sing it alone. She felt sick and her mouth clamped shut as if defiant about letting any notes out. Her jaw ached from the tension.

'Lulu, do you want to start for us?' Liam said.

Lulu nodded and stood graciously, taking her time to get

into position before she began. When Liam started playing, she sang through the piece perfectly, having thought about how she would stand and gesture to put on a convincing performance. There was something about her that commanded respect and you could see she was embracing every minute, performing as if she were at the Albert Hall with an audience of thousands. Liam smiled as she sang. It made Sophie's anxiety rise further. How could she compete with that?

At the end, Lulu took a slow, theatrical bow and even gestured towards Liam and the piano as if they should applaud his musicianship too, like you would in the theatre.

'Great job, Lulu. That was wonderful!' Liam said, clapping as she finished.

'Thank you,' she said, sitting down to watch the others take their turn.

Albert from the rotary club was next and he sang the entire piece an octave too high, his eyes bulging as he realised the top notes he'd need to reach. It was tuneful but very, very high. By the end he was standing on tiptoes to get the notes out. Nevertheless, he too performed as if his life depended on it and even did a little tap dance during the four-bar instrumental.

When he finished, he curtseyed and Liam said, 'That was . . .' He grappled for the right word, 'an excellent effort. The dance was . . . inspired.'

'Thanks,' Albert said, grinning. He flushed with pride and sat down next to Lulu. They held hands, waiting for Greg to take his turn.

Greg's voice was lovely, but it was the voice of an older man, thin and tired. Sophie willed him to do well – he was one of the nicest people she knew – but she had to admit, it wasn't the best singing she'd ever witnessed. Poor Greg – he'd tried so hard.

Sophie was so busy congratulating Greg on his efforts when he came to sit back down that Liam's voice startled her.

'Miss Law . . . I'm mean Sophie.' She looked up at him as he held out his hand to offer her the stage.

This was it. She tried to ignore the fact that her legs were wobbly and stood up, making her way over to the piano. Slowly, she turned to face her audience of Lulu, Greg and Albert. Each one of them was grinning and she could feel the encouragement coming off them in waves. But the butterflies in her stomach were having a Christmas party, and she was genuinely concerned that she might just be sick right there on the floor in front of them. Her palms were warm and sweaty and her throat was dry. This was going to be a disaster.

The sentiments her friends had said as they left the hall echoed in her head. They all had faith in her; they knew they could count on her. Why couldn't she have the same faith in herself?

Her right knee was shaking out of control, and she swallowed a thousand times as Liam played the opening chords. She was determined to be ready and give a good performance. She just hoped her voice would hold out and not give away her fear. Opening her mouth, she began to sing.

A tiny sound came out. It was in tune and in time. Sophie was pleased that her voice remained even. By the end of the line, she had even started to relax.

'Come on, honey, give it some!' Lulu shouted.

Sophie hesitated but closed her eyes and imagined she was in the flat alone. She sang a little louder, and she surprised herself when it sounded good. The echo in the empty hall enhanced her natural singing voice and it sounded better than she expected. She sang louder still, letting herself go and relaxing into the music until she sang with complete abandon and enjoyed every single second, hitting the final high note with all of her power, the finishing echo causing everyone to wait in silence until the final reverberation had disappeared.

Albert's mouth dropped open. Lulu grinned from ear to ear and gave Sophie a thumbs up before applauding loudly and whistling through two fingers. Greg nodded in the way a father might to show how proud he was of his daughter. Liam didn't take his eyes off her. She knew she had impressed him. And she was glad. It was about time that she said or did something he couldn't argue with.

She realised she had tears in her eyes. She was truly proud of what she'd done. And judging by her audience's reaction, she'd done something right. They'd descended into cheering and whooping, and Lulu gave her a standing ovation.

'Well done, everyone,' Liam said. 'That was excellent.' He flicked through a notebook he had balanced on the top of the piano. 'Are you happy for me to email out the results this evening? It'll probably be about half past ten by the time I get home.'

Everyone nodded their agreement, and Liam wrote a note to himself in his book.

'Great,' Liam said. 'I'll see you all next week. Thank you for your auditions.'

Sophie stacked the four chairs up and put them against the

hall wall, while Lulu, Albert and Greg gathered their belongings and made for the door, chatting amongst themselves.

'Soph, have you got a minute?'

She turned at his voice, tidying the last chair away before she looked at her watch. She might have time, but she wasn't prepared to use all of it talking to Liam Hawthorn, especially if their conversation descended into anything like their other meetings had in the last week.

'Yes,' she said finally.

Liam put down his music and baton and walked over to her. He pushed his curls back from his face and looked at the floor. When he looked back up at Sophie, his eyes were bright. 'I just wanted to apologise for the way I behaved the other day at parents' evening.'

Sophie nodded, but didn't know what to say. She was taken aback by his apology – it was completely unexpected.

'And the time we met before that,' he added with an endearing, lopsided grin.

Sophie couldn't help but smile. 'You could have behaved better, perhaps, yes.'

'I know you were only trying to do your job.'

'I really was. But I won't push it again. You know Cassie better than I do. And I guess if you need my help, you know where you can find it.'

'I appreciate that.'

Liam made eye contact with her and for a moment, neither of them spoke. Sophie tried to stop herself from getting lost in his eyes, from noticing the crinkles in their corners. She shook herself out of it.

'Yes, well,' Sophie said, buttoning up her coat. 'I'll see you next week, Liam.'

'See you, Soph,' he said as she turned to leave.

Sophie found herself smiling, and she felt a little lighter as she walked down the street and along the brook back to her flat. Despite wanting to do some serious damage to Kate and Lulu for signing her up for the audition, she was a tiny bit glad that they had. Once she'd overcome her initial pang of terror, she'd actually quite enjoyed herself. And it was quite nice to think that she'd not done a terrible job of it either.

Her imagination flickered to the night of the concert: Sophie standing centre stage. Through the bright lights she could just make out her mother and father seated in the front row, applauding wildly at the end of her performance, pride written across both their faces. She'd pass her mother a wodge of cash from the ticket sales and they'd hug. It would be nice. She reminded herself that it was unlikely she'd get the solo, but smiled as she let herself into the flat at the thought of the possibility.

Sophie switched on the Christmas lights and made herself a hot chocolate. Something about her good mood made her decide to phone her mother and clear the air. They'd not spoken since their argument after school the other day.

After several rings, her mother finally picked up the phone.
'Hello?'

'Hi, Mum,' Sophie said. 'It's me,' she added unnecessarily.

'It's a bit late, don't you think?'

'Sorry. I thought you would probably still be up – which I guess you are seeing as you answered?' Her voice went up as if she was asking a question, lightening the grump her mother seemed to have answered the phone in.

'Well, yes,' June said, 'I suppose we are.'

Her mother was as stilted as Sophie had expected her to be.

'Look, Mum,' Sophie said, playing with a loose thread at the bottom of her cardigan. 'I actually phoned to say I'm sorry.' She gave her mother the opportunity to respond, but there was nothing. 'I don't want to fight with you.' She wanted to get the apology out of the way and hoped her mother would give up her uppity tone sooner rather than later.

'I appreciate that.' No apology. 'I don't want to fight with you either.'

Sophie smiled. That was as close to an apology as she was ever likely to get, and she would have to live with it.

'So, how are you and Dad?'

'Good thank you,' June said, her tone instantly more relaxed. 'We've had an excellent day today organising some of the big fundraisers for the new year.'

'That sounds exciting. I put the finishing touches to our flyers and posters today for the concert and added the charity name.'

'I hope they're finished and printed in time.'

Sophie ignored June's negativity. She was feeling happy, and she was determined not to let her mother get the better of her. 'We normally make quite a bit of money during the Christmas concert,' she continued. 'So I'm hoping we'll have a sizable donation for you before the end of the year.'

'That's kind of you, love.'

'Well, it's important to both of us, isn't it?'

'It is,' June said.

'I'm just glad I can help you out,' Sophie said. And she realised she meant it. The charity might have meant something to Sophie, but so did her mother's approval.

'It's much appreciated. It's nice to know we've got guaranteed money coming in.'

'I did something crazy this evening,' Sophie said, changing the subject.

'Oh yes?' June's interest piqued.

'I auditioned for a solo in the concert.'

'You did?' Her mother sounded surprised.

'I did. Well, I didn't plan on it, but a couple of my friends from the choir had signed me up behind my back, so I just sort of went for it. It was great.'

'Well,' June said after a long pause. 'That's very unlike you, Sophie. You do know that if you get it, you'll actually have to sing in front of people. Maybe hundreds of them.'

'I know.' She realised she hadn't thought about it all the way through to its conclusion.

'Anyway, it's getting late, love, and me and your dad are far too old for staying up past our bedtime.'

'Sorry, Mum.'

Silence.

'Mum?'

'Yes, love?'

'Can I come over for dinner soon? I've got a real hankering for one of your roasts.'

It had been over a year since she'd stepped foot in the family home. She hadn't been back since it had happened, but something had shifted and she felt like maybe it was time.

'Of course, love.' Sophie could hear the joy in June's voice. She was trying to play it down, though, as expected. 'We'd love to have you for dinner.'

'Great,' Sophie said, feeling pleased to have built a bridge with her mother.

'Good night, love. Good luck with the audition. Let us know how it goes.'

'I will. Night, Mum.'

June hung up the phone, and Sophie put hers down on the sofa. She smiled, pleased at herself for being the adult, apologising and making the first move in putting the past behind them, mending the relationship. And June had sounded like she genuinely cared about the outcome of the audition and – dare she even think it? – was proud of her for giving the audition a go in the first place.

Sophie allowed herself to dream and smiled at the thought of getting the solo. It wasn't the thought of singing in front of people that made her want it. No, that part terrified her. It was the thought of the applause and the acceptance afterwards that she really craved. She imagined the dust motes dancing in the lights that blinded her as she bowed to the crowd after a successful performance. Her fantasy in slow motion, she hoped it wasn't going to be too dreamlike. For a moment, she hoped it might come true.

Startled back to reality, Sophie reached for her phone again, where an email had popped up:

*Dear Soph,*

*Congratulations on a fantastic audition today. If I could have given you all a song, I would have done, but after much thought and a tough decision, I've decided to award the solo to Lulu.*

*Thank you for taking the time to audition for me. You were great.*

*Thanks,*
*Liam Hawthorn*

*Well, there goes my dream,* thought Sophie.

# Chapter Eleven

Sophie supported Kate as she lowered herself into the comfy chair by the window at the front of the coffee shop. In Kate's own words, she was the size of a whale and moving in general wasn't particularly easy or attractive. Once she knew Kate was comfortable, Sophie dropped her bags by the table and went to stand in line.

'Hi, Greg,' Sophie said as she neared the counter.

'Afternoon, love. What can I get you?' Greg slid his glasses up his nose and pushed his baggy sleeves up over his bony elbows.

'I think you mentioned something about a hazelnut mocha last week.'

'Ah yes, just a minute.' Greg turned to make the drinks and Sophie watched as a little girl of no more than two toddled around the sofas, wobbly on her legs. Her mother was busy talking to a fellow mother friend amidst the chaos of a very busy Friday afternoon in the coffee shop.

'Oops,' Sophie said as the little girl fell to her bottom. She looked up at Sophie, dazed, and held out a hand. Sophie took the girl's tiny, perfect hand in her own and pulled her up. 'There you go,' she said, as the little girl found her balance and toddled off again.

The mother looked around and called her daughter over to her, a tight smile on her face. Sophie opened her mouth to explain, but the mother was already cooing over her little one and adjusting the butterfly clip in her hair, while she texted using her free hand.

Sophie swallowed and bit her lip, turning at Greg's voice.

'Here you go, Sophie love.' He slid the two mugs over, both piled high with squirty cream and marshmallows. If she'd been paying more attention, she might have asked him to hold the cream. As it was, she'd had a trying week. Maybe cream and marshmallows were exactly what she needed.

'Better have a couple of those mince pies, too,' Sophie said on reflection. She placed everything on a tray and pushed her way through the crowds to where Kate was waiting at their usual table.

'So,' Kate said, her voice thick with pastry from the mince pie she'd just taken a huge bite of. 'Been on any dates recently?'

Sophie shook her head and then sipped her mocha. 'Nope. I'm still recovering from Balloongate. And look where that's got me. I don't think I could cope with any more complications or date-based coincidences in my life at the moment.'

Kate smirked. 'It will make a good anecdote, though.' She took a sip of her own drink. 'You know, when all the embarrassment isn't raw any more and you can talk about it without wincing.'

Sophie laughed. 'I'm not sure I'll ever get over the humiliation. Everywhere I go Liam pops up as if from nowhere. He could be here, right now, watching me!'

Kate snorted into her mocha, causing some to splash over the edge onto her skirt. She looked down at the stain and back up at Sophie.

'I suppose I'd better get used to being covered in stuff – it'll be all sick and poo next month!'

'Lovely.' Sophie pulled a face. She curled up on the chair as if she was in her own living room. The easy-listening Christmas songs that underscored the bustle of the coffee shop made her feel at home.

'He's not a stalker,' Kate said, returning to their previous conversation as she dabbed mocha from her clothes.

'I know,' Sophie said, as if Kate's comment was serious. 'It's just made me a bit wary of dating for now.'

'You can't stop dating for ever,' Kate said. 'You'll never find a boyfriend!'

'You sound like my mother,' Sophie said, her eyes flicking to the ceiling.

'I'm practising,' she said with a playful wink and a hand on her enormous belly.

'I guess I'm not that interested at the moment.' Sophie wrapped both hands around her drink and brought it close to her face for warmth.

'Any particular reason why not?' Kate raised her eyebrows so high they disappeared underneath her fringe.

'I don't know what you mean.' Sophie narrowed her eyes and spoke through clenched teeth, a warning to Kate to cease that line of questioning at once.

'Did you hear about how the audition went?' Kate asked, taking the hint.

Sophie had kept quiet about the email she'd received late Tuesday night. She was embarrassed to tell Kate that she'd been unsuccessful.

'Lulu got it,' she mumbled.

'Ah.' Kate smiled a smile of conciliation. 'Well, Lulu was a Hollywood star.'

'It's true,' Sophie said, laughing off the dull feeling of disappointment. If she was organising the concert – and she was – she'd probably have chosen Lulu too. Her name alone would get people through the door and they'd raise lots of money for charity, which was the important thing.

'Are you sure that there isn't any other reason you might be off dating?' Kate said. She narrowed her eyes and pointed accusatorially in Sophie's direction.

'I thought we'd moved on from this,' Sophie said.

'You might have done.'

'No. There's no reason why I might be off dating.' She painted on her best poker face.

'Sophie!' Kate said, a little louder.

Sophie blushed. 'No!' She laughed, knowing full well it would imply her guilt. She couldn't help it; Kate's third degree was making her squirm.

'I think the lady doth protest too much!'

'You made me protest by keeping going on about it!'

'About what?' Kate asked.

Sophie opened her mouth, nearly falling into Kate's trap. She closed it again. 'Nothing.' She groaned and rolled her eyes, shifting in her chair to give herself something to do.

'What about Liam?' Kate asked.

There it was. The elephant in the room. Brash as ever, Kate said it outright.

'What about him?' Sophie asked innocently, her poker face back, but her mind was wandering. There had been a few occasions now when his eyes had caught her off guard.

'Do you still fancy him? Even a little bit?' Kate said, bringing

Sophie back to their conversation and away from her scandalous thoughts.

Sophie screwed up her napkin and threw it across the table at her. 'No. There's no gossip here, if that's what you're after. It doesn't matter how I feel. Liam Hawthorn is emotionally unavailable, he has a child and I'm pretty sure he hates me. So, however I feel, it doesn't really matter, does it?'

'So you do fancy him?'

Sophie shook her head. 'Drop it, Kate. It's never going to happen.'

'OK.'

It always frustrated Sophie when Kate did that. An 'OK' from Kate was never the end of the conversation.

'I don't fancy him,' Sophie said again. 'I thought I might once, when it was possible the hideousness of the first date was a fluke. But since then, every time I've bumped into Liam Hawthorn everything has gone terribly wrong. I'm not sure that's a good basis for any kind of relationship.'

Kate acknowledged her point with a nod and Sophie felt like she'd won – this round, at least.

Until from the table opposite, Liam Hawthorn put down his newspaper and stood up, wrapping his scarf around his neck.

'Afternoon, ladies,' he said with a smile as he squeezed past them to leave.

'Do you think . . . ?' Sophie said.

'Almost certainly.' Kate nodded emphatically.

Liam smiled to himself and hummed a Christmas tune as he walked across town to pick up Cassie from her friend's house. He had to admit, Sophie wasn't the only one who'd been thinking that way recently. After rehearsal on Tuesday night, Sophie had made her way into Liam's thoughts more than once, and he found himself looking out for her now that he was going to pick Cassie up from school more regularly.

He'd not felt like this since Emily had died. And while Sophie's presence in his life made him feel lighter somehow, it was always accompanied with a tightness in his chest from the guilt. Finding someone like Sophie was surprising and sudden, which might explain why he was so horrible to her nearly every time he saw her – self-preservation and all that.

He thought about how embarrassed she must be feeling right now, thinking he'd heard everything she and Kate had been saying about him – which, of course, he had. He could imagine her flushed cheeks and she'd be nibbling her perfect bottom lip like she did when she was nervous. But it was nice to know, although it saddened him that she thought he hated her. Now maybe he could just relax around her and see what happened, perhaps go out of his way to be nice to her once in a while. He was definitely interested. The thought surprised him.

Cassie came bounding down the garden path as Liam made his way towards the front door to knock.

'Cassie,' he said as she ran into his arms. He pulled her back from him to see her face was covered in tears, her eyes red and cheeks blotchy. 'What's wrong?' Liam looked back along the path to see her friend's mother standing at the door. 'Jen, what happened?' Liam stood and walked Cassie back towards the house.

'I don't know,' Jen said. 'One minute she was fine, and the next she was upset. Amy says that Cassie tried to take something from her but I don't really know what's happened.'

'That's a lie!' Cassie said, the full force of her frustration coming out in a scream.

'OK, OK, love,' Liam said, stroking her hair. She shrugged him off. 'What did Amy have that you wanted?'

'You always side with everybody else!' she screamed, running away from the house and sitting against the garden wall. She hid her head between her knees.

'God, I'm so sorry, Jen,' Liam said, running his hand over his stubble. 'I don't know what's got into her recently. I'm really sorry if what Amy said is true. I'll try to get to the bottom of it tonight. And if she's taken anything, I'll make sure Amy gets it back. Sorry.'

Liam didn't get embarrassed very often, but he could feel his face getting hotter. He didn't know what was worse, Jen thinking that Cassie was a thief or Jen thinking he was a terrible parent. At this rate, Jen would think both.

'It's no bother. They've been upstairs playing together fine until about five minutes ago. I would've phoned, but I knew you were on your way.'

'Thanks,' he mumbled, and she closed the door, heading back inside to deal with her own distraught daughter, he guessed.

'What happened?' he asked Cassie again as he rounded the gate to where Cassie was sitting with her head in her hands.

Cassie sniffed. 'Nothing,' she said. Then she got up and began walking towards home.

'Come on, love, something must have happened for you to get so upset.'

'It's nothing, Dad.' She quickened her step and walked slightly ahead of him.

'Why can't you talk to me?' he snapped, his tone clipped and voice raised.

'I don't want to talk to you.' Cassie matched his tone and quickened her pace.

Liam knew that was the end of the conversation. And so he just followed her home. Helpless.

When they arrived at the farmhouse, Cassie went in first, took off her shoes, and went straight upstairs. Liam heard her jump onto the bed and then stay there for a long time. He hated that he couldn't do anything more. He knew she wasn't going to speak to him about whatever had happened. And even if it was just a falling-out or she had tried to steal something like Jen had suggested, it saddened him to think that Cassie didn't want to tell him or talk about it with him. What was he doing wrong as a father?

Sophie would know what to say. She would be able to get through to Cassie and he wondered whether working with her rather than against her on this one might help Cassie open up. Maybe he should apologise again and admit that, actually, she might be able to do something with Cassie that he couldn't. God knows she needed a mother figure in her life. He loved his mum, and she did everything she could to support them, but it wasn't the same.

His breath caught as he realised what he was thinking, and he made a silent apology to Emily.

When he checked on Cassie later, he found she had fallen asleep face down and fully clothed (*another parenting fail*, he thought). He'd not realised that as Cassie got older, parenting might become more difficult. Or rather, he had realised that; he had just been in denial and hadn't realised it would become so hard so soon.

# Chapter Twelve

Four weeks until Christmas

Sophie reread Kate's text message:

*Knackered after the check-up and final scan, so giving rehearsal a miss. Here's a picture of peanut so you don't hate me!*

Kate was right. The grainy black-and-white photo removed some of Sophie's hate. The outline of Kate's baby, the tiny hands clenched into little fists, one thumb in its mouth, thawed Sophie's initial wave of frustration. It didn't change the fact that Kate was sending Sophie to rehearsal without her sidekick, though. The possibility that Liam had heard their entire conversation on Friday in the coffee shop was racing round Sophie's mind and churning in her stomach.

To avoid festering in the flat alone as she waited for rehearsal to begin, Sophie went to the pub, ordered her usual chicken burger and Diet Coke, and sat reading until it was exactly half past seven. There was no way she was going to arrive at rehearsal until she absolutely had to. She was mortified that tonight's rehearsal meant dealing with the fact she'd not got the solo *and* the possibility that Liam had overheard their conversation the other day at the coffee shop. Even the thought of it being a possibility made Sophie feel physically sick with nerves. Her stomach flipped as she shuffled out of the booth and got ready to leave the pub.

Walking across the village green in the frosty November air, Sophie was met with the drifting sound of the choir warming up. If she went in now, she could slip into a chair at the back and go unnoticed. A shiver accompanied her cringe. She took a deep breath and pushed the door open. It creaked loudly as it closed behind her at the exact same moment that everyone was sitting down, and a sea of faces glanced in her direction. Including Liam's.

'Hi, Soph,' he said, standing poised to start at the front of the hall.

Sophie raised a hand sheepishly and gave a little wave before finding a spare chair at the back of the hall to sit on. Her coat stayed firmly zipped up in a subconscious attempt to keep herself hidden from view.

'I hope you don't mind us starting. It's just, you weren't here. Did you need to do any announcements or anything?'

Sophie shook her head. She didn't know what was worse: Liam taking charge of her rehearsal or everyone looking in her direction while he questioned her. She felt like all the things that could embarrass her were tattooed onto her face.

'OK. Let's start with "Gaudette" again today then.' Liam lifted his baton and the choir turned back to him. Sophie let out a breath she'd been holding, and everyone started to sing.

Sophie found her voice to be croaky, having not warmed up. Not only that, but her whole body was tense and uneasy.

That horrible feeling was lying in the pit of her stomach again. She felt like the embarrassment was eating her alive.

To make matters worse, Liam looked good tonight. He wore a Christmas jumper, which some may have deemed cheesy, but for Sophie only made him more attractive. He hadn't shaved for a few days, she noticed, and he was developing a darker shadow of stubble on his chin.

Across the room, his hazel eyes met hers frequently. He was looking at everyone, of course. But she became acutely aware each time they made eye contact and it made her shiver.

Oh God. Kate was right. She did fancy him a bit – as if she needed anything else to add to the discomfort of the situation. She couldn't focus when he was around, she'd become obsessed with his eyes and he featured in far too many of her conversations, even when he wasn't around. Sophie realised she was in trouble.

He occupied her thoughts until it was break time, the singing part of the evening passing by in a blur.

'Congratulations, Lulu,' Sophie said, reaching past her for a polystyrene cup of tea during the break.

'Thank you, honey,' Lulu said, enveloping her in a huge cuddle, tea spilling everywhere.

This week, Lulu's coat of choice was a bright yellow mackintosh that crinkled up and poked Sophie in the face as they hugged – but at least it wasn't a carcass and it was waterproof enough that the spilt tea ran right off it.

'You were fabulous too,' she said, releasing her.

'Well,' Sophie said, sipping her tea to hide her flushed cheeks. 'Not as fabulous as you.'

She realised just how disappointed she was, having missed

out on something she'd not even wanted in the first place.

Greg smiled sympathetically at Sophie through the serving hatch, as Lulu's attention went to someone else congratulating her for the solo. 'You were wonderful, love,' he added quietly.

'Thanks, Greg,' Sophie said, deciding that today was definitely a day for adding an extra sugar to her tea. She plopped one in from the plate on the side.

She wasn't really in the mood to talk to anyone, but Liam seemed to be doing the rounds and speaking to everyone as he sidled over for a hot drink of his own. Sophie ducked out of the hall and found her way to the toilet, locking the door and sitting down for no other reason than to escape the furore. Only when the noise had died down did she creep back into the main hall and take up her place at the back. She could do this; only a little while longer and she could escape.

'We're just going to go through the notes for the harmonies in "O Holy Night",' Liam said. 'And then, Lulu, would you be happy to stay and learn the solo music? We can put the two bits together at next week's rehearsal.'

'Wonderful,' Lulu said, looking around to soak up the adoring smiles she undoubtedly expected every time anyone mentioned the fact she was the soloist.

Every concert was the same. Sophie didn't begrudge Lulu her success. She'd worked hard for it over the course of her lifetime and she'd be sure to bring in a huge audience, all making donations to the charity. Plus, it was a minor triumph that Sophie would be able to escape rehearsal sooner rather than later.

'Soph?' Liam's address startled her. 'Would you mind coming round the front and joining the altos again? With Lulu singing solo, we could really do with a voice like yours to strengthen that middle section.'

She smiled at his half compliment and shuffled through the row of seats, avoiding the gaze of everyone as they turned to watch.

'Perfect.' Liam smiled at her and she averted her eyes. 'So, seeing as you've just made all that effort, let's begin with the alto line and we can build it from there.'

Sophie nodded. Her new seat was right next to where Liam was conducting from. She was so close she thought she could almost smell his aftershave, all pine cones and spice. His proximity meant that for the rest of the rehearsal, Sophie's head became a jumble of emotion. One minute she was feeling the flush of embarrassment and the next the heat of something else, something new. At no point did she manage to focus her attention on learning the alto line.

Just as she was thinking about how good he looked in his jumper, she dropped her music on the floor. It glided across the surface and landed at Liam's feet. She leant forward to pick it up as he reached down to retrieve it for her, and their hands brushed.

'Thanks.'

'You're welcome.'

Those eyes.

She sat back in her chair, again feeling the warm flush of embarrassment, her hand warm where he'd touched her.

She was glad when he announced that the main rehearsal was over and that he'd be working with Lulu for the rest of the evening.

'See you on Friday then, Sophie love,' Greg said once he'd

wrapped himself up in his coat and scarf. He picked up his chair to put it away. He only managed to lift it slightly and it dragged on the floor.

'Here, Greg. Let me do that.' Sophie took it from him and piled it on top of her own to ensure the room was put back to rights before anyone else used it the following day.

'Soph.' Liam pushed through the choristers getting ready to head out into the cold on their way home.

'Liam,' she said, lifting and moving the chairs across to where the rest of them were piled up next to the wall. He followed her.

'Perhaps this isn't the time or place to ask.' He held the back of his neck with one arm and looked uncomfortable.

'It sounds like you're going to ask anyway.' She didn't mean to sound defensive, but somehow it came out that way.

'I think you may be right that something is wrong with Cassie. In fact, I know there is.' He looked thoughtful. 'She's been behaving strangely for a while now, especially since we moved back.'

Moved back? That was new information. Sophie hadn't realised Liam had lived here before.

'I've noticed it more and more too, even since we last spoke.' She didn't want to think back to parents' evening, but it was true. Cassie had got into a few disagreements since they'd last met.

'Is there any chance we could have a proper conversation about it at some point this week? Maybe after school? I promise not to get angry and shout.'

There was definitely the hint of a cheeky smile, and Sophie relaxed a little. Despite everything, it appeared Liam was making an effort so that things weren't awkward between them. Maybe he hadn't heard everything she'd said in the coffee shop after all.

Sophie smiled. 'I could do next Monday at pickup time,' she suggested. 'Sorry, I'm a bit busy until then.'

'Monday's great,' Liam said, looking instantly relieved. 'I'll see you then.'

He gestured over to the piano where Lulu was flamboyantly singing through scales despite the lack of audience or accompaniment. 'I'd better . . .'

'Of course,' she said as he walked away. 'Bye.' She scolded herself as she realised she was looking at his bum.

Well, at least they'd broken the ice. That was something to take away from the evening. And twice now Liam had acted almost pleasantly. As Sophie glanced over towards where he was playing arpeggios on the piano, their eyes met briefly and he smiled, lifting his free hand in a slight wave goodbye.

Feeling better, Sophie made her way out into the night. She didn't want the solo really, anyway. It would mean more rehearsal time, more exposure to the audience. It would have been nice if Liam had thought she was up to it, but really, she'd dodged a bullet. Yes, it was definitely best that she wouldn't be singing anything by herself.

When Liam had finished rehearsing with Lulu, he packed up his stuff and walked back to the farm. He often regretted his decision to walk everywhere at this time of year, but it was his thing and he did it regardless. It was particularly cold that night and he had come with far too much stuff to carry it comfortably across town and down the lane to the family farm by himself. While it was a tiring walk, he enjoyed the fact he could see the stars once he'd left the glare of the town's Christmas tree. It was the thing he liked most about living out in the sticks.

While his conversation with Sophie had been short, he played it over again in his head. In the movie of his mind he couldn't help but focus in on her full lips as they curved into a smile, her faint blush as she coloured at the memory of their previous encounters, the way she tucked her hair behind her ear when she got nervous. She wasn't the same woman who'd been on that horrific date with him only a couple of weeks earlier. She was someone new, someone exciting, someone who made his heart race every time he thought of her.

It had been a trying time since their date. It wasn't just Cassie who'd been playing up recently. He had behaved awfully towards Sophie, too. He wondered whether it was coincidence or whether he'd been trying subconsciously to fend her off once he realised he liked her. It was the first time anyone had stirred him since . . . What were the chances that his child's teacher would not only be in the choir he'd offered to help out at the last minute, but also be the woman he'd been on his first date in five years with only a fortnight ago? His whole body cringed at the memory.

The balloon thing had seemed like a novel idea at the time. He was sure any girl would have been flattered to receive a gift on a first date, especially something so different and imaginative, thoughtful even. That's what he'd been going for, anyway. It was the last time he'd take advice from Cassie, even if he'd only used the conversation as a way of getting her to talk to him.

He regretted his decision the minute he saw her shivering

at the top of the hill near the car park. Her face was seared in his memory. He noticed how beautiful she was at first, and then how disappointed and confused she looked when she saw the gift afterwards. It only got worse in the pub, which was ridiculously busy and full of people. Balloons were not a great idea in such a small space. But it was too late by then. He'd made his balloon-based bed . . .

The conversation had been dire. Not because either of them was short on the personality and conversation stakes – he knew that now; Sophie was full of personality. But, because he'd spent the entire time cursing himself for thinking that a balloon bouquet would be a good idea and worrying about where the helium buggers would float next, he'd been too preoccupied to really show Sophie what he was about. He feared that she probably felt the same sense of anxiety, or worse, embarrassment. She mostly eyed the balloons warily. It had led to a stilted conversation where Liam couldn't focus on impressing Sophie with his usually dazzling wit and charm.

He'd certainly never expected to see her again at Cassie's school. He'd behaved appallingly, and he cringed again at the thought of his behaviour. She was only trying to help. Shaking his head in the darkness of the lane, he made a silent promise to behave better at their meeting next week and to be nice to her when he saw her. He really should stop pushing her away.

What he had to admit to himself now was that he quite liked her – and that voice! Wow! As an MD he had heard his fair share of singers, but Sophie's voice was something else. He felt bad not giving her the solo, but she was right, she'd be far too busy essentially stage managing the concert. Besides, Lulu van

Morris would definitely draw in a crowd and raise lots of money for Sophie's charity, which she seemed to be so passionate about. He just hoped he'd made the right decision – he didn't think she'd signed up for the audition herself. From the look on Lulu's face, and the fact Sophie's name had been scrawled in the same flamboyant hand and gold pen as Lulu's, he was pretty sure she'd been coerced.

Dumping his bits and pieces on the floor, he unlocked the front door to the farmhouse.

'I'm home,' he whispered, falling in through the door with his belongings.

'Hello, dear.' His mother's voice came from the kitchen.

'Hi, Mum.' He walked round to her and planted a big kiss on her cheek. 'Thanks for this evening.'

'It's no trouble, love. Cassie was an angel,' she said, drying up the last of the crockery.

'How much did Cassie pay you to say that?' he asked with a laugh.

'Can't say.' She mimed locking her lips.

'Well, thank you, anyway. She loves spending Tuesday evenings with you. I just wish she could be that happy all the time.'

'She is, love. She's just working through some stuff,' Barbara said, untying her apron and hanging it on the back of the kitchen door. 'I'd better get back to your dad,' she added through a stifled yawn.

'All right.'

Liam followed Barbara out to the front door and hovered in the doorway, shuffling his feet while she put on her coat and scarf.

'What's up, love?' she asked.

'Nothing. Why?'

'You're all nervous and on edge. What's going on?'

Liam swallowed. 'Do you think Emily's up there watching down on us all? Do you think she sees Cassie growing up? Does she see . . . me?'

'I'm sure she does, love. If there's a way she can look down on you both, she will be.'

Liam looked at his feet.

'What's this really about?' Barbara asked.

'Nothing. I just think about her sometimes and wonder what she's doing.'

'That's only natural.' Barbara reached a hand up to his cheek and kissed him on the other one.

'Do you think if it had been the other way round, Emily would have . . .' Liam considered the right way to phrase his question. 'Moved on?'

Barbara thought about her response for a moment, making eye contact and looking deep down into Liam's soul – the way that only mothers can. 'Would you have wanted her to?'

'You know, I genuinely don't know the answer to that question. I would want her to be happy but the thought of her and Cassie being part of a family with someone else . . . it breaks my heart.' His throat ached as he spoke, and his eyes pricked with tears.

'No one will become part of the family in the way that Emily was, love, no one. But families shift and they change. They evolve. But only after enough time has passed. And when enough time has passed, that evolution comes naturally.'

Liam nodded as he processed what Barbara had said.

'Come here,' she said, pulling him into a hug. 'The fact you're even asking means you're healing, that you're moving forward. You don't need to forget. You don't need to even get over what happened. But moving on with your life, bringing what you and Cassie need into it, that's important.'

'You're right.'

'I know. It's my job to be right.'

'Thanks, Mum.'

'Are you going to be OK?'

'I'll be fine. Love you.' He kissed the top of her head and watched her safely to her front door on the other side of the courtyard.

Then, after locking up, he slid a couple of his bags into the living room with a booted foot. He left them not quite in the middle of the floor, gave up, and went to the kitchen to get a beer from the fridge.

Flopping down on the sofa, his mind wandered to thoughts of Sophie. He was glad they'd spoken earlier that evening so that she didn't feel embarrassed about what he may, or may not, have overheard in the coffee shop last week. He was pleased they'd managed to have a civil conversation, too. Most of all, he was happy that they'd arranged to meet to talk about Cassie. Despite it only being a very tiny bit of a plan, he gave himself some imaginary good dad bonus points for the effort and settled down for the evening, trying not to think about the lightness he felt in his heart at having carved out some time to spend with Sophie alone.

# Chapter Thirteen

'Sophie!' June sounded surprised to see her daughter, despite dinner that weekend having been arranged. 'Come in, come in. You should have used your key.' She waved her hands as she spoke. Her cheeks were rouged from the heat of the kitchen, and the hair around her face stuck to the clammy skin at her temples. The heat from the hallway rushed out into the cold.

June pulled the door wide open and hurried back through the hallway into the kitchen, flinging a tea towel over her shoulder.

'I forgot it, sorry.' Sophie closed her fingers around the key in her hand and dropped it into her bag. 'Dad.' She smiled.

David filled the living room doorway, where, behind him, the TV was on, casting its dancing shadows over the walls.

'Sophie. How are you, love?' He stepped forward and drew her into a hug.

'What took you so long?' June's voice travelled from the kitchen down the hallway.

Sophie pulled away, and David gave her a knowing look as she traipsed into the kitchen.

'Sorry.'

'Better late than never, I suppose,' she said.

'The Tube took longer than I thought it would.'

Her mother tutted. Sophie took a deep breath. It wasn't like she'd missed the start of dinner. The kitchen was a discordant arena of chaos. Used pots and pans teetered on the edge of work surfaces, and the tap in the sink ran while the bubbles grew precariously close to the edge. The fan was on so that her mother was forced to shout every word. Sophie reached over, opened the window and turned off the tap.

'Is there anything I can do to help?'

'No, no. I've got it all under control.'

It didn't look like it. The oven beeped, and there was a faint smell of something catching on the bottom of a saucepan.

'It'll be five minutes. Why don't you go away and help your father lay the table?' June didn't turn around. Instead, she bent down to look through the oven door and waved her hand around behind her.

Sophie composed herself with a deep breath and went through to the living room. David was in his chair, which over the years had become fitted to the shape of his body. Even the arm rests had little divots where he liked to rest his elbows while watching his favourite programmes.

'She kick you out too?'

Sophie opened the drawer of the great Welsh dresser at the back of the room and took out the cutlery she needed. 'Afraid so.'

'Lucky escape if you ask me.'

They shared a conspiratorial smile.

He settled back into his chair and turned the TV up to signal the end of their conversation.

'Right, here we go.' June whirled into the room carrying

three plates with the salt and pepper caddies hanging from her forearm.

Sophie took the plates from her and set them on the table. 'Dad, it's ready.'

David struggled up from his seat with a grunt and settled himself at the table. Sophie passed him the third plate and took her own seat between her parents. It had always been this way. This was a house of predictability.

'How's work, Dad?' Sophie asked, reaching for the gravy. She poured a healthy portion into the centre of her plate and as it crept towards the edge, she willed it to stop. Out of the corner of her eye she could see June watching too as she settled into her seat.

'Not too bad, love. Same old, really.'

Sophie was relieved when the gravy came to a stop, millimetres from the edge of the plate. June relaxed too and the three of them set to eating in silence.

'And how are the concert rehearsals going?' June asked after a minute.

Sophie forced down her mashed potato, slightly on the lumpy side, with milk that was not fully mixed in.

'They're going OK.' She smiled across the table at her mother, whose eyes narrowed.

'Just OK?' She put her fork down to rest against her plate.

'Uh huh.' Sophie shovelled in another mouthful of the lumpy mash. If her mouth was full, she couldn't answer any more questions.

'You're hiding something.' She waved her knife in Sophie's direction.

119

'Not really. It's going well, honestly.' She spoke with her mouth full and nodded emphatically, struggling to swallow her latest mouthful. 'I didn't get the solo, though.'

'Never mind, love. I'm sure you did really well.' David smiled across the table at her.

'Thanks, Dad.'

'Well, who did? Who could be better than my daughter?'

'Lulu van Morris, actually. She often gets the solo in concerts. She's been performing for such a long time.'

'Hmm.' June didn't look up from her dinner, spiking pea after pea on her fork.

'She'll be good for fundraising. She's basically a celebrity and people will pay to see her.'

That caught her mother's attention. 'That's good, I suppose.'

'It is.' Sophie didn't know why she felt the need to labour her point.

'It's a shame you couldn't do it, though.' June smiled, but it didn't reach her eyes, her thin pink lips stretching across her face instead.

'Would anyone like something more to drink?' Sophie stood and reached for the now empty water jug in the middle of the table and didn't wait for a response.

While she waited for the tap to run cold, she rested her head on the work surface, the small, cool patch that wasn't covered in dirty dishes. Once the jug was full, she splashed some water on her forehead and neck, drying off the excess with a tea towel.

'Here we are.' She placed the jug in the middle of the table.

Her mother held out a glass. 'Aren't you going to pour?'

'I'll do it,' David said. He filled the glasses.

'I saw Jordan shopping in town with his mother last week.'

Sophie fought the urge to put down her fork. 'Oh?'

'They were Christmas shopping together. Isn't that lovely? Pam can't make it into town and back by herself any more. Such a caring boy.'

June stood to collect the empty plates. Sophie wished she'd put her fork down when she'd had the chance so that she now wouldn't be gripping onto it so tightly that it was hurting the inside of her clenched fist.

'Are you finished with that?' June nodded towards the fork.

'What? Oh, yes. Sorry.' Sophie dropped it down with a clatter.

'Do you ever think you'll speak to him again? Anything to rekindle?'

'Absolutely not.' Sophie pushed her chair back slightly from the table and folded her arms, digging her nails into the top of them.

'Hmm. Shame.' June carried out the dirty plates and returned with a huge trifle.

'God, Mum. There's only three of us.'

June placed the trifle down on the table triumphantly, and Sophie panicked for a moment that someone else might join them. Jordan? Surely her mother wouldn't be that outrageously stupid?

'Here you go.' June dished out huge portions of fruit and jelly and cream.

The room filled with the sickly smell of sugar. Sophie was already full and gagged at the thought of eating anything else. But it was trifle. And she knew full well that June wouldn't let her go anywhere until she'd eaten her bowlful.

'This is great, Mum.' And she meant it. It was all of her childhood birthdays and Christmases at once.

'We were thinking of redecorating upstairs,' June said after they'd eaten in silence for a minute or two, David making appreciative murmurs every time he put a spoonful of trifle in his mouth.

'That sounds exciting.'

'We thought we might turn your room into a gym.'

God, her mother was dropping bombshells all over the place tonight.

'What?'

Sophie had moved out of the family home over a decade ago, but it didn't stop her from feeling it in the pit of her stomach. Upstairs, her childhood bedroom was still exactly as it had been all those years ago. The wallpaper was covered in tiny pink flowers that matched the duvet set, which always graced her bed when she visited. The cupboard was plastered in every sticker she'd ever received from a successful visit to the dentist or doctor, and underneath the bed was a box of tickets and programmes and frayed friendship bracelets that took her back to that time. Even the smell of the trinkets when Sophie opened that box made her feel at home.

'Well, you know, love,' David said, 'you've been gone such a long time, and now that you've moved away from London too . . . we just felt it was time to spruce the place up a bit.'

The feeling in the pit of her stomach strengthened as she realised her father wanted to change it all too. It felt like she was being punished for something.

'We're going to put in a gym. Keep me and your father nice and trim in our old age.'

An image flashed into Sophie's mind of the pair of them in sweatbands, huffing and puffing their way through a weights session, and she felt an inexplicable urge to cry.

'Excuse me.' She pushed back her chair and left the room, June and David continuing to eat their ridiculous portions of trifle.

As was habit, she ran her fingers over the embossed wallpaper in the hallway as she climbed the stairs. In the bathroom, still a retro shade of avocado, she sat on the edge of the bath. It felt damp in there and Sophie realised that the old place probably could do with a renovation. But her room? It felt like such an invasion.

She went into her bedroom. The carpet was a deep purple, worn bare in places where she'd sat and played as a child. Sitting on the edge of the bed, she reached one arm underneath and felt around for the shoe box. It was a little dusty on top, so she ran a thumb over it.

It read, *Sophie's Stuff. Keep Out.*

All over the outside of the box was a combination of *I heart Jordan* and scribbles of *Mrs J Hummel*, where she'd been practising her signature should she and Jordan have ever married. It made her sick now to think of it. She didn't know whether the churning in her stomach was relief to have escaped such a heartless man, sadness at his having left her, or the aftereffects of June's trifle.

She lifted the lid and laid it gently on the flowery bedspread. Inside the box were torn cinema tickets, a couple of badges, notes she'd been passed at school. And the one thing she'd been avoiding for over a year.

Sophie picked up the grainy black-and-white scan photo and ran a thumb over the white shadow in the middle.

'Sophie, are you OK?'

She turned, surprised to hear her mother's voice.

Sophie nodded. June came into the room and sat on the edge of the bed next to her daughter.

'I just feel a bit sad that my old room won't be here any more, that's all.'

'I'm sorry, sweetheart. We didn't think it would bother you so much.'

'Neither did I.'

'It's just been such a long time since you've been here and things are gathering dust. We just thought . . .'

Except it hadn't been that long. She might not have lived here properly for over a decade, but she'd been to stay often and even moved in once or twice for short bursts. And the memories of the last time she stayed were still so vivid.

Sophie swallowed to compose herself and reached for her mother's hand. 'It's fine. And you definitely need to sort out that bathroom. *Homes Under the Hammer* would rip that right out.'

Her mother laughed and squeezed Sophie's hand. 'I'm sorry, we didn't think. I know that sometimes I don't think before I say these things. I just get so carried away with planning and things. You know me.'

Sophie squeezed her hand back.

'What's going on here?' David appeared at the door.

'The *Antiques Road Show* starts in five minutes and you know you want to see if there's a hidden gem worth thousands of pounds.' He turned and left – the expectation for Sophie and June to follow.

'Come on.' Sophie stood and pulled June up with her. She hid the photograph under some old cinema tickets and put her shoebox of trinkets back under the bed.

'Well,' declared her mother as the credits rolled. 'I'm stuffed. I'm growing my very own food baby right here.'

Sophie flinched.

'Another drink, love?' David asked.

Sophie shook her head, stood up, and stretched. 'No thank you, Dad.' She kissed him on the head. 'I have to get going. It'll take me forty minutes to get across town to the train station and I don't want to miss the last train.'

'I really wish you wouldn't gallivant around on public transport in the middle of the night, Sophie,' June said.

'It's nine o'clock, Mum.'

'Even still.' She set about puffing cushions and straightening the throw now that Sophie had stood. It was like she'd already left.

'Bye, Mum. Thank you for dinner. It was lovely.'

'You're welcome, sweetheart.' June leant a little closer and kissed the air on either side of Sophie's face.

By the time Sophie had hopped on two separate Tubes and emerged into the open air of Paddington station, it was cold enough for her to see her breath. She slipped on her gloves and shoved her hands firmly into her pockets for added warmth. She'd need a coffee if she was going to stay awake on the train back to Oxford.

She saw him just as she turned around to look at the departures screen. Across the platforms, on the other side of a slow-moving train, he appeared in between each of the carriages as they pulled out of the station. She pushed past the crowd of people staring up at the screen and when the train left, she could see it was him for sure. He had the same crop of jet-black hair and his signature long, dark trench coat. His briefcase, the one Sophie had bought him for his birthday two years ago, lay on the floor, resting against his shin. He was with another woman – a woman who looked vaguely familiar.

But the most surprising thing of all was that Sophie felt nothing. Her eyes didn't prick with unexpected tears. Nor did she feel the urge to race across the platform and throttle him. And there was no lurch from her heart, either.

Jordan was there, ripe for confrontation. But Sophie didn't care any more, and it made her feel a little lighter.

# Chapter Fourteen

Three weeks until Christmas

It was duty day again. Sophie hated doing duty twice a week enough as it was, but now, in the very depths of December, it was freezing. For as far as she could see above the houses, in every direction, the sky was grey and dull. The rain was sort of coming down – it was half sleet, almost snow, but not really enough to gather up the entire school and allow them inside. That would be even more chaotic than allowing them to frolic in it outside. Miss Davies, the headteacher, insisted it was good for them. It might be good for them, thought Sophie, but it was hideous for her. She pulled her coat around herself more tightly and checked that the zip was up as high as it could be for the hundredth time. She loved Christmas but relished the indoor activities that involved roaring fires and hot chocolate with marshmallows. Unless there were Christmas lights or mulled wine, the outdoors wasn't really her cup of tea, even at Christmas time.

Her strategy to keep warm in the predictably inclement weather was to walk in a figure of eight around the playground and the school building. Not only did she look like she was doing an excellent job of being on duty, but it also helped her to reach 10,000 steps on her Fitbit and build up a bit of body heat at the same time. If it worked for the children who ran around like greyhounds all lunchtime and then came into the classroom sweating and red, then it could work for her too. She didn't want to go too mad, though; being sweaty and red wasn't really the look she was going for, especially since her meeting with Liam was scheduled for today. But, of course, it really didn't matter what she looked like for that, did it?

As she rounded the corner to the main yard area, Sophie spotted a lonely figure on the friendship bench. Whoever it was, they were hunched over, staring at their shoes, while the wind whipped around them and all the other children ran past without a second look. Sophie made her way across the playground and sat down next to the child on the bench. When she did, they looked up and Sophie saw it was Cassie, hiding behind her hair.

'Hi, Cassie,' Sophie said.

Cassie didn't reply, and they sat there together for a couple of minutes in silence. Cassie shivered.

'I was wondering whether you might be able to give me a hand with something in my classroom,' Sophie said.

Cassie shrugged. 'All right.'

'Come on, then.' They walked together into the school building, Cassie dragging slightly behind her. It was only a few minutes until the bell and Sophie could see there were enough staff outside for her to disappear for the final few moments of lunch.

'Why don't you sit there next to the radiator?' Sophie suggested as she shook her coat off. 'I'll just go and get what we need.' She went into the cupboard and reached for the craft boxes, which she laid out on the table between them. 'I've been making some Christmas decorations for the class Christmas tree ready to decorate it on Wednesday. I've been a little busy, though, and I don't think I'll finish. Do you think you could help me?'

Cassie nodded but didn't say anything, her expression giving nothing away.

'You just need to do this.' Sophie took a red and a white pipe cleaner and twizzled them together until they were wound around each other. Then she bent the top over so that they looked like a candy cane and tied a thin piece of silvery thread to the top as a hook.

'Do you think you can do that?' she asked, passing her example to Cassie.

Cassie took it and rolled it between her fingers, considering the task. 'I guess so,' she mumbled.

Cassie took off her coat and scarf, Sophie was pleased to note. She hoped it was because she felt a bit more relaxed than she'd looked outside on the bench. They worked in companionable silence for a few minutes, twisting pipe cleaners together, looping the silver thread and making a pile of completed candy canes.

'How come you were sitting on the friendship bench today?' Sophie asked after a while.

Cassie shook her head. 'No reason.' She focused intently on the candy cane in her hand, bending the top over so that it curved perfectly.

'Cassie. Come on, you can tell me.'

'I'm fed up with everyone in this school, all right?' She raised her voice and looked down again as soon as her brief outburst was over.

Sophie gave her a second to recover. She could see Cassie's shoulders were tense and her mind was racing.

'What do you mean?' Sophie asked.

'No one wants to be my friend since we moved back.' Cassie sighed and took a deep breath. 'Everyone in our year is scared of Lily. If she doesn't like someone then everyone stays away from them.'

'And she doesn't like you at the moment.'

'Nope.' Cassie sighed again and put her finished candy cane in the pile.

Sophie didn't know what to say. How had Lily come to gain so much power in a primary school playground? And how hadn't she seen it before?

'Lily's the popular one,' Cassie continued, unprompted. 'When she says something, everyone does it.'

'That's sad,' Sophie said without thinking. 'I mean, it's unacceptable. Leave it with me. I'll sort everything out, I promise.' She realised that she'd come across as more emotional than she'd intended. 'I'll speak to Lily later today.'

'I thought someone might come and talk to me if I sat on the friendship bench.' Cassie bent the candy cane over that she'd just twizzled together. 'But they didn't.'

'Lucky I found you, then,' Sophie said, smiling at her.

Sophie thought she saw a small smile play at the corner of Cassie's lips, but it faded as soon as she'd noticed it – if it had ever even been there at all.

They continued to work together in silence. She felt rather than saw Cassie glance in her direction a couple of times. The third time, she said, 'Lily told everyone that I didn't have a mum and they all laughed at me.'

Sophie was always caught off guard when a child shared

something like this. It always surprised her how cruel the other children could be and how honest they were about things that had happened. Maybe this was her chance to get to the bottom of what on earth was going on with Cassie and why she'd seemed so out of sorts recently.

'What happened?'

Cassie didn't respond but continued to wind pipe cleaners around each other in silence.

'Cassie?'

'She told everyone Mum died,' Cassie said finally, putting down her decoration and picking at a fingernail. She wiped a sleeve across her face, and Sophie could see that she'd started to cry.

'I'm sorry, Cassie.' For once, Sophie didn't know what to say, and her throat tightened with emotion. There wasn't anything in the teacher handbook for how to deal with this. It saddened her to think that both Cassie and Liam had been forced to deal with such a tragic event.

'It's OK,' Cassie said. 'It happened before we moved away. I don't know why Lily is being so mean about it, though. I thought everyone would have forgotten. Why does she think it's funny?' she asked. Her nose crinkled up with incomprehension.

'Sometimes people laugh when they don't really understand something,' Sophie explained, bending her own candy cane over and cutting a length of the silver thread. 'It's because they don't know how else to react.'

'But it's not funny.'

'I know it's not, sweetheart. But to everyone else it's a difficult thing to talk about and so they might laugh to avoid talking about it.'

'Oh.' Cassie picked up some more pipe cleaners and twirled them again. After a minute or two she said, 'Why are you being nice to me? All I ever do is get into trouble.'

'Cassie.' Sophie stopped what she was doing and turned to face Cassie, making eye contact before she continued. 'It's OK to be angry sometimes. It's all right if sometimes you have arguments, if you get sad or upset, or even if you make mistakes. We all do it. It's how people deal with their emotions. And we learn from everything that happens to us, every decision we make. Nobody's upset with you for not always doing the right thing. We just want to know why and make sure that you're OK,' she explained.

Cassie blinked back her tears. 'These are pretty,' she said, holding one of the candy canes up to admire it.

'You've done a great job!' Sophie said, accepting that Cassie had listened but wanted to move on. 'Would you like to take one home for your tree?'

Cassie shook her head. 'No, thank you.'

'Are you sure?' Sophie raised her eyebrows.

'We don't put a tree up any more.'

'You don't?' Sophie put down the candy cane. She could barely disguise the surprise in her voice.

'No, not since Mum died.'

Sophie's heart broke for Cassie. Her mother had died, and she'd been denied the one time of year where magic happens, where everything could seem like it was all right. She felt a wave of anger directed at Liam, but it subsided as quickly as it had arrived. There was no way Sophie could ever comprehend how or why someone might act like that under the circumstances.

'That's a shame,' Sophie said. She felt desperately sad inside but didn't want to let Cassie see her judgement. If that's what Liam needed to do to cope with what had happened, then who was she to say otherwise?

'I can't remember before Mum died,' Cassie said. 'Not really. So, I'm not missing out on anything. Lily was mean about the Christmas tree thing too,' she added.

'I'll speak to Lily later today,' Sophie promised. 'You did the right thing to walk away and find the friendship bench.'

Cassie smiled and continued to bend over her candy cane. Her tongue poked out of her mouth as she concentrated.

'You know I'm meeting your dad after school, don't you?'

Cassie nodded.

'I'd like to talk to him about some of the things you said today. Is that OK?'

'Yes, that's OK.'

'Will you bring him into the classroom at the end of the day?'

Cassie nodded.

The bell went and the sound of cold, damp children coming in from the playground made Sophie spring into action.

'Why don't you take a candy cane anyway and you can hang it from a door handle or something?' Sophie suggested.

Cassie looked pleased and placed one in her coat pocket.

'Now go and pop your coat on the peg and we can start this afternoon's lesson.'

Cassie did as she was asked, just as the hordes came tumbling in through the door, ready for geography.


The afternoon rushed past, despite the children being slightly giddy at the prospect of snow and slightly irritable because of their clothes and hair being wet through. Sophie was pretty sure that they'd learnt something about precipitation, even if it was just through their lunchtime experience of it.

At the end of the day, she went out to the playground as she always did. Across the way, Kate was saying goodbye to her own class. She made a T shape with her hand and Sophie replied by holding up her entire hand to show she'd be five minutes. Kate raised an eyebrow and gave a knowing nod as Cassie led Liam by the hand over to Sophie.

'Hello again, Miss Lawson,' he said.

She liked that he kept it professional where his daughter was concerned. She had to admit, it sent a wave of something through her body when he addressed her so formally.

'Are we still OK to have a chat now?' he asked.

'Of course,' Sophie said. 'Shall we sit in my classroom and get out of the cold?' She'd popped out for her end-of-day duties in just her cardigan and was regretting it.

'No problem.' Liam held out his hand to indicate she should lead the way.

Sophie went inside, her cheeks burning and her whole body aware of Liam's presence behind her. She could feel him looking at the back of her head, her neck warm, and somehow her art of conversation, or even small talk, ceased to exist.

In the classroom, the three of them sat down around one of the desks, knees hunched up on the tiny chairs once again. This time, though, it didn't seem as funny. Liam fiddled with his coat and then his hands as they settled. He looked worried, a wrinkle in his forehead as he waited for Sophie to begin.

'So, Cassie was a little upset today,' Sophie said.

'Oh?' Liam looked at his daughter, who, for some reason, was looking at the floor and seemed to be ashamed. He brushed her hair away from her face. 'What happened, sweetheart?'

Cassie said nothing.

'Another child, I'm afraid to say Lily again, was being unkind to her.' Sophie paused. She was worried about giving him the details because she knew it might hurt him, and she didn't want him to react badly and walk away from the conversation again. What if it really upset him? Selfishly, and a little surprisingly, Sophie didn't want to see how he felt about another woman. After a second, she said, 'She was making fun of Cassie's mother.'

Liam nodded. 'I see.' He closed his eyes for a moment and when he opened them, he looked down at the table in front of him. Sophie searched his face to try and work out what he was feeling, but his expression was even, his hazel eyes glazed over slightly as he processed what she'd said.

'It doesn't matter, Dad.' Cassie broke the silence. 'Miss Lawson said that sometimes when things are difficult, people laugh because they don't know how to be.'

'Is that right?' Liam said. He looked up at Sophie and smiled, his face changing completely. 'Well, Miss Lawson is right. They probably think it's a horrible thing to have happened and just don't know what to say to you.'

He held Sophie's eye contact. His smile had reached his eyes. The tiny crow's feet at the corners crinkled with relief.

'Cassie was great today,' Sophie said once she'd found her voice. 'She sat on the friendship bench so I knew she wanted to talk and then we came in here and she helped me to make the Christmas decorations for the class tree.'

'You did, did you?' Liam put his arm around his daughter.

'Look,' Cassie said, getting her candy cane out of her pocket and holding it up to show him.

'That's lovely. Very good!' Liam took it and held it up to get a better look. 'Well done, sweetheart.'

'I hope you don't mind. I said Cassie could take that one home,' Sophie said.

He didn't know that she knew about their lack of Christmas tree, but she hoped that she wouldn't offend him with the gift.

'Of course not.'

'Miss Davies, the headteacher, is meeting with Lily and her parents now about what's happened over the past week or so. We don't tolerate bullying here. We will probably get the girls together next week for Lily to apologise to Cassie. I hope that's OK?' Sophie spoke tentatively, hoping that Liam would be satisfied they were doing all they could to keep Cassie safe and resolve things with Lily.

'That sounds great. Thank you for looking after her today,' Liam said.

'Of course. It was my pleasure.' Sophie felt lighter at his reaction, relieved that he trusted she was doing all she could, given the situation.

'Cassie,' Liam said. 'Why don't you just wait outside a minute so I can have a private conversation with Miss Lawson?'

Cassie looked up at her dad, slight concern written on her face about what they might say.

'Don't worry, I won't say anything too embarrassing,' he joked, tousling her hair. She got up and left dutifully, closing the door behind her.

Sophie found her mouth dry and could feel her blood

pumping. They were alone. Normally when this happened at school, he shouted at her. Today, something had shifted between them, but the uncertainty of how it was going to play out sent Sophie's heart racing.

'Thank you for today,' Liam said.

'That's OK. I was worried about her. It must have been a really tough time for you both.'

'It was over five years ago now,' Liam said, as if explaining it away.

'Still . . .'

'What I mean is, we dealt with it and we've moved on as much as you can after something like that. I think Cassie may be dealing with some delayed grief, though, and moving back here has brought it out of her over the past few months. I'm worried about her.'

Liam was suddenly vulnerable to Sophie. The worry was written in the lines on his face. Sophie felt as though she wanted to comfort him and take the worry away. It surprised her to feel so strongly that she wanted to make it better for him and Cassie.

'That's what I wanted to discuss with you today,' Liam said. 'How can I help her?'

'She'll be OK in time. It might be tough for a while but children are resilient. And we'll do everything we can do here to support her. She might make it challenging for you, but talk to her. And if she's reluctant, let her know that you're there to listen, whenever she's ready – even if it's in the middle of the night, or maybe several months from now.'

Liam raised an eyebrow. 'Months?'

'It can take time for a child to deal with grief. Actually, it takes a long time for any of us to deal with grief.' She swallowed to get rid of the slight tightness in her throat. 'It can be hard. But when she's ready to talk, she just needs to know that you'll be there.'

Liam nodded. 'That sounds doable.'

'I don't really feel like there's anything any of us can really "do" at the moment but it would be good if you could keep in contact with us about any changes or anything you notice at home and we can do the same.'

'That sounds perfect. Really, thank you,' Liam said and looked at her with those hazel eyes that made her insides feel funny.

'It's nothing.' Sophie smiled, suddenly nervous.

Liam stood to go, and she followed suit, opening the door to let him out.

'Thank you, Mr Hawthorn,' Sophie said, holding out a hand for him to shake. He took it, dwarfing Sophie's hand in his own. She noticed Kate lurking in the hallway, and, wanting to divert any suspicions she knew she'd have to deny once Liam left, she withdrew her hand quickly.

'Thank you, Miss Lawson. Really, thank you,' he said, his voice sounding lower and more serious than she'd heard it before.

Sophie returned his smile. 'Bye, Cassie, see you tomorrow,' she called.

'Bye, Miss Lawson!'

'Come on, you,' Liam said, scooping her up off the chair and heading out of the school building. Sophie watched them go.

'Staffroom, now, please! I want to know everything!' Kate said, pointing first at Sophie and then into the staffroom.

'Give me a minute,' Sophie said, ducking back into her classroom for a couple of deep breaths. She felt a little lightheaded and needed a moment. She looked at her hand where Liam had shaken it and tried to reconcile her feelings with the man who had been nothing but mean to her until recently.

'Right, you,' Kate said, crowding Sophie the minute she entered the staffroom. 'Sit there,' she said, pointing to the faded orange woven chair. 'And tell me all of it.'

'There's nothing to tell,' Sophie said, ready to deny everything. 'We met to discuss Cassie, and that's all we talked about. I think she's working through delayed grief.'

'Come on, Sophie. Don't change the subject. What's going on between you two?' Kate asked, ignoring Sophie's last comment and taking a softer approach.

Sophie knew what she was up to. 'Nothing, honestly. He asked me on Tuesday to meet with him today to talk about Cassie. He finally acknowledged that something's wrong with her.'

'That's good, I suppose,' Kate said, appearing to give in. 'Tea?' she asked, pouring herself a cup.

'Mmm, please.' Sophie studied the notice board while she waited and tore down a few out-of-date posters.

'It's nice that he's stepping up a bit. He's been collecting Cassie after school recently instead of leaving it up to grandma, hasn't he?' Kate said, passing Sophie her tea.

Sophie ignored the question. 'I don't think this is him stepping up.' Her clipped tone on 'stepping up' came out harsher than she'd intended.

The way Kate had spoken implied that until now Liam simply hadn't cared about Cassie. As far as Sophie could see, that wasn't the case. Liam wanted to be a good father; he was just struggling to know quite how to do it at the moment.

'I think he's finally able to acknowledge that Cassie's working through some stuff and he wants to support her,' said Sophie after some thought.

'It's taken him long enough,' Kate said, flopping down into one of the staffroom chairs.

'I think it was hard for him to admit that there was a problem.'

'It sounds like maybe he didn't want to admit it,' Kate said. 'These days, parents are so busy with their own lives that they just don't see their children or their issues.'

'I think, *actually*, it might be more to do with the fact his wife died, and he's having to deal with his own grief as well as Cassie's.' Sophie could feel her blood pressure rising. Kate was beginning to wind her up.

'His wife died?' Kate said, sipping her tea.

Sophie nodded.

'Wow, that's awful.'

'Yep, five or so years ago now.'

'You'd have thought he'd be a little more adjusted to it, though, if it was that long ago.'

'Kate!' Sophie put her tea down on the coffee table a little too forcefully and it sloshed over the edge.

'Well, you know. He's got a daughter to worry about. Maybe he needs to work through his own grief so that he can support his daughter through hers.'

'That's so unkind,' Sophie said.

'Is it? Sorry.' Kate rubbed her hand over her stomach.

Kate's apology seemed genuine, like her comments might have been the product of a tiring day. But Sophie's heartbeat throbbed in her ears and her eyes stung with the threat of tears.

'It takes a long time to get over something like that.'

'I know, you're right. Sorry, that was insensitive. This pregnancy is throwing me off. I'm just so tired and irritable all the time,' Kate said, laughing off her comments.

'It's not funny. The man's wife died. Sometimes people never get over something like that.' Sophie's voice was getting louder, and she thought her tears might actually come. She wasn't sure she could hold them back any longer.

'I'm sorry, Sophie. I didn't mean to . . . are you OK?'

Kate made to stand up, but Sophie shook her head and wiped a sleeve across her face.

'I'm fine.' She ran out of the staffroom and, for once, left school on time.


'So, do you want to talk to me about what happened today?' Liam asked as he and Cassie drove home in the Land Rover. Sophie's advice about being ready to listen was fresh in his mind, and he was eager to let Cassie know he was there for her.

'It was just what Miss Lawson said.' Cassie shrugged. She looked out of the window, deliberately avoiding eye contact with her father.

'I know what Miss Lawson told me. I just wanted to hear your version.' He indicated into the single-track lane that would take them back to the farmhouse.

Cassie shuffled in her seat and eventually turned so that Liam could just about see her face if he took his eyes off the road.

'Lily and a couple of the other girls were being mean about Mum. They were laughing at how we don't have a Christmas tree. They thought it was funny, that was all.'

Liam's heart twisted in his chest. This was his fault. The first year after it happened, he hadn't felt like putting up the Christmas tree, and Cassie had been too young to notice. After that, it had kind of become their own tradition. Emily had been the one who loved Christmas, and it hadn't felt right to celebrate it in the same way since she died.

'Do you want to put up a Christmas tree?' Liam said.

'Don't mind,' Cassie mumbled. That was code for yes. Liam knew his daughter, and if she avoided a question, then the answer was probably yes.

'Well, maybe we could put one up this year,' he said.

Cassie turned to look back out the window again. Every time Liam thought he'd made some kind of breakthrough with her, she pushed him back, and he felt as though he was starting again.

He tried a different tactic. 'Miss Lawson was helpful today, though, wasn't she?'

'Miss Lawson is always helpful, even though I'm not always very nice to her,' Cassie said, continuing to look out the window as they pulled into the courtyard of the farmhouse.

'What do you mean?'

'You know.' Cassie shrugged. 'Like with the fight and stuff. She never gives up on me, even when I'm naughty.'

'I'm glad you feel like she's there for you,' Liam said, putting the handbrake on.

He got out and walked around to help Cassie out of the vehicle. She reached for his hand and jumped down onto the muddy ground.

'You know I'm here for you too, right?' he said, bending down to hug her.

Cassie nodded. 'I know,' she said, before wiggling out of his grip and trudging over to the front door. Liam reached over her head to unlock the door, and they both went into the hallway and removed their shoes.

'Spag bol for dinner, sweetheart?' he asked.

'Yum,' Cassie said, smiling at last. Liam smiled back at her.

'Why don't you do your homework and I'll call you when it's ready? I'm sure Miss Lawson has set you something to get on with.'

'I have to practise the twelve times table for a test and there's some art stuff,' Cassie said, passing Liam her coat to hang up and bounding off up the stairs to get on with her homework.

Liam went into the kitchen and dropped his stuff onto the kitchen table. He began gathering the ingredients for dinner from the fridge and the cupboard while Sophie occupied his thoughts.

Sophie Lawson was burrowing her way firmly into every aspect of their lives. In the past, Liam would have been wary of such things, but there was something about Sophie that meant he didn't really mind. She had been nothing but kind to Cassie. While he knew Cassie wasn't wholly happy at the moment, whatever Sophie was doing, it was helping his daughter get through it. The fact they'd almost had a full conversation on the way home that evening was proof of it – and he was thankful. Sophie Lawson was in their lives and here to stay. Surprising himself, Liam was all right with that.

# Chapter Fifteen

Sophie woke up feeling wretched. Her argument with Kate had brought things to the surface she'd not had to confront for a long while and once home, she'd had a good cry and an early night.

She rolled over to check the time on her phone. One missed call from her mother and four texts from Kate. But more worryingly, she was running late. Throwing her phone face down on the bed, she jumped out and went to have a quick shower. She'd have to make do with third-day-unwashed hair.

She raced down the stairs, and into the underground car park, where she had her allocated parking space. Sophie threw her bag onto the passenger seat, quickly followed by her lunchbox, which had stubbornly refused to fit into the bag. On impact, the lid sprang off and salad and dressing flew everywhere. Sophie swore under her breath and then jumped into the car and sat, trying to calm down for a couple of moments. *It's just a salad*, she told herself, and put the key in the ignition.

When she turned the engine on, it grumbled for a few seconds before it popped and a plume of smoke, or steam, or something, drifted up from the bonnet. She turned the key again, but it just chugged and then cut out. Sophie swore again – at the car this time – and thumped the steering wheel before plonking her head down on it in exasperation. The horn beeped, and she jumped back up, the noise echoing around the underground car park.

Sadly, there was no one to call who could get there in time to help, so there was nothing for it. She would have to walk. She pulled on her bobble hat and did her coat up to the very top before calling school and leaving a quick message to explain the situation. Hopefully, someone would pick it up before her class came in and ran riot without her.

Sophie quickly learnt that the only thing more frustrating than your car breaking down, or blowing up, on a frosty December morning was being put on hold when you try to phone the garage. She had hoped to get through to them so she could arrange for them to meet her later when she got home. Having to listen to the deceptively calming music for the entire time it took her to get to school was intensely frustrating.

To make matters worse, it was cold and grey, and rain or sleet were likely on the cards. The thought of the forty-five-minute walk to school didn't appeal at the best of times, but when the first drops of sleet began to mottle Sophie's woolly scarf, she gritted her teeth even harder, her jaw aching from the tension and the cold.

By the time she reached school, she was seething, and an ever so slight headache had kicked in.

'Good morning, Miss Lawson,' the headteacher said as Sophie raced into her classroom. Her voice was laced with faint contempt.

She couldn't believe that the only person available to cover the first few minutes of the day was the headteacher. Sophie's cheeks flushed.

'Thank you for looking after my class, Miss Davies,' she said, taking off her coat and hat and hanging them in the craft cupboard. 'I can take it from here.'

Miss Davies nodded and Sophie made a mental note to try and do something to impress her later this week, when she wasn't feeling quite so hideous.

Sophie studied her class, their expectant faces looking up at her brightly. She had no idea where Miss Davies had got with them and realised that she would be winging literacy that morning.

With Cranswell Primary being such a small school, Sophie only just managed to avoid Kate all day. She didn't know if she still felt angry with some of the things Kate had said, or whether she felt embarrassed at her reaction and just wasn't ready to talk to her yet. Either way, she'd decided that avoidance and the silent treatment were the way to go, however petulant. She couldn't help the way she felt.

Avoiding Kate at rehearsal that evening was going to be trickier. At least she was singing alto now, so she had a legitimate reason to sit away from her.

At the end of the day, Sophie wrapped herself up warmly in her coat and bobble hat for the walk to the town hall from school. Rehearsal would begin shortly. When she arrived, she shrugged off her layers and laid them out on her chair to make it comfier.

'You look cold,' Greg said, pointing out her nose, which had grown so red in the freezing evening air that Sophie could see it shining if she looked down and went slightly cross-eyed.

'I had to walk from school. My car broke down.'

'Oh dear,' Greg said. 'I'd offer you mine, but I've not driven it for years. The old eyesight's been playing up for a while now.' He lifted his spectacles and wiggled them as if to demonstrate his point.

'Oh, Greg.' Sophie smiled and squeezed his arm. 'Have you seen Lulu?'

Sophie was aware that the seat next to hers was empty, and she hadn't heard Lulu yet, which was odd, because if you hadn't seen her, you could normally hear her. She looked around the room at everyone settling into their positions, ready for rehearsal to begin, but Lulu was nowhere in sight. Come to think of it, now she was looking, neither was Kate. Sophie felt a flash of relief and then an instant wave of guilt that she was pleased with her friend's absence.

Liam came in with his music stand, songbooks and other paraphernalia, and dumped them on the ground by the music cupboard before wheeling out the piano. He looked like he'd walked to get to rehearsal too and had carried with him rather too many things. Once the piano was in place, he fussed with them, opening up the music stand and sorting out music books.

'Evening, everyone,' Liam said once the noise had died down. He rolled up the sleeves of his burgundy jumper and pushed his dark curls back off his face. Looking a little ruffled, he flicked through one of the music books. 'Soph, are we OK to get started?'

She nodded.

'Excellent. Let's begin with a warmup, shall we?' He looked around the room and smiled. Sophie caught his eye and glanced down at her music, her heart giving a little lurch. She felt his gaze linger on her, and she tried to shake all thoughts of him out of her head. Absent-mindedly, she plaited the fringe on her scarf.

Greg pulled on the shoulder of Sophie's sweater, bringing her suddenly out of her daydream, only to realise that everyone else was standing and singing '1,2,3,4,5' to the tune of 'Knees Up Mother Brown' as a warmup. She stood slowly, in an attempt to stop Liam from noticing she'd missed the beginning – but of course he did.

When they'd finished, everyone sat down again and flicked through their music to find the first song. A low mêlée of chatter rippled around the room.

'So,' Liam said. 'We've got a bit of a problem.' He placed his hand on the back of his neck and pulled it forward, stopping to play with his ear.

At his words, Sophie snapped up to look at him. Silence descended on the rest of the group too, eager to hear what he had to say.

'What is it?' Greg asked, when Liam wasn't as forthcoming as he'd have liked.

'Unfortunately, our Hollywood star has had a fall and spent the last couple of days in hospital. She's fine,' he added quickly as the choir murmured their concern. 'But the doctor doesn't think she'll be able to do the solo, or even be in the concert at all.'

There was a collective gasp from the choir as they looked to each other for answers, or comfort, or something. This was a huge blow. Lulu's voice held the choir together. Without her, Sophie was loath to admit, they were just a group of misfits who got together for a bit of a singsong once a week. Sophie bit the corner of her nail while she worried about what they would do. Why hadn't Lulu phoned her?

'It's OK, though,' Liam said, louder now over the chatter. The panic died down. 'I've got a plan.' He winked dramatically, and a group of the elderly sopranos giggled together. 'So, for now,' he continued, 'we're going to do an hour of chorus bits and then, Soph, if you don't mind, I'd like you to stay for a while longer so we can work out what to do next. Is that OK with you?'

'Of course,' she said, pleased that Liam recognised she was organising the concert and that he'd need her help. She ignored the butterflies that were rousing from their sleep, keen to spend more time in Liam's presence.

'Excellent. Right, everyone, turn to page twenty-two.' Everyone shuffled through their music and Liam cued them to sing.

Hang on a minute. The solution didn't include Sophie singing a solo, did it? Surely not. She swallowed anxiously and dismissed the notion, her voice suddenly wobbly and unable to hold a tune.

The hour flew by as Sophie knew it would. By the time they had run the Christmas numbers, Sophie was convinced that Liam was going to ask her to do the solo. Part of her wished Kate was there and that they were talking. She'd know what the solution was. Or at least she'd help her find a willing victim – sorry, volunteer – to take Lulu's place. Instead, she spent the coffee break attempting to talk various people into it. She started by sowing the seed of an idea, but after ten minutes began asking fellow choristers outright. By the end of the coffee break, people were actively avoiding her as word spread of her mission.

'I'll see you on Friday,' Greg said as he packed up his music and put on his coat. 'We've got mint choc chip hot chocolate as a special and I'll throw in a candy cane biscuit too,' he added with a wink, leaving quickly to dodge Sophie before she could ask him to get involved as well.

'Sounds delicious,' Sophie said with a sigh. She knew what was coming.

Taking Greg's chair from where he'd left it, she piled it on top of the others, sliding a tower of them to the edge of the town hall to clear the room before everyone left.

All too soon, the hall was empty of people, but to Sophie, it felt fuller than it had ever done before.

'Are you OK?' Liam asked, leaning on the edge of the piano.

'Is Lulu all right? I'm surprised she didn't phone me.'

'She asked me to let you know, but the number didn't work. I must have written it down wrong.' He looked away when he realised he was vaguely referencing their date, where Sophie had given him her number in the first place.

'Oh, right,' Sophie said, equally embarrassed. She'd given him a fake number, and he'd tried to use it. A nervous laugh threatened to bubble up and out of her mouth. 'So, when you asked me to stay behind earlier, it sounded like you had a plan,' she said, changing the subject to avoid addressing the mysterious phone number situation. She sat on one of the chairs that had been left out, and Liam settled himself down on the piano stool.

'I have,' he said, avoiding Sophie's eye contact and tidying his piano music on the stand instead.

'Care to share?' Sophie asked when he'd not answered for a moment.

'How would you feel taking the solo?' He stopped what he was doing and looked up at her.

Despite knowing it was coming, Sophie had spent too much time trying to find an alternative soloist instead of thinking of a suitable response for when Liam asked her to step in.

'I know it's a bit awkward,' Liam said. 'You know, because you didn't get the solo in the first place.' He leant forward with his hands on his knees and grimaced.

'It's awkward *now*,' Sophie said. 'I'd not even thought of that.'

'Your audition was great. It makes perfect sense.'

'The thing is,' she said, unravelling the braid at the end of her scarf she'd plaited earlier, 'when I didn't get the solo before, it felt like a bit of a lucky escape, to be honest. I'm not sure I want to do it any more.'

'You didn't want the solo?' he asked, his forehead wrinkling. He ran a hand through his curls, looking frustrated and sexy.

'Not really. I didn't want to do the audition. You know Lulu and Kate made me,' she said, biting the corner of her nail. 'They signed me up while I was organising something else, and when you read my name out, I couldn't think of an excuse not to. You'd just turned up, and I didn't want to let you down. I didn't want to let the choir down. I don't know. It sounds silly now I say it,' she said, shrugging.

'But your audition was great,' Liam said again, smiling at her.

Sophie glanced up to meet his eyes. 'OK, so there may have been a moment where I thought it might be exciting to do a solo, but it was only for a moment, and now I'm back to not wanting to do it. Besides, you're right, you gave the solo to Lulu. There must have been a reason why I wasn't good enough.'

'I thought that with Lulu starring in the concert we might make more money for your mum's charity. She'll bring in the crowds.' He pulled out a piece of sheet music. 'Your voice is amazing.'

Sophie swallowed uncomfortably. He'd given Lulu the solo so they'd make more money for the charity. He'd seen how important it was to her. The butterflies in her stomach awoke a little more and hovered off the floor.

'What about Greg? I didn't have time to ask him this evening.'

Liam shook his head.

'I know a music teacher who comes into school on a Thursday who might help us out,' Sophie suggested, her voice full of desperate hope.

'There's really no one else who can do it,' Liam said, shaking his head again. 'You know the music, and your voice is strong. I want you.'

Liam was right, and Sophie knew it. She ran through the choir in her head, and there wasn't anyone else who could do it. Singing the solo might be the only way the concert could go ahead.

'All right,' Sophie said uncertainly. 'Maybe we could give it a go.'

'Have you got time now?'

He knew she had because they'd expected rehearsal to go on until ten. She couldn't lie and escape. Reluctantly, she nodded.

'Let's make a start.' Liam settled himself on the piano stool.

'OK,' she mumbled, suddenly very aware of the moisture levels – or lack thereof – in her throat. She swallowed again.

'Why don't you come and stand over here by the piano? Then you can follow the music as I play.'

Sophie made her way over to where he was sitting and stood slightly behind him. She had her own score and didn't put it down. It was always good to have something to hold when you felt nervous to stop you from fiddling. And Sophie knew she was a fiddler.

'OK, so let's go from bar fourteen, which is where you would come in. Here's your note,' Liam said, playing it for her.

He began the accompaniment, but Sophie didn't come in on her cue. Something stopped her from singing. Her throat felt tight, and her voice was stuck somewhere behind it.

'Let me just get a drink,' Sophie said once Liam had paused the music and looked round at her.

He smiled. 'No problem.'

She walked over to her bag. Sophie's hand trembled as she opened the water bottle. She knew that from across the room Liam could see she was nervous. The thing was, she didn't know whether it was because of Liam or because he was expecting her to sing alone. It was probably because she'd had about thirty seconds to consider whether or not she was happy to take Lulu's place and sing the solo. The audition had been one thing, but things had become very serious, very quickly. She made a mental note to kill Kate for getting her into this – and Lulu too, once she was feeling better. Then, thinking that death might be too serious, she vowed never to make either of them a cup of tea again.

'Ready?' Liam asked as she walked back over to the piano.

'Ready,' she echoed. She didn't feel ready.

Liam counted her in and played again. This time Sophie came in but pitched her first note wrong. Liam stopped playing.

'God! Sorry.' Sophie hid her face behind her hands. It was too embarrassing for words.

'Look,' Liam said, standing to face her. He put a hand on her arm.

Sophie tried not to flinch.

'If I didn't think you could do it, I wouldn't have asked.'

'But you didn't ask,' Sophie said. 'You gave the solo to Lulu. I'm just here now by default.'

'That's a good point. But I'm going to ignore it,' Liam said, his face breaking into that full lopsided grin that made Sophie smile. 'You can do this.'

A moment passed between them. Sophie could smell his aftershave and see the flecks of gold in his eyes. She wanted to reach out and run a hand through his curls. She wanted to close the space between them.

'All right. Let's go again,' she said, taking a deep breath.

'Why don't you close your eyes?'

'I'm sorry?'

'Close your eyes. Pretend I'm not here,' Liam suggested. 'That way, you won't feel embarrassed. Pretend you're singing in the shower or the car or something.'

Sophie did as he'd suggested. But instead of feeling more confident, it worried her more not being able to see his face or reaction. She took some deep breaths and opened her eyes again. She could do this. She didn't need any gimmicks or strategies.

She knew she could sing this song. She'd been singing it in the shower for weeks.

This time, when Liam began to play, Sophie sang. She started quietly but confidently, her voice strong and even. The slight vibrato on the long notes brought something more to the melody. It was going well, and she began to relax.

Sophie closed her eyes as she reached for the final top note, but missed it, her voice breaking at the pivotal moment. A silence followed as Sophie gave herself a second to recover from the embarrassment. Liam stopped playing.

'Wow,' Liam said. 'That was amazing. For a first rehearsal that was outstanding. It was supposed to be a sing-through but you've already got it, you know that?'

Sophie opened her eyes and looked down to where Liam was sitting at the piano.

'It was horrible. I missed the last note, and that's really all anyone is coming to hear.'

'Don't be so hard on yourself. It was just a run-through, Soph. You didn't hit the top note because you're nervous. The rest was beautiful.'

'You have to say that,' Sophie said. 'Because you need me!'

'Not true,' Liam said, flipping the pages of his music back to the beginning again. 'Well, a little bit true, but I'd have said it anyway.'

'Hmm,' Sophie said. She wasn't convinced.

'Right, let's do it again. But this time, let's try to add in some nuance. Like this bit here.' He pointed at some of the notes on the page. 'Let's leave this bit slightly quieter, so that when you reach this note, you can really go for it. Happy to run this section again and try it?' he asked, showing her what he meant on the music.

Sophie nodded, took another swig of her drink, and held one of her clammy hands in the other while Liam played the intro again. She felt dizzy as he got to where she was supposed to open her mouth and sing. She joined in late and fumbled her way through the bit Liam had directed her in, stopping halfway through.

'Sorry.'

'Let's do it again, shall we?' He pointed to the same bars on the sheet music.

But Sophie didn't think she could take the shame. She knew her face was red with embarrassment and her heart was racing so fast she was struggling to catch her breath. She was mortified that she couldn't just sing the song like he was asking her to. What was she thinking? There was no way she could ever do a solo. She'd been kidding herself.

'I'm sorry, Liam.' She grabbed her coat and bag from the chair. 'I can't do this.'

'Soph, wait.'

She heard him push the piano stool back and stand.

'Sophie!' he called out.

But she had already crossed the hall and fled.

# Chapter Sixteen

The cold air rushed at Sophie's face, knocking what little breath she had left out of her lungs. She hurried across the green and along the edge of the brook towards her flat, desperate to get in there and hide.

The muffled sound of steel drums rang out from within her bag. With an aggravated sigh, Sophie stopped, leant her bag on the top of some fencing and rifled in it to retrieve her phone, with only the light of the screen to guide her.

'Are you OK?' Her mother sounded concerned when she finally answered.

'Yes, fine. Why?'

'You sound a bit out of breath.'

Now she came to think of it, Sophie did feel breathless. She rested her arms on the fence and held her head in her hands.

'I'm fine, really,' she lied. 'Are you OK? Why are you calling?' She didn't mean to sound rude, but her tone was off and she knew it.

There was a rustling at the other end of the phone, and Sophie found herself feeling annoyed that her mother wasn't just getting on with it.

'How's the fundraising going?' June said, once the rustling

had stopped. There it was. There was always an ulterior motive with her mother. This was a business call, not pleasure.

'Slowly,' Sophie said carefully. Still acutely aware of her breathing, she stood and waited for the spots before her eyes to clear, using her free hand to squeeze her temples.

'Have you raised anything?' June's voice grew a little higher. 'Anything at all?'

'Well, you know, it's just . . .'

'Sophie, we're banking on a big donation. It's part of our plans for fresh initiatives in the new year.'

Despite taking deep breaths, Sophie was struggling to fill her lungs. Her mother's call was an ambush, and she wasn't mentally or emotionally prepared after the day she'd had. She wished she hadn't answered the phone at all.

'We'll raise plenty,' Sophie said, rubbing her eyes, tired. 'Historically, most tickets get sold on the door, so we'll do the bulk of our fundraising on the night itself.'

Her mother breathed a sigh of relief. 'That's good then. Have you got anyone sponsoring your programme or flyers or anything?'

Another question Sophie didn't know how to answer.

'We did have but there were a few issues, so I'm in the process of finding a couple of new companies and getting the flyers reprinted.'

'You mean advertisers pulled out? Or didn't you check the flyers before you sent them over? That's a costly mistake, Sophie, don't you think?'

The chastisement took her back to her childhood.

Sophie's temples throbbed. 'It wasn't my fault, Mum. They

changed their minds. Besides, Albert from the rotary club is in charge of publicity.'

'It rather sounds like he shouldn't be.'

'I can't do everything.' Sophie was annoyed on Albert's behalf, protective over her friend. She could almost hear her mother's lips purse together over the phone as she judged her.

'Well, hopefully with your Hollywood star doing the solo, you'll get a sizeable audience, which will help.'

Sophie swallowed uncomfortably and blinked back the tears that lurked just below the surface. There was no way she was going to drop that one on her mother just yet. She didn't need to know about her absent soloist until it was absolutely necessary.

'Yes, it should be great,' she lied, controlling her voice and keeping it even, too afraid to reveal the truth. 'Anyway,' Sophie said, before her mother had time to respond. 'I have to go. I'm nearly at my front door.'

'OK, love. Let me know how it goes. I'm happy to get involved if you need me to. Maybe I could be there on the night as a kind of representative?'

'Maybe,' Sophie said, not believing for a second that her mother would ever make it to something she was organising. 'Bye, Mum.'

She held the phone to her ear until June hung up. Her breathing had returned to normal, but it had been replaced with a tightness in her chest and she felt warm despite the freezing temperature. Her mum really knew how to press her buttons.

She let out a growl between clenched teeth and mimed throwing her phone over the fence. It slipped out of her gloved hand and she watched as it flew several metres and landed in the grass on the edge of the brook.

Sophie swore under her breath. There was only one thing for it. She crouched down to climb through the fence and padded along the bank. It was muddy underfoot. She knew that her beautiful shoes were going to be ruined.

Moving away from the fence, which she held with her fingertips for balance, she let go of her grip. After a few steps, she tripped on the uneven ground and fell in the mud. Her head landed on something sharp, and she watched as her phone slid further out of reach and into the water.

She blinked a few times, her vision a little fuzzy. Bringing her hand to her face, she felt warm blood coming from a cut. The skin was already tender around it. Cursing, she pushed herself up and waded into the water, reaching her hand into the murky depths to retrieve her phone. She was sure she'd read somewhere that an airing cupboard and rice could fix it once she'd made it back to the flat.

Footsteps came towards her down the path. Sophie knew she looked a mess and didn't really want to explain to anyone why she was wading in the brook and covered in mud and blood. She crouched down, realising too late that the cold water was deep enough to soak through her trousers and knickers, freezing her bum.

The figure walked past, a figure that she would have recognised anywhere. The silhouette of Liam's curls and the low hum of a melody as he passed gave him away instantly.

Sophie felt herself crouch lower still. There was no way she wanted to be found like this by him. She'd already embarrassed herself in front of Liam Hawthorn enough this evening. She didn't know if her heart or her stomach could take any more.

When the coast was clear, Sophie raced along the path to her flat and once inside set to covering her phone with rice and placing it on top of the boiler in the airing cupboard.

Moving to the bedroom to get out of her wet clothes, she caught sight of herself in the mirror. What a mess. A muddy tide line marked itself across her thighs, her shoes, trousers and coat ruined. Around her face, her hair hung in limp clumps, still dripping with muddy water. The mud on her face made her look like a marine, camouflaged, but not at all ready for battle. After the day she'd had, all the fight had gone. Her cheek was grazed. Tiny flecks of blood pooled where the rough ground had broken the skin. She sighed.

She wanted to call someone, but she had no phone. And even if she did, who would she speak to? Her parents wouldn't be interested, and Kate wasn't talking to her. And then there was . . . no one else.

# Chapter Seventeen

It was the light creeping through her curtains that woke Sophie rather than her alarm. It probably meant she had overslept . . .

It probably meant that she'd overslept! Again.

Cursing under her breath, she sat up, rubbing her face and realising too late that it had grown incredibly sore during the night. The brook, her phone, Liam, the solo. It all came rushing back to her and made her head hurt even more.

Stumbling to the bathroom, she looked at her watch. It wasn't as late as she'd feared, but she didn't have long to get ready and leave for school. The mechanic still hadn't been out to look at her car. And now she didn't have a phone to use to deal with the situation.

Her head throbbed like she'd downed a bottle of wine the night before. She felt hard done by to be experiencing the symptoms of a hangover without having enjoyed the merriment of wine the previous evening. It wasn't fair. Rubbing her head in a lame attempt to get rid of her headache, she took a quick shower and readied herself for school.

She rummaged around in the pile of rice in her airing cupboard to discover that the rice thing was a myth, before opening her laptop and finding five minutes to cancel her phone and order a new one. Thankfully, they would deliver it tomorrow, and she'd still have her old number.

The world outside was far brighter than Sophie felt. It was still dark, and the way was lit with Christmas lights illuminating shop windows, the winter sun just making its slow ascent above the horizon. It was quiet, but the few people who were already braving the cold were wrapped up warm, their faces ruddy and smiling.

Sophie pulled her scarf up a little higher to mask the bruise that had spread across her cheek from the evening before. It smarted, and she wondered what she was going to tell people at work. The truth was far too ridiculous.

Turning the corner, she almost tripped over an old, greying Labrador. The owner was a homeless woman, wrapped up in layers of tatty, old fabrics and sleeping on a pile of cardboard boxes. Sophie was surprised. You didn't see homeless people in Cranswell.

The Labrador stirred from its slumber and languidly raised its head to look at her before nestling back down again. The old lady reached out a gloved hand and rested it on her companion.

Sophie pulled a five-pound note out of her purse and rolled it up, placing it in the woman's hand. It was freezing, even in her coat and scarf, and she couldn't bear to see the woman suffering.

She heard a muffled, 'God bless you,' as she continued on her way.

Arriving at school, Sophie raced across the playground, keen to get to her classroom and set up for the day. Yesterday had not gone as planned, and she craved the normality of a problem-free school day.

A cry stopped her in her tracks. She turned, noticing one

163

of the reception children on the floor, hands out in front and looking stunned. She spun around and went to help.

'Goodness me, that was quite a fall.' She put on her cheery voice as the child pushed themselves up off the floor.

Their face was covered in an unpleasant mix of tears and gravel from the ground.

'Come into my room and we'll get you cleaned up.'

The child said nothing, but offered his hand. He snivelled and choked on his tears as Sophie led him into her room.

'You might get to be in this classroom when you get up to juniors,' she said, sitting him down and reaching for the first aid kit. He had stopped crying and Sophie was sure she caught a hint of a smile playing at the corner of his mouth and thought that his injury didn't look as bad as she'd first thought.

She was right. Once she'd wiped away the gravel from his face and hands, there was little damage done. But the shock must have surprised him. She found a Mr Men plaster and stuck it on his hand, even though it wasn't really needed.

'Good news,' Sophie said, standing up. 'You're going to be fine. Shall I take you through to the reception classroom?'

The boy nodded and Sophie walked him through to his classroom. As soon as he entered the door, he skipped off, saying, 'Thank you, Miss Lawson. You're the best.' Sophie smiled at that, the comment taking the edge off the past twenty-four hours.

Her spate of good deeds meant she was running very late, and she hadn't set anything up in time for the morning bell. She raced back to her classroom, flung her coat into the craft cupboard and began welcoming the children into her room. She played with her hair and arranged it so that it covered most of her face when she realised the children were noticing her bruised cheek. She wasn't entirely sure what her story was going to be, but by the time she saw another adult she'd have figured it out.

At break time, Sophie was pleased to find the staffroom empty. She'd spent the morning torturing herself with reruns of the rehearsal from last night and let herself fall into a grump. Boiling the kettle, she looked out the window at the children, screaming, running about carefree. When had she turned into a proper adult, and why was it so hard?

She jumped as someone came in the staffroom and turned around, brandishing a teaspoon.

'It's only me,' Kate said, holding up her hands to profess her innocence. 'God, what happened to you?' she asked.

Sophie adjusted her hair to hide the graze on her face and hoped that her blushing cheeks wouldn't draw attention to it like a neon bar sign.

'Nothing. I'm fine.'

'Come on, Sophie,' Kate said, taking a few steps across the room towards her, their argument forgotten, and lifting her hair to see what was lurking underneath. 'What happened?'

'I fell into the brook.' There, she'd said it.

'What?' Kate's tone said concern. The grin that spread across her face was the precursor to mirth.

'I tripped and fell by the flat.' Even Sophie smiled a little when she heard the ridiculousness of it all.

'You fell *into* a brook?' Kate snorted and laughed for a long time. Tears pooled in the corners of her eyes and she held on to her rounded tummy with one hand and leant on the counter edge with her other.

Sophie was laughing too.

Kate wiped her eyes with the back of her hand. 'How the hell did you end up *in* there?'

'I dropped my phone and tried to get it and one thing led to another . . .'

Cue another bout of laughter from Kate. 'Oh, Sophie! You do get yourself into some scrapes. Is your phone all right?'

Sophie shook her head. 'No. I covered it with rice and everything but I had no joy. I've ordered another one to arrive tomorrow.'

Kate laughed again until it subsided. Then she reached across and squeezed Sophie's shoulder and they settled into silence. 'I'm sorry about what happened the other day.'

'You don't need to be sorry. I shouldn't have got angry with you.'

'Maybe. But I think I was pretty insensitive. This pregnancy is turning me into a monster. I just didn't really think about what I was saying. Of course it's awful what Cassie and her dad had to go through. I don't know why I reacted like I did.'

'It wasn't all your fault. I shouldn't be so sensitive about these things.'

They shared a look, and Sophie felt guilty that she was keeping things from her friend.

'Do you want to talk about it?'

Sophie shook her head. 'Not yet.'

'OK,' Kate said, looking at her watch.

Sophie was grateful for Kate not pushing her. Since they'd

met, Kate had always been there for her. She hoped that would never change. Kate wouldn't disappear when she needed her in a time of crisis – not like Jordan.

'Time to teach.' Sophie returned her unused tea bag and mug to the cupboard.

'Wait. Before you go, you won't have seen this.' Kate pulled her phone out of her pocket and waved it in front of Sophie's face. 'Your mum's on Facebook.'

'Oh God.' Sophie took the phone from Kate and swiped through June's profile, already inundated with posts.

Her mother, who had only recently learnt about social media, let alone started to use it, had already posted three times since nine o'clock that morning. Once with a real-life story of someone who her charity had helped and two pleas for fundraising events and donations.

Sophie swallowed a lump of guilt. She'd expected cat videos and misspelt musings about breakfast foods, but June had used her profile to promote the charity and extend her reach. Sophie sighed. Without Lulu to sing the solo, the Christmas concert may not go ahead and she wouldn't be able to raise the funds her mother needed – and expected – from her. And even if it went ahead, their big named star wouldn't be there to drive sales. Sophie already knew how to solve the problem and she knew she'd need to step up and take the solo, even if it made her feel a bit sick.

# Chapter Eighteen

'Mr Hawthorn.' She could see Liam at the front gate, and Cassie hadn't made it out of the classroom yet. She took her chance and hurried across the car park.

'Soph . . . Miss Lawson,' Liam said, turning to see her racing towards him. 'What have you done to your face?' He lifted his hand towards the graze on her cheek before lowering it again, without following through with the gesture.

'Nothing, I'm fine,' Sophie said, brushing his question away. There was no way Liam would ever find out that she fell into the brook – worse still, sat down in it to avoid being caught by him. 'I'm sorry about the rehearsal last night.'

'That's OK. I know I sprang it on you. I didn't mean to—'

'I'll do it,' she interrupted him. She was breathless, the freezing air rouging her cheeks in the cold.

'You will?' A smile spread across his face.

'I will,' Sophie said, returning his smile. 'I'll just need a bit, or rather a lot, of practice.'

'That's no problem.'

'But we've only got a couple of rehearsals left.' Sophie bit her lip. 'Do you think we can make it work?'

'What if you came over to the farm at the weekend for an extra rehearsal?' He looked away.

Sophie felt her stomach twist and her heart do a double beat.

'Cassie won't be there,' Liam added.

Surprised at the invitation, Sophie said nothing for a second. Liam was inviting her to his house. OK, perhaps it was just for a rehearsal; it was business, if you like, but nevertheless, Liam Hawthorn had invited her over to his house. In fact, he'd said 'farm', hadn't he? She pictured him sitting next to a log fire or perhaps riding horses over the fields with Cassie at the weekend.

Liam took the decision out of her hands. 'Look, I have your number. Let me give you mine and you can text me to let me know later.'

'I haven't got a phone at the moment,' Sophie said quickly. Actually, he didn't have her number. He had the fake one that she'd given to him at the end of their terrible date. He'd already used it once, and it hadn't worked.

'Oh.' He glanced at her bruised face again and narrowed his eyes as he looked to be connecting the two.

Sophie would be surprised if he guessed right.

'Are you sure you're OK?'

'I've got a new phone coming tomorrow and my number will be different. Here.'

She took a pen out of her pocket and wrote down the number – her real number – on a scrap of paper. Liam tore a bit off and scribbled his own on it before passing it back. Thankfully, this way, he'd never know she'd given him a fake number to escape their original date. It was a silver lining in an odd sort of way. Thank goodness she'd fallen into the brook.

'Think about it and text me later this week if you think you'll have the time at the weekend. No pressure,' Liam said.

It wasn't the time she was worried about. It was the singing – and the being alone with Liam – that terrified her. She blushed and couldn't take her eyes away from his for a moment. There were so many reasons why it wasn't a good idea. The fact he was so very good-looking and a wonderful father and a musician weren't one of them.

'I'll think about it,' Sophie said, putting Liam's number safely inside her coat pocket.

Liam smiled. 'I'll speak to you tomorrow.'

The following evening, Sophie plugged in her new phone and left it to charge fully. As she sat reading next to the window, it vibrated right off the edge of the windowsill. Picking it up from where it dangled on its charger, Sophie swiped to read the message:

*Let me know if you're up for Saturday. I hope you're OK? L*

Sophie smiled as she sipped her hot chocolate. She used the message to save Liam's number as a new contact in her phone, then read for a little longer until she realised that she'd read the same page three times and still didn't know what had happened to Oliver Twist. She put her book down and reread the message. Three times. And then read two further pages of her book that she would need to reread again at a later date.

She wanted to go over to Liam's on Saturday afternoon to rehearse. There was no doubt about it. The problem was, Liam had ended his message with a question mark, which meant she'd have to reply. She was still worried about committing. After a moment she typed:

*I'm fine, thank you. I'll let you know about rehearsal. S*

Sophie read and reread the message several times before she pressed send, hoping that it sent friendly but not too friendly vibes. Once she'd sent it out into the ether, she sat back and finished her drink, checking her phone every thirty seconds for a response. A tick showed that he'd read it, but no reply. She read both messages again. There was no reason for him to respond.

Another hot chocolate was required. And more marshmallows. Oliver Twist would have to wait.

# Chapter Nineteen

Sophie picked glitter off her cardigan as she walked up to the staffroom. While she loved Christmas, school went a little to the extreme. She had glitter and glue everywhere and the kids were getting excitable with a fortnight to go until they broke up still. She was also getting a bit sick of the nativity. If none of the kids turned up, Sophie could perform it as a one-woman show, glitter and all.

'Here you go,' Kate said as Sophie entered the staffroom. She put a warm cup of tea into her hands.

Sophie took it gratefully, still wrestling with a stubborn sequin that appeared to be glued in her hair.

'Thanks, you're a star,' she said, and sat down next to Kate on the comfy chairs.

'Did you tell anyone else you fell in the brook?' Kate asked, giggling again the instant she'd said it.

'Kate! It wasn't that funny,' Sophie said, watching the tears roll down Kate's face.

'Ooh, but it was,' Kate said, barely able to control her voice.

'Actually,' Sophie said, despite Kate's giggles, 'I need your advice.' She turned in her chair to sit opposite Kate, face on.

Kate leant forward. 'I can help.'

Sophie smiled. 'Liam has asked me to do the solo at the Christmas concert. Did you hear Lulu's had a fall?'

'Yeah, I did. Is she OK?' Kate looked genuinely concerned.

'Fine, I think,' Sophie said.

'Are you going to do it? The solo?'

'I said I would, yes.'

'Wow, that's great, Sophie,' Kate said, a smile spreading across her face. She sipped her tea and then said, 'So what advice do you need if you've already said yes?'

'Liam asked me to go over to the farm at the weekend for an extra rehearsal.' She blurted it out and then hid in her mug, drinking half of her tea while she waited for Kate's inevitable reaction.

Kate let out a yelp. 'What?'

Sophie wondered whether she should have mentioned anything at all.

'It's just a rehearsal,' Sophie said. But inside, talking about it to her made her feel excited. She couldn't help but smile.

'Will Cassie be there?'

'No, she's away this weekend. I think she might be staying at her grandma's house.'

'So, it'll be just the two of you?' Kate asked, apparently thrilled with the turn the conversation had taken.

'Yes, but it's nothing,' Sophie protested. 'Remember, he's got a lot of baggage with past relationships. And, of course, a daughter who's in my class. I don't want to get involved in any of that and he's probably not really in the place for it either.' Sophie knew she wasn't justifying it to Kate; she was trying to convince herself why starting something with Liam would be

173

wrong – and that was just everything that he brought with him. She daren't think about Jordan or how she was terrified that the same thing could happen again. Even the memory of the pain physically hurt her.

'So, are you going to go?' Kate asked.

'I think I'd like to,' Sophie admitted, despite her worries. 'But only because I've got a lot to learn to be as good as Lulu would have been in the concert.'

'And that's the only reason,' Kate said, downing the dregs of her tea and getting up to rinse her mug.

'Yes. That's the only reason,' Sophie said decidedly.

Kate smirked. 'Of course it is.'

The bell went and Kate put the rinsed mugs upside down on the draining board. 'This conversation's not over,' she said, pointing a finger at Sophie in mock threat. 'I've got to run to nativity rehearsal now. But we definitely need to catch up about this again before the weekend.' She winked.

'All right.'

Sophie decided she would think carefully from now on about what to share in the future. She liked the feeling of her having something secret and precious of her own.

She thought for a moment back to how things had ended with Jordan, how it had taken her months to recover – physically and emotionally. Could she really let herself get involved with someone again? But then, every time she had a wobble about her feelings for Liam, she thought about his kind heart, his hazel eyes . . . and suddenly the worries she had dissolved and she felt happy. It had been a long time since she'd let herself feel like this.

She glanced down at her phone again, like she'd done pretty regularly since Liam's original text. But there was nothing. She felt deflated, but then remembered what the weekend might bring. The only problem was that he'd asked her to text him, to let him know, and the thought of it filled her with dread. She knew full well that the message, were she to send it, would have at least three rewrites and several edits. There were published books out there that would be less well written. Maybe she just wouldn't go. She pushed the thought to the back of her mind and turned into her classroom, ready for the afternoon session, which seemed to last for ever.

When the bell went to signal the end of the school day, Sophie led her class out to the playground and watched as they found their families and ran off to go home with them.

'Bye, Miss Lawson,' shouted one boy as he whipped off across the yard.

'Bye, Harry,' Sophie said, waving behind him.

'Bye, Miss,' said another.

'Thank you, Miss Lawson,' said the mother, looking exhausted from having spent the day caring for her other two toddlers. Her hair was dishevelled, and she had a Peppa Pig sticker attached to the sleeve of her cardigan.

'You're welcome,' Sophie said with a smile. 'See you tomorrow, Tallulah.'

'Miss Lawson?' Cassie sidled up to her and tapped her on the arm.

Sophie looked down at her and smiled.

'My dad's over there,' she said and pointed across the playground.

Liam leant on the fence, wrapped up in a dark jacket, scarf and hat. Sophie's stomach flipped.

'Off you go then.'

Cassie walked across the yard to where her father stood, waiting.

Liam looked up as Cassie arrived and caught Sophie's eye. She held his eye contact for a moment and then smiled, looking down shyly as he held up a hand to give a slightly self-conscious wave. He wrapped his arms around Cassie, who seemed to be a bit happier than in recent weeks. Sophie thought for a moment too long about what it might feel like to have Liam Hawthorn's arm around her own shoulders.

'You guys,' Kate said, rolling her eyes and breaking the moment.

'You guys, nothing, Kate. There's nothing to tell.'

Kate nodded, exaggerating her agreement. 'Of course not.'

As they bickered, Liam made his way across the playground.

'Miss Lawson,' he said.

As usual, his use of her full name made her feel giddy. There was something so Regency about it.

'Mr Hawthorn.'

He stood to the side, inviting Sophie to join him slightly away from the crowd of teachers and students waiting for their parents. He'd left Cassie sitting on a bench by the school gate.

'So, have you thought any more about rehearsing tomorrow?'

'Erm . . .' Sophie babbled uncertainly, acutely aware of Kate's proximity. Behind Liam, Kate's eyes had widened as she did an exaggerated nod and mouthed, *Say yes!*

'I was hoping you might have texted me again by now,' he joked, sensing how uncomfortable she was and playing with her.

'I . . . it was . . . I . . .' Where were the words? Sophie was never lost for words. She wanted to go, so why couldn't she just say so? This wasn't about feelings or romance. This was about the concert and making sure the solo happened so that she could raise money for her mother's charity.

'Look, how about I pick you up at around 2 p.m.? We can rehearse and then have a coffee or something afterwards?' Liam said, his eyes bright and his face smiling.

How could she say no? Now if only she could find the words to say yes.

'All right,' agreed Sophie eventually. 'But I can drive; you don't need to worry about coming to collect me.'

'No, no. It can be treacherous on the roads in these conditions. I'd rather know you were safe.'

'OK, well, thank you,' Sophie said, thinking how nice it was that he wanted to ensure her safety.

'Text me your address so I know where I can get you,' he said. Then, looking around to see Kate, he added, 'Thank you for your help, Miss Lawson,' and winked at her. 'See you tomorrow,' he whispered.

Sophie smiled. She was a schoolgirl excited about a first crush.

# Chapter Twenty

Sophie's flat was tiny. Having spent the last few hours attempting to make a critical fashion decision, she had now covered the place in discarded outfits and accessories. Sophie had every single pair of shoes that she owned out on the bed and a dozen dresses and tops hung up on any and every surface available that would take a coat hanger. Her cheeks were red and her hair a mess, having brushed it back off her face a hundred times in the process. She opened a window out into the December air. She didn't care that they were in the throes of winter. Sophie was warm. Really warm. And she needed to cool down – in more ways than one.

Lifting various items and accessories, Sophie searched for her phone. She found it under a pile of cardigans and scrolled through to find Kate's number.

'Kate!' She almost screamed when she heard the sound change and guessed that Kate had answered.

'Sophie. Are you OK?' Kate sounded genuinely worried.

'Yes, yes,' Sophie said, waving her hand about and then feeling foolish that Kate wasn't there to witness her body language. 'Look.' She sat down on the bed. 'I know I've been playing everything down until now, but Liam is due to pick me up in an hour, and I don't know what on earth to wear. I want to look nice,' she admitted pathetically.

'But it's just a rehearsal. What are you worried about?' Kate's voice was laced with faux concern.

Sophie could hear the glee dripping through the phone. Kate wasn't going to make this easy. Sophie would have to admit what was really going on here before she handed over any advice.

'All right.' She'd succumbed far quicker than she would have liked, but Liam would be there to pick her up soon. She was running out of time. 'I like him. This rehearsal is important to me, even if it just puts my feelings to bed.'

'Interesting choice of phrase,' Kate said, her smirk reaching Sophie through the phone.

'Oh, shut up!' She threw one of the tops she had already decided against onto the floor in mock frustration. 'Please help me! I'm all flustered and I don't know what to wear!'

'Just go smart-casual,' came the unhelpful response.

'I was kind of hoping for something more than that,' Sophie said, particularly disappointed given her admission only seconds earlier. She thought the trade was worth slightly more than that. 'I didn't just tell you I like Liam for your advice to be "smart-casual"!'

'I'm not sure I can really help. Just wear something that you're comfortable with and be yourself. Liam has invited you over for one of two things. Either he genuinely wants to rehearse, in which case you've got nothing to worry about. Or he already likes you too, in which case you've got nothing to worry about. He sees you all the time. He knows what you usually wear, so yes, go smart-casual. What you wear isn't going to have an impact either way.'

'You're right,' Sophie said, lying back on her bed. Her breathing noticeably slowed again.

'Of course, you probably want to wear something easy to get on and off and that you won't mind doing the walk of shame in.' Kate laughed wickedly.

Sophie groaned. 'Goodbye, Kate. Thank you for not being useful at all!' She hung up, putting her phone down on the bed beside her.

All she'd really learnt from her conversation with Kate was to be herself, which was not at all helpful. Being Sophie was to be a little awkward and a bit anxious all the time, and she couldn't help but think that wasn't particularly attractive to a member of the opposite sex.

No, she thought. She could do this. It wasn't a blind date from the internet this time. This was Liam. She sort of knew him. And he sort of knew her. And he knew what kind of clothes she wore and what her hair looked like normally, so there was no need to worry. He'd seen her covered in glitter and at her most embarrassed. It couldn't get any worse, could it?

Whatever she was using to justify things to herself, the truth was, time was passing, and she had no choice but to make some kind of decision – any kind of decision so that she didn't end up going over to Liam Hawthorn's house in her pants and bra. She shook a fleeting notion of what that could lead to out of her mind.

Sitting up with a groan, she brushed her hair and straightened it. She decided that jeans and a jumper would be laid-back and help her feel relaxed in what, for Sophie, would definitely be a stressful situation.

Time flew past far too quickly for Sophie's liking, and before long, her phone buzzed. Liam's text simply said:

*Downstairs.*

She told herself that she didn't have time to analyse the message and that one word really didn't warrant analysis, anyway.

Running the brush through her hair one last time, she grabbed her coat and doubled back on herself three times to check and check again that she'd turned her straighteners off before locking the door behind her as she left.

Liam was waiting at the front of her block of flats in his Land Rover. It was one of the big ones, where you had to go up a couple of steps to get into it. The sides were splattered with mud and Sophie could see from where she stood on the pavement that it was battered and well used. Standing on her tiptoes and peeping through the window, she gave a little wave. Liam popped open the door.

'I almost didn't see you there,' he said, laughing as Sophie held on to the door and threw herself up into the passenger seat. It wasn't a brilliant start. She couldn't imagine that there was a graceful way to get herself into a vehicle when the passenger seat was on what felt like the second floor, but she'd given it her best shot.

'Hi,' she said finally, once she'd settled into the seat and adjusted her clothes.

'Hi,' he replied, smiling. 'I'd have helped you in if you'd waited.'

Sophie grimaced – her first faux pas – she hoped not the first of many, although past experience didn't fill her with confidence.

'It's fine,' she said. But it wasn't. She'd literally launched herself into the car. She hid her embarrassment behind her hair.

Reaching for the gearstick, only centimetres from Sophie's knee, Liam put the Land Rover into first and pulled off, looking carefully in all of his mirrors as he did so. He noticed Sophie watching him.

'You can never be too careful.'

He seemed borderline obsessive of road safety. As they drove, Sophie tried to decide whether it was endearing or a little frustrating. It would have been a lot less stressful simply to drive herself over to the farm this afternoon. She wouldn't have embarrassed herself by jumping into his car for a start.

They drove for several minutes through the town in what Sophie hoped was a companionable silence. She glanced over at him and noticed the muscles in his arms tensing as he controlled the vehicle. He'd shaved that day and his hair was less unruly than it normally was. She desperately wracked her brain for something witty or interesting to say. Her heart was pounding in her chest and her throat was getting dry so that even if she could think of something to say, she was sure it would come out all croaky.

'Thank you for picking me up,' she said after a while. It was the best she could do.

'That's no problem,' Liam said, taking his eyes off the road for a moment to smile at her before looking back ahead.

'I would have driven myself, you know.'

'I know. But it's fine. Like I said, the roads can be

treacherous around here – especially the single-track ones near to the farm,' he explained. 'They get icy and never thaw out because of the hedgerows.'

'Well, thank you, anyway.' Then, after a moment, she said, 'How was Cassie after what happened the other day?'

'Fine, thanks to you. She really likes you as a teacher, you know,' Liam said. 'She might be going through a tough time at the moment – delayed grief or something, the doctor said. But she trusts you and is happy to talk about those difficult things with you, which I'm so grateful for. It's tough for her, not having a mother figure to talk to or guide her.'

'Well, I'm glad I could help,' she said after a moment, pulling at a thread at the end of her coat sleeve. 'I didn't know you were planning on talking to a doctor.'

'It felt like it was time.'

'Was it helpful?'

'I think so. It helped to put a few things in perspective, manage our expectations, that sort of thing.' He smiled a sad smile and glanced at Sophie, his eyes softening when he met hers. 'I didn't think moving back would be so difficult for her.'

They pulled into a single-track lane where the hedgerow was laced with frost. The ice hadn't yet melted, and the road was covered in lumps of mud thrown from tractors. All around there were fields, desolate and barren for now, hibernating and ready for spring to arrive. It was a pretty scene, though, and Sophie sat up straight to look out the window and get a better view. She seldom ventured out of town in this direction and she didn't realise how beautiful the landscape was out here.

'I can see what you mean about the roads,' Sophie said. 'Did you live on the farm before you moved away?'

They pulled left through an overgrown hedgerow and into a courtyard. Liam parked next to the farmhouse and turned off the engine. 'All my life,' he said, jumping out of the vehicle and making his way around the other side to help Sophie out. 'I grew up here, helping Dad on the farm and running riot in the fields with the animals.' His eyes brightened at the nostalgia, and he smiled. She realised she was staring.

Opening the passenger door, Liam held his hand out for Sophie. She took it and a wave of warmth rushed through her like they were conducting electricity. He helped her down to the ground and let her hand drop. She found herself looking at his lips and realised her own were slightly parted, too.

'Thank you,' she said.

He swallowed, then stepped back and held out his arm to indicate that she should lead the way.

'Have you always lived round here?' Liam asked. 'You don't seem the Cotswold market town type.'

'What on earth do you mean?' she asked, pretending to be shocked.

Liam laughed. 'Well, you don't look like you've ever been to a farm before for a start,' he said, looking down at her entirely unsuitable choice of footwear. Heeled suede boots weren't the best decision she'd ever made in her life. But then, after all the faffing and worrying, she'd not really had time to think rationally about her footwear before she'd left. She made a mental note to throttle Kate when she saw her next.

'No, I guess not,' she said. 'I moved from London last year. I was a city girl at heart, but now I love living here. It was definitely the right thing to do, moving to the countryside.'

'What was it that made you move?' Liam asked as they walked towards the farmhouse.

Sophie hesitated. 'My job.' She added, 'Mainly.'

'Come on in.' He held the front door open for her.

Sophie stepped past him and silently inhaled a breath of his aftershave. His hand brushed hers. An image of Jordan flashed into her head, changing the fluttering in her stomach into a feeling of nausea. What was she doing? She needed to stop this. It was a rehearsal, and that was all, she reminded herself. The Christmas concert was in a couple of weeks, and Sophie was getting nervous. She had the final flyers to get printed and distributed, fundraising pressure, and now she had to learn a solo, by heart, in about a fortnight. She didn't have time for anything else. She spent a moment steeling her resolve and telling herself to focus on the task at hand. And to stop fantasising unhealthily about Liam Hawthorn.

The house was empty and completely devoid of anything to do with Christmas. With a log burner and a voluptuous sofa in the living space, it still felt homely, but Sophie felt sad that Christmas hadn't arrived there yet. She imagined how beautiful it could look with all the festive trimmings. She remembered Cassie had said that they hadn't really decorated since her mother died.

Liam looked around the empty room and seemed to be embarrassed. 'I've not got around to decorating yet.' He unwrapped his scarf and discarded it, along with his gloves, on the back of the sofa. 'Tea?'

'Yes, please.' Sophie added her own jacket to where Liam

had laid his. She followed him into the kitchen, which centred around a hefty oak dining table and a dark green Aga, wondering whether to say anything else about the lack of Christmas decorations. She felt like she had an unfair advantage, having been told the reason by Cassie only the other day.

'Actually,' Liam said, filling the kettle with water, 'I was thinking about putting the decorations up tomorrow.'

'Oh?' That was new.

'Yes, well, I've been a bit of a Scrooge since Emily passed and Christmas hasn't really been that high on my list of priorities.'

'I'm sorry,' Sophie said, instantly feeling stupid about her pathetic attempt at sympathy. He must have heard it a million times.

'It's fine. It was a long time ago. This year I feel like things have changed a bit and, you know, might be getting back to normal.' He ran a hand through his dark curls. 'Sorry, you don't want to hear all this.'

'It's fine, honestly,' Sophie said.

Liam avoided eye contact by fussing with the kettle and mugs. Sophie watched him move around the kitchen while he talked a bit about the house and his childhood. He was nipped in at the waist but broad across his shoulders: the kind of man who could carry you out of a burning building.

'Here.'

Sophie smiled as Liam brought two mugs over to the kitchen table and they sat sipping them quietly for a moment. She realised she'd not been listening to him while she thought about him rescuing her from a fire.

'Shall we go and set up at the piano?'

Sophie nodded, and they went back through the living room to a door that opened into a music room on the other side. There were floor-to-ceiling windows and the winter sun shone through them, glinting off the shiny grand piano that stood in the centre of the room.

'Wow,' Sophie said, stepping into the room and feeling as though she shouldn't touch anything. The space was full of different instruments. Guitars hung from the three walls that weren't windows and a cello or double bass – Sophie didn't know which – stood upright in one corner. All of them looked terribly expensive.

'It was my grandfather's,' Liam explained.

Sophie turned, taking in the room, and dropped her gaze to the great expanse of a grand piano that filled the centre of the space.

'Is that where you got your musical talents from?' she asked.

'It's where it started, yes.'

He reached for two coasters and put his tea down on one. Sophie followed his lead.

'Right, let's warm up.'

Sophie stood, and Liam came to stand in front of her. He lifted both of his hands and put them close to her shoulders.

'Do you mind?' he asked, his eyes never breaking from hers.

She shook her head, and he rested his hands gently on her shoulders, pushing them back slightly so that her posture improved.

'Make sure your feet are wide so that you have a firm base and a strong core,' he added, pressing his hand on her abdomen.

When he released her and sat back at the piano, she could still feel the warm imprint of his hands all over her body.

'Is this OK?' she asked.

Liam looked at her and nodded. 'Perfect. Let's start with breathing and enunciation.'

They spent the next ten minutes with Sophie singing scales while making ridiculous animal sounds. She felt stupid, but it didn't take long for her to relax. There was something about Liam that made her feel calm, especially when he was in his element like this. It was the same trust she'd put in a professional, like a doctor.

'Why don't you sit while we talk through what I'd like to do with the song?' Liam offered, gesturing to the other half of the piano stool.

Sophie looked from the stool, looked at Liam and looked again at the stool, before sitting down next to him. It was tiny, and she found herself close to him, their arms and thighs touching. She breathed in his scent – a little too heavy almost, she thought, but it was so very masculine and something flipped inside her stomach again.

'Let's go from here,' Liam said, pointing to a bar on the sheet music. 'We can just sing it roughly through.'

'OK.' Sophie swallowed nervously. She hugged her arms across her chest.

'Don't forget you'll need the space in your lungs to sing.'

She uncrossed her arms and sat on her hands instead.

Liam smiled and started playing.

Sophie opened her mouth to sing, but her voice wobbled, even though she persevered through to the end of the song.

'What's wrong?' Liam asked after she had finished and he'd stopped playing.

'What do you mean?' Sophie said, her voice still cracking when she spoke.

'You don't sound like yourself.'

'I'm just a bit worried about doing this solo, I think,' Sophie said. A nervous laugh came from nowhere.

'You don't need to be anxious about it.'

'I can't help it,' Sophie said. 'Every time you play, my throat gets tight and my mouth goes dry and it's a miracle that anything comes out at all.' She sighed and let her chest fall. She looked at her shoes, her hands clasped tightly together on her lap.

'If what I heard at your audition is how you sing when you've got all that going on, I'd love to hear you when you're feeling relaxed.'

Sophie looked at him and smiled. He angled himself to face her and at this range she could finally see his face close up. The hazel eyes that had popped into her thoughts so often over the past few days were flecked with light gold and dark brown and his face was etched with age, but they were the kind of wrinkles that suggested a lifetime of laughter and smiles, despite what he'd been through.

'You don't need to be nervous.'

Sophie didn't know what he was talking about now. She guessed it was probably her impending performance at the concert, but they were so close that if either of them moved just a little closer, they would be close enough to . . .

Liam shifted on the stool and moved forward slightly, but Sophie turned to face the piano and cleared her throat. She couldn't do this. This was a parent who she'd already attempted to date. She knew she had nothing in common with him. But then Liam was so far removed from her memory of the hideous balloon date, she had to keep reminding herself he was the same guy.

'Let's sing it again,' Sophie said, turning the score back to the start. She stood, partly to improve her lung capacity and partly to break the spell of the moment. The piano stool was simply too small for them to share comfortably and risk-free.

Liam cleared his throat. 'All right.'

He played again and Sophie sang, better this time.

Liam's acceptance was enough to give her the confidence boost she needed to sing her best. She just hoped that her confidence stuck around for long enough to reach the day of the concert.

When she'd finished, Liam said, 'That was awesome, Soph. When you relax and nail it, you really are amazing.'

'Thank you.' She sat back on the stool next to him, making sure that there was a little more space between them this time. She desperately needed to calm the butterfly acrobatics that were going on in her stomach.

Liam went on to point out some areas that they would need to fine-tune and a couple of places where he wanted to mix up the dynamics.

'I was also wondering whether you'd like to sing this,' he said, pulling out some more sheet music from behind 'O Holy Night'.

Sophie took it from him and looked through it. '"White Christmas"?' It was a song from one of her favourite Christmas films. She'd watched it repeatedly with her father when she was little and they used to sing 'Snow' together, putting on all the individual voices. It brought a smile to her face.

Liam nodded. 'It's my favourite Christmas song and I think you could sing it really well. We could finish the concert with it. You could sing the first verse and then in the second verse the choir and the audience could join in. What do you think?'

'I don't know,' Sophie said, biting her bottom lip. 'The concert is less than two weeks away. Two or three rehearsals might not be enough to get both songs ready.' The familiar feeling of fear crept into her mind – and her gag reflex – again.

'I think you'd do a great job,' he said.

It wasn't much of a reason, but it annoyed Sophie by how much she wavered just because of his confidence in her.

'Can we try it at least?'

Sophie pulled a face. It was a bit of an ask and she would usually shy away from such a public responsibility. For some reason, though, she'd let herself get in too deep and she'd have to go with it now. There were too many people she might let down.

Liam said, 'You'll be fine. Ready?'

'As I'll ever be.' She stood and felt that familiar feeling of her throat tightening and her heart beating faster. It was any wonder she remembered how to breathe once the panic set in. How would she ever get through a real-life concert?

Liam played once again, and Sophie sang. It might have been a first attempt, but it was pretty much perfect. Of course it was. She'd been singing along to it for decades. She knew the words by heart, and the nuance of Bing Crosby was in her muscle memory. Singing 'White Christmas' was like pulling on a worn, old but cherished Christmas jumper. When she finished, they remained silent as the final reverberation from the grand piano strings echoed away into nothing.

'Do you have any idea how good you are?' Liam asked.

Sophie blushed and folded her arms.

'We're going to have to work on your confidence. You come alive when you sing and hide away when you've finished as if the audience is going to judge you harshly.'

'That's what an audience does, though,' she said. 'They judge you.'

'They won't be judging you harshly, though, Soph.'

The way he said her name, so casual, so familiar. It made her breath catch.

'They'll be overwhelmed by how wonderful you are.'

She smiled and unfolded her arms.

'That's better,' he said, turning back to the piano. 'Shall we try it again? This time I want you to really focus on your intonation.'

'OK.' She nodded and began to sing.

'Posture,' Liam prompted, and she stood like he'd shown her before.

The afternoon flew by in Liam's company and before long the sun was setting and the music room grew dark. Liam got up and turned on the lamp that sat on the sideboard.

'Thank you for this afternoon,' Sophie said. 'I'm feeling much better about the whole thing and we've still got a couple of weeks' practice.'

'You're going to blow everyone away on the night.'

'I hope so.' She moved across towards the window to look out over the fields as the sun cast its long shadows across the icy furrows. 'I suppose I ought to get going,' she said, a little disappointed that the day had passed so quickly.

'You don't have to,' Liam said.

Sophie turned to face him.

'I thought maybe you could help me decorate the tree,' he added.

She was surprised by his proposal. 'Don't you want to wait and do it with Cassie?'

'Cassie's having a sleepover at Mum's until tomorrow afternoon and if I don't get it done before then, the run-up to Christmas is insane. We'll never get it done. Besides, it'll be a nice surprise for her when she gets back tomorrow.'

Sophie pretended to think it over for a moment. Then said, 'All right. I'd love to.'

'Would you like a drink first?'

'I'd love one, thanks.'

Liam led the way back through to the kitchen. 'Tea?'

Sophie nodded, and Liam set to putting the kettle on.

'How is your cut?' he asked, indicating Sophie's face.

Self-consciously, she pulled her hair forward. 'Fine now, thank you,' she said.

'How did you manage that?'

Sophie weighed up the possible responses. How could she answer him without telling him the whole ridiculous, embarrassing story? Her mind went blank. No other lies presented themselves; she was going to have to do this.

'I fell on my way home from rehearsal the other evening, down by the brook. Actually, I fell *into* the brook.' She waited for him to laugh, but it didn't come.

'Does it hurt?' he asked, turning to face her.

He brushed his thumb lightly over the cut, which now was little more than a yellowing bruise that Sophie had covered generously with foundation. She didn't recoil from his touch, despite the shock of it. Instead, she let him touch her and savoured the feeling, suddenly becoming a little light-headed. She swallowed nervously.

'A little.'

'So you fell into the brook.' His mouth curved into a slight smile.

Sophie nodded.

Liam's smile grew a little wider. 'Is that where your phone went?'

Sophie nodded again. Liam pressed his lips together.

'You can laugh, you know,' Sophie said, and he did.

'Oh, Soph. That's awful.' He said it through his laugh, a laugh that made Sophie's heart soar.

She joined him.

'Are you sure it doesn't hurt? It looks really sore.' He rested his hands on her shoulders and looked closely at her face.

'Not any more,' she said once she'd recovered from his proximity. 'It was a shock at the time, but I'm fine.'

'You say that a lot, you know,' Liam said.

'What?'

'That you're fine.'

'I am, though.'

'It's OK not to be, you know?' He smiled again and held her eye contact.

Sophie smiled. 'I know.'

It was refreshing that, although they'd laughed together, he still genuinely cared that she was OK.

'That's partly why I've agreed to do this terrifying solo.'

'What do you mean?'

'That whole day was awful. My car broke down, rehearsal was crap, I lost my phone to a brook, a brook that I also fell into. It was a horrific end to a hideous day, so when I saw you waiting at the school gate the next afternoon, I knew I had to say yes. Besides, everyone's counting on me and it might be the only way to save the concert. My mum's depending on me.'

'That's a lot of pressure for one person to carry on their shoulders.'

Sophie shrugged. 'I just want everything to go well and for us to raise lots of money.'

'You are a good person, Sophie Lawson.'

Her heart fluttered.

'Come on,' she said, changing the subject. 'Let's get this tree decorated.'

There was nothing Sophie loved more than Christmas, and decorating the tree in the low glimmer of fairy lights was one of her favourite parts of the festivities.

Liam led the way out of the kitchen and back into the living room, where several boxes were already laid out on the floor. Sophie hadn't noticed them when she and Liam had walked through the room before, but they sat on the other side of the sofa, covered in a thick layer of dust.

'I have no idea where to start,' Liam said, hands on his hips.

'Where's the tree?' Sophie asked.

Now this was something she was good at. Liam wouldn't have to tell her to find her confidence here.

'Over here.' He pointed to a box on the floor.

Sophie stepped over the others and opened it, pulling out the central piece of the tree and holding it upright. 'If you hold this, I can fit the base on.'

Liam did as he was told and held on to the centre of the tree as Sophie screwed the base onto it. Then they added the branches, Sophie instructing Liam to fold them out to create a 'fuller tree'.

'I'd forgotten how lovely putting up the Christmas tree could be,' Liam said, lifting another box onto the sofa and opening it to reveal carefully wrapped decorations. They picked them out one by one and unwrapped them before hanging them all over the tree.

'Wait, there's one more,' Liam said as they neared finishing.

He rushed upstairs while Sophie stood back and admired their work. It was dark outside now and the only light they were working by were the fairy lights that sparkled and twinkled all over the tree.

Liam came back into the room with the candy cane that Cassie had made with Sophie. 'She's had it hanging on her bedroom door ever since she brought it home that day.'

Sophie smiled. It was nice to think that she'd made a difference – even if it was just a small one. That was, after all, why she'd gone into teaching in the first place.

'It looks great,' Sophie said.

'It really does,' Liam said, stepping back to join her, their arms touching. Neither moved away.

'Wait!' Sophie said, suddenly jumping away from him. 'We've not put the star on top.'

'Oh yes! Here it is.' He rifled around in the box on the sofa and pulled out a gold metallic star. 'Care to do the honours?' he asked, holding it out to her.

Sophie took the ornament from him and balanced on her tiptoes, reaching to put the star at the top of the tree. She just managed to place it over the very top branch when she lost her balance and saw branches racing towards her face. With lightning-quick reactions, Liam put both hands on Sophie's waist and pulled her back, stopping her from crumpling to the floor in a heap. She turned to face him, but he didn't take his hands away.

'That was close,' he said, his voice suddenly gruff.

'A bit too close,' Sophie said, acutely aware of how close he was to her.

She should have broken eye contact and stood up, but she didn't. She took in every detail of his face and realised that she'd put her own hands on his arms to brace herself for impact when she'd fallen. Before she could release him and step backwards, Liam leant down and brushed her lips softly with his own.

He pulled back, gazing into her eyes. She realised he was waiting for an invitation to kiss her again. Moving her hands further up his arms was all the invitation he needed and this time, when he leant forward, Sophie did the same and their lips met again. She moved her arm up to loop around the back of his neck, her fingers in his hair. His hands rested on her waist, pulling her close to him.

Sophie's mind cleared. She didn't think about Jordan or heartbreak. She didn't think about school or concerts or Cassie. It was just her and Liam, enjoying the most intense kiss she'd ever had in her life. Her blood pressure rose, and she could feel her heart pumping furiously in her chest. Pulling away, they looked at each other, breathless.

'I'm sorry, I . . .' Sophie said.

'Don't be sorry,' Liam said, kissing her again lightly. 'I've been wanting to do that all afternoon.'

Sophie smiled, her body relaxing. 'How did you know I'd kiss you back?'

Liam lifted his hand and ran it along her collarbone. Sophie held her breath.

'I heard you and Kate talking in the coffee shop.'

'Oh God!' Sophie grimaced and hid her face behind her hands.

Liam moved her hands away, pulling her closer, and he kissed her again. There was something romantic about the Christmas lights and having just decorated the tree. There was something romantic about Christmas. Their kiss grew deeper. Sophie's heart pounded in her chest and her skin burnt wherever Liam put his hands, leaving a scorching trail all over her body. He placed a hand on the base of her back and let it graze the skin in the space between her jeans and jumper. Sophie felt her head grow dizzy, her breath shallow.

She jumped back. 'Sorry, I can't.' She looked down at her feet and focused on breathing.

'That's OK.'

She could feel him looking at her, but she didn't dare look

at him. Where was this going? What was she thinking? There was no way she was ready for this. She wrapped her arms around her stomach where the ache was strongest.

'No, it's not OK.' Sophie shook her head and adjusted her clothes where Liam had displaced them. 'I'm sorry, I should never have . . .'

She knew she liked Liam and the entire week had been building up to this moment. But something felt wrong. It was the first time she'd got close to anyone since Jordan. And suddenly the thought of it terrified her. Surely she would only get hurt? Her breath felt thin, and her heart throbbed. But it wasn't because of their kiss any more. It was sheer panic. She clutched at her chest.

'Are you OK?' Liam asked.

'I'm fine.'

Liam bit his lip, as if to hold back something he wanted to say. 'Maybe I should take you home,' he said eventually.

She nodded. Her body prickled as the adrenaline that had rushed through her only seconds earlier drained away. She shivered. Remembering she hadn't driven over herself and that Liam would now have to take her home in the Land Rover filled her with dread. She didn't know if she could deal with the awkwardness.

She let Liam guide her out of the house in a daze, handing her coat to her as he ushered her out the door. He gave her a hand up into the Land Rover and the same heat passed between them. But instead of reacting to it, Liam looked down at his feet and walked around to the driver's side. Sophie fought to hold back tears. What had she done? She attempted and failed to stop the catastrophising part of her brain from working overtime.

Sitting close to the car door, Sophie pressed her hands together on her lap. She forced herself to keep her eyes on the barren landscape out the window. She knew that if she turned even a little, she would see Liam glancing her way as he drove. Twice he cleared his throat as if about to speak, but twice he seemed to change his mind. She swallowed painfully, the lump in her throat and the tears in her eyes threatening to betray her.

Sophie opened the passenger door as soon as Liam pulled up outside her flat. He hopped out of the driver's side to help her, but Sophie had jumped out herself before he could make it round to the passenger door. She twisted her ankle as she landed.

'I'm fine, thank you,' she said, righting herself quickly and walking past Liam, purposely avoiding eye contact. He stood and watched her unlock the front door, not leaving until she was safely inside the building, she noticed.

Once she was inside, hot tears rolled down Sophie's face. She made her way painfully up the stairs and along the corridor to her flat. Her ankle smarted with each step she took. When she got in, she double-locked the door and added the chain. She didn't bother with the Christmas lights, turning her phone off and heading straight for bed.

Throwing the clothes she had left all over her bed earlier that day onto the floor, Sophie crawled under the covers and let herself sob. She felt damaged and foolish. She cursed the impact that Jordan had had on her and how she was letting it interfere with what could have been something special. Not any more. She'd well and truly blown it. Liam probably wouldn't come anywhere near her now. Except, of course, she would have to see him at the school gates every day. And at rehearsal. She groaned and pulled the duvet up over her head. She was alone again, and it was just over two weeks until Christmas.

Liam's language was pretty colourful on the drive home. He'd messed that up horrifically. Sophie was the best thing that had happened to him in such a long time and now she was sitting upstairs in her flat, alone and upset. She should have been sitting in Liam's arms enjoying the Christmas tree that they'd just decorated or sharing a hot chocolate before he drove her back home or . . . Liam shook his head. This reality was so far removed from what he'd envisaged the evening becoming, and it was entirely his fault.

And that kiss! Liam hadn't dared to think he would ever be allowed to kiss Sophie, but he had, and it had been perfect. He grimaced at the memory of her freaking out and how appallingly he'd handled it. Why did he have to go and offer to take her straight home? If they'd talked, perhaps he could have worked out what was wrong and then made her feel better about it. Perhaps she would have stayed. He hated himself.

What was he thinking? The afternoon had gone exactly as he'd imagined it would – it had been perfect. He had no idea where Sophie's wave of panic had come from when they were kissing. One minute it seemed like she couldn't get enough of him; she was so close he was inhaling the smell of her shampoo and feeling the curve of her back. And then . . . the look on her face was etched in his mind – an abject look of terror or panic.

He didn't know what he'd done wrong. All he'd wanted to do was to take her in his arms and make it all OK, but for some reason, he was the problem.

He couldn't wipe the picture of Sophie's dejected expression from his mind. She had looked so small and vulnerable. He wanted to protect her from whatever it was she feared. Liam reran the scene over and over in his head. How could he have handled it better? He hated to think of her up there in her flat, alone and upset. If only he'd said or done the right thing in the moment. If only he'd known what the right thing to say or do was.

The biggest surprise was that Emily hadn't crossed his mind at all.

# Chapter Twenty-One

Two weeks until Christmas

Sophie drifted through Monday in a daze and it was home time for the children before she knew it. She asked her teaching assistant to watch her class during collection to avoid seeing Liam. She was in limbo, both painfully embarrassed at what had happened but desperate to see him, to speak to him and try to work through whatever had stopped her when they kissed. Hiding in the staffroom, she made herself a hot chocolate – it had been that sort of day – and ran back to her classroom to hole herself up and do some planning, undisturbed.

After working through the literacy prep for the coming week and tidying up the Christmas poetry display, she thought she'd got away with it too, but just as Sophie was beginning to relax, Kate came around the door.

With only a couple of weeks to go before she popped, Kate was a giant. A ten-year-old child's seat just wasn't going to cut it, so Sophie watched as she risked flopping down onto a beanbag in the book corner. She didn't crack a smile despite how ridiculous Kate looked.

'So, I'm guessing your radio silence means it didn't quite go as planned?' Kate said, breathless from her seating ordeal.

'Not quite, no.' Sophie stapled things aggressively to the wall without turning to look at her friend.

'Do you want to talk about it?'

Silence.

'No, not really.' Sophie cut a length of border paper from the roll, then climbed up the stepladder and attached it along the top of the display with more angry staples – an appropriate fiery red. She'd been aiming for festive.

'Well, I do,' Kate said. 'What happened? Or didn't happen?' There was a mischievous tone in her voice.

Sophie could see that Kate was trying to lighten the mood and calm her down.

It worked. Sophie sighed, her shoulders sagging. She turned and joined Kate in the reading corner, slumping down into the other beanbag. She let out a deep breath and stuck out her bottom lip like a child.

'Oh God. You've got it bad,' said Kate. She looked concerned and reached across to squeeze Sophie's knee. 'What happened?'

'It started well,' Sophie said. 'He picked me up. We rehearsed all afternoon, and the songs were sounding great. In fact, I'd say I almost felt confident about the concert.'

'That's a big deal coming from you,' Kate said seriously. 'Where did it all go wrong?'

'We put up his Christmas tree – the first time he's done it since his wife died.' Sophie looked away from Kate's face, her eyebrows rising higher and higher on her forehead. 'And then he kissed me.' Sophie dealt the final blow and waited for Kate's reaction.

Kate's mouth opened, then closed. Then opened again. With a sharp glare from Sophie, she shut it and mimed locking it with a key, which she threw out of an imaginary window.

Sophie continued. 'And then I stopped kissing him and ran away.'

Kate tutted involuntarily and put a hand over her mouth. 'Sorry.'

'I panicked,' Sophie said. 'And then he said he should take me home. Which he did.' She looked down at her hands and picked the quick of one of her nails.

'Oh,' Kate said, looking down too.

It was an anti-climax Sophie hadn't wanted to share, and Kate probably hadn't wanted to hear.

'What happened? Why did you freak out?'

Sophie shook her head. 'I don't know. I spent all afternoon wanting to kiss him and when we did, I just panicked. I kept thinking back to my ex-boyfriend, back to what happened.'

'Because you still love him?' Kate asked, sounding uncertain.

Sophie hadn't brought up her previous boyfriend with Kate. Her one serious relationship had ended before they met, and she'd left it to her past. The reason she'd moved to Cranswell was to escape what had happened.

Sophie shook her head. 'No.'

'Do you want to talk about it?' asked Kate gently.

'I don't know what to say, really. Jordan left me because I wasn't enough for him. When things got tough, he didn't want to stick around.' She paused and swallowed. 'It was all a bit of a mess.' Her eyes stung with the tears building up behind them. 'I couldn't give him what he wanted and when he realised that, he left. It was quick. One day he was there, our life just beginning, and the next day, everything was gone. It broke me.'

'But that was Jordan,' Kate said. She gave a sympathetic smile. 'You can't think that every guy out there will do the same thing. Especially not a good egg like Liam.'

Sophie relaxed when Kate didn't press her further. 'I know. But I don't know if I'm strong enough to get through that kind of hurt again,' she said. 'It changed me.'

Kate was silent. They didn't talk about serious things like this. Kate was her carefree, laugh-a-minute, drinking wine kind of friend. They didn't talk about the past, about feelings. Or perhaps that was just Sophie's way of handling what had happened.

'I guess if things are over with Liam, at least you don't have to worry about another bouquet of balloons turning up on your doorstep for Valentine's Day.' Kate smiled and gave Sophie's knee a playful nudge.

Sophie returned the smile, but recoiled at the thought of the balloons. A tinge of sadness lingered, despite Kate's attempt at a joke.

'That's true,' Sophie said. 'I may have sidestepped another balloon situation, but I have made things very awkward for the concert. I wish I wasn't doing the stupid thing any more.' She shook her head at her own stupidity.

'Take that back,' Kate said, pointing an accusatory finger at Sophie. 'The Christmas concert is not stupid. Rehearsals are the highlight of your week.'

'All right, all right,' Sophie agreed, holding up her hands to surrender. 'But it's still going to be pretty rubbish for a while. Not to mention awkward and tense.'

'Agreed,' Kate said, 'but it won't last for ever.'

'Thanks, Kate.' Sophie's eyes glazed over as she replayed the kiss again. Before she'd been an idiot and run away, it had been intense, perfect. She'd not felt anything for Jordan when she'd spotted him at Paddington. So why did she care so much now? Why was he making her behave like a fool? It wasn't Jordan that was the issue, though. She was pretty sure it was the fear of someone – anyone – having the power to break her heart again.

She picked mindlessly at a thread on one of the reading corner beanbags.

'Fancy going into London tomorrow for a bit of Christmas shopping?' Kate said.

Sophie looked up at her friend. 'What?'

'I know it's a Tuesday, but it's the report-writing and wellbeing inset day and I know for a fact that you have finished your reports. You always do them early. So let's do a bit of Christmas shopping. You could do with a day out and I've still got Christmas presents to buy.'

Sophie frowned. The rule-follower in her told her it was mischievous to go shopping on what would ordinarily be a school day. The inset did have 'wellbeing' in the title, though . . .

'Come on,' Kate said. 'It'll cheer you up and stop you moping around your flat for the day thinking about how much you're in love with Liam.'

'I'm not in love with Liam.' She threw a cushion at Kate's head.

'Come on.'

Sophie thought for a second longer. 'All right.' Her expression remained distrustful.

'Yay!' Kate clapped her hands together.

'OK, so now that you've got the gossip you came for and you've enticed me to skive off work . . .'

'Wellbeing day,' Kate said, her finger in the air.

'OK, wellbeing day. I need to get on. It's rehearsal tomorrow evening, so I've got to plan maths for the rest of the week before I go home.' She stood up from the beanbag and smoothed down her skirt.

'You're going to have to shoehorn me out of this beanbag first. Otherwise, I might have to take up residence,' Kate said, trying and failing to push herself up from the floor.

'Come on, you.' Sophie grabbed Kate by the hand and used her entire body weight to counterbalance and prise her up from the ground.

'Will you be OK?' Kate asked once they had both regained their composure.

'Of course,' Sophie said. 'I'll be fine. Just hold my hand tomorrow night at rehearsal,' she added.

Kate laughed. 'Of course I will. It'll be all right.'

Sophie didn't know if it would be. All she knew was that it would inevitably 'be'. And before she even had time to worry about it, Tuesday night would come racing around the corner.

# Chapter Twenty-Two

Sophie was pretty sure that a forty-minute train journey followed by London Underground adventures and being on her feet all day probably wasn't the best plan for Kate in her present condition, but despite Sophie's initial concern, Kate had shouted her down and found herself on a Great Western train pulling into Paddington station the very next morning.

As with any school trip, whether or not there were children with them, calories definitely didn't count and before they'd even arrived in London, they'd already consumed a hot chocolate, croissants and an obscene amount of Haribo. Sophie gathered up their rubbish and took it with her as they made their way to the door of the carriage.

A few feet below them, the platform stretched out with people scurrying about, wrapped warmly for the cold weather and carrying laptops, suitcases and bags. Some of them looked like they were genuinely travelling to do business, but as always, Sophie wondered what the other people were up to and why they weren't cooped up in an office somewhere. Is this what the world was like when she was a prisoner in her classroom all day, every day?

She helped Kate down from the train and waited while she

went for her fifth wee of the journey so far, but only after Kate had grumbled how far away the toilets were from their platform.

Then, they caught the Tube to Oxford Street. They climbed the stairs, Kate huffing and puffing behind her, and Sophie emerged from the station, breathing in the cold air and the familiar sight of Oxford Circus.

Before moving to Cranswell, Sophie had lived in London her whole life. The bustle and the lights and the noise felt like home and Oxford Street at Christmas was just beautiful. Everything was so much bigger than the real world. Shop windows stretched up over two or three floors of the department stores; Christmas trees were decorated with baubles the size of footballs; lights sparkled everywhere you looked. The doormen at Hamley's were dressed up like Cinderella's footmen, and the windows of Fortnum & Mason showcased luxurious hampers, everything dappled with gold leaf. For Sophie, Oxford Street was the epitome of Christmas.

'Right,' Kate said, catching her breath from the steps up to ground level. 'Where shall we begin?'

'I was hoping to buy some extra-special things from Harrods or Selfridges' food hall. You know, something nice for Christmas day, maybe some cheese. And I still need a present for my mum. I just don't know what to get her. What about you?' Sophie asked.

'I agree. Something tasty for the Christmas evening buffet would be nice. Some cheese for when I can eat it again would be perfect too,' Kate said, rubbing her belly. 'Also, I still need to buy for Gav and I want a new scarf. Ooh, and I need to buy something for my TA,' she added.

'Just a small list, then,' Sophie said, laughing. 'Let's go to the food hall first, shall we? Maybe I could buy Mum a hamper or something.'

'Sounds like a plan. But just so you know, I'm about fifteen minutes away from needing another wee.'

Sophie shot her a look of disbelief.

'I can't help it. This baby is sitting right on top of my bladder.'

They started in Fortnum & Mason. The window display was too enticing for them to pass without going in for a look – forest creatures wrapped up in coats and scarves, carrying piles of wrapped Christmas gifts through the trees. It was like a fairy tale. Sophie loved how once you were inside, it felt like you'd stepped back in time – the lead window frames and food stands that sold various delights by weight. Gorgeous.

'This would be great for Mum and Dad,' Sophie said, holding up a wicker basket. Inside there was a selection of biscuits and crackers, along with some preserves. It was the perfect present for the two of them.

'Looks great,' Kate said. 'You keep looking. I'm just going to pop to the toilet.'

Sophie tried not to roll her eyes. She felt for Kate, but this was ridiculous.

'No problem,' Sophie said. 'I'll go and pay for this and then meet you by that exit over there.' She pointed over the top of people's heads to show Kate which exit she meant. They'd easily lose each other without a clear plan – the place was heaving with Christmas shoppers.

'OK,' Kate said. 'See you in a minute.' She waddled off in the direction of the bathroom, parting the crowds like a desperate and hormonal Moses.

Sophie wandered over towards the checkout, stopping to admire the grand Christmas tree that stood proudly in the middle of the hall. It was at least eight feet tall and there were decorations on almost every single branch. You could barely see the boughs for baubles. She realised that this was how Fortnum & Mason had showcased some of the decorations they had for sale, noticing that they each had little price tags. Sophie took a closer look. They were all glass baubles, each with a tiny scene recreated inside. Some were famous literary scenes; others seemed to illustrate a particular pastime or interest. Some were of coloured glass and empty; others were blown into interesting shapes.

One in particular piqued her interest. It was a medium-sized glass bauble, with a treble clef and musical note made of shaped silver wire, and the whole bauble worked like a snow globe. Sophie picked it up and turned it over. When she turned it back, the tiny particles of 'snow' fell slowly through the bauble, reflecting the light as they caught it. Sophie smiled sadly. She knew exactly who she would have bought this for. It matched the rest of Liam's Christmas decorations perfectly. Would it be strange to buy it for him still, even though things had gone spectacularly wrong? Perhaps a peace offering like this could help them become friends again, which was going to be especially important given that Liam was destined to be in her life for a while yet, romantically or otherwise.

She rolled the cool glass between her fingers, the tiny particles of snow floating languidly in all directions. She would buy it. She may never give it to him, but she didn't have time to think about it too much. She resumed her efforts to get to the checkout. Kate took a long time in the bathroom these days, but she didn't have all the time in the world.

'Sophie, love!'

Sophie turned at the sound of her mother's voice. Through the crowd, she could see her waving wildly.

'Hi, Mum.' She stood – spotted – as June made her way towards her. There was no escaping now.

'What are you doing here?' June asked. 'Shouldn't you be at work?'

'It's an inset day.'

She wasn't sure what else to say. Last time she'd spoken to her mother, she'd been so annoyed she'd thrown her phone in the brook and they'd not spoken since. Was her mother really that oblivious to how Sophie felt after their last conversation? She shifted the hamper, which was getting heavier the longer she stood there holding it.

'No wonder you teachers get a bad rap, using your training days to go shopping,' June said, tutting. She put her basket down on the floor.

Sophie sighed. So they were going to have a proper conversation.

'Well, actually, Mum, I've already completed all the work we were asked to do today, so I thought I'd use the opportunity to get a bit of Christmas shopping done while it was quiet. It seems like everyone else had the same idea, though.' She looked around at the chaotic scene. The place was full of shoppers and the claustrophobia was making Sophie overheat.

She tucked her hair behind her ear with her free hand, half holding and half hiding the hamper she'd picked up as her mother's Christmas present.

'What have you done to your face?' June asked, noticing Sophie's partially healed cheek.

'Oh, nothing,' Sophie said, blushing.

'Sophie, it looks really sore. What happened?' her mother persisted.

'I'm fine. I just took a fall,' she said. 'Into a brook.' It didn't sound so funny this time.

Her mother pressed her lips together, and she could see she was being judged.

'Goodness,' said June, putting her hand to her mouth as though she was in a silent movie. 'Whatever did you do that for?'

'I didn't plan for it to happen.' Sophie couldn't believe she was having to explain this.

'Gosh. Well, I don't suppose anything like that would have happened had you stayed in London. So much for moving away, eh?' She smiled as if she'd made a joke.

Sophie pressed her lips together. She just couldn't help herself, could she?

'I'm fine anyway,' Sophie said in an attempt to move on from that particular topic.

'I'm glad to hear it,' said June. 'Any luck with getting those flyers sorted?'

'We're getting there,' Sophie said, shifting her weight to try and accommodate the awkwardly shaped hamper that seemed to be growing heavier still. She didn't want to shatter Liam's bauble either.

'The concert's getting close, though, isn't it?' A look of genuine concern drifted across June's face. Didn't she know the date of the concert by now? That was surely a clear sign she had no intention of attending.

'It's Christmas Eve, so I've got a bit of time to play with,' Sophie said.

'Fingers crossed you get them printed properly, then.'

'I will,' Sophie said. She was getting to the point where she wanted the conversation to be over so that she could go and find somewhere she could get a drink – preferably alcoholic. It was all right to drink on a school day if you weren't technically at school, right?

'Anyway, I must dash. Your father's in here somewhere buying pants and I'll need to make sure he's got the right ones before he takes them to the tills.'

'Bye, Mum,' Sophie said as her mother lurched forward for a couple of air kisses.

'Bye, Sophie love,' June said. She turned and made her way through the crowd, disappearing into the throng.

As always, Sophie was left feeling like she'd been hit in the face with a shovel. She took a deep breath, suddenly far too hot, and finally made it over to the tills to pay. By the time she got to the agreed meeting place, Kate had texted her to say she'd gone to the coffee shop next door.

'Sorry,' Sophie said, rushing through the door and flopping down onto a sofa opposite Kate.

'Where did you get to?' Kate asked, sipping her already half-drunk tea. Sophie didn't realise she'd been so long.

'Sorry,' she said again, redoing her ponytail and peeling off as many layers as she could to try and cool down. 'I bumped into Mum.' Her eyes flicked to the ceiling.

Kate smiled knowingly. 'And how is the lovely June?'

'As encouraging as always.'

Kate slid a cup over to Sophie. 'Help yourself.'

Sophie took the teapot and poured herself a drink. 'Thanks.'

'What did she hound you about this time?'

'Flyers, skiving off school, moving to Cranswell . . .' Sophie trailed off to signal the list could go on for ever.

'Makes you sound like a teenager.' Kate laughed and rubbed her belly.

'I know,' Sophie said, relaxing with a sip of her tea. She shuffled down into the sofa a bit more and made herself comfortable. 'I can't do anything right. I just want her to be proud of me for something. Something where I haven't failed, and it doesn't go catastrophically wrong. Even falling into the brook was entirely my fault, it seems.'

Kate snorted. 'Sophie, you are a successful adult with a good job and a flat of your own. You've not failed at anything.'

Sophie tilted her head. 'I suppose.'

'You're not talking about Jordan again, are you?' Kate asked, surprising Sophie.

'No. Maybe.' Sophie struggled to find the words. 'That whole thing messed me up pretty badly,' she said finally.

'But none of it was your fault,' Kate said. 'Besides, Liam likes you now.' She wiggled her eyebrows playfully.

'Kate,' Sophie warned.

'Even if you freaked out, he still likes you. He can't just turn that off.' Kate's reasoning did kind of make sense.

'True.' Sophie smiled at the thought of Liam having some sort of feelings for her. The truth was, she liked him too and as time went by, she regretted running out on him more and more.

'It's not over, you know,' Kate said, almost reading her thoughts. 'You can still salvage something.'

'I don't know. Maybe. At the very least, I need to apologise.'

'And rehearsal tonight will be the perfect opportunity for you to do that.'

'It will,' Sophie said, already worrying about just how awkward that might be.

# Chapter Twenty-Three

Sophie wasn't surprised to hear that Kate had overdone it being on her feet all day in London. She passed on dinner at the pub and went home for a nap instead. At least she'd not bailed on rehearsal completely. For Sophie, it meant heading back to the flat after school and stressing over what to wear again. The town hall was so cold that she rarely removed her coat anyway, but Liam would be there, and she couldn't help but care. She didn't know if she'd apologise to him; she didn't really know if she'd even talk to him – or him to her. From experience, it was likely she'd avoid him all evening – anything to sidestep an awkward conversation.

She ran the straighteners over her hair, brushed her teeth and put on her favourite light blue jeans and a festive yet subtle jumper. Looking in the mirror, she liked what she saw. She just hoped that if there was anything left to salvage, Liam would too.

'Ready for this?' Kate said when they met outside the town hall. She squeezed Sophie's hand.

'As I'll ever be.' She hung back as Kate led the way into the building.

'Come on. You've got this.' Kate reached back and grabbed Sophie's hand, dragging her into the hall and choosing seats for them towards the back. Sophie appreciated the gesture, which of course Kate had intuitively known to make.

They arrived just as rehearsal was starting. Sophie felt her cheeks colour when she clocked Liam across the room. She looked away as he looked in her direction, and Kate squeezed her hand again.

'You've got this,' she repeated under her breath.

'Right,' Liam said, bringing the choir to attention. The hubbub of the group petered out into mumbles before, eventually, they were quiet enough for him to say something else. Sophie's heart was thumping. She was convinced that everyone else in the room could hear it too. She slouched a little lower in the chair and folded her arms, picking at the fabric of her jumper at the same time.

'I thought we could begin with "White Christmas",' Liam said. Sophie took a shaky breath. Surely he wasn't going to make her sing in front of everyone? He knew she wasn't ready. They'd talked about it.

'Our new last-minute soloist will be singing the first verse. The idea is that the rest of the choir and the audience join in after that. It'll be the finale of the concert. Let's run the choir's section first.'

Sophie's mouth hung open. The ominous 'first' convinced her he was about to ask her to sing. How dare he?

The choir stood around her and Sophie joined them, her arms folded across her chest. Out of the corner of her eye, she was aware Kate was looking at her. She avoided eye contact until Liam began to play the accompaniment on the piano and everyone sang. One of Sophie's legs refused to stop shaking.

When they finished the sing-through, a couple of the sopranos on the front row turned to look at Sophie expectantly. In her mind, she'd stumbled back, sliding chairs to either side, and was running away. In reality, Liam was saying something, and she was ignoring him.

'Sophie?' It definitely sounded like it wasn't the first time he'd said her name. People were looking in her direction. 'You don't need to come up to the front, but would you mind singing your verse so that everyone knows when to come in?'

Sophie nodded and a very tiny 'Yes' came out of her mouth, her voice cracking.

Liam moved to the piano while Greg gave Sophie an emphatic thumbs up. She swallowed several times during the introductory melody, her throat dry. She just knew her voice was going to break. After a deep breath in, she sang.

When she finished her verse, she looked up from the floor to see smiling faces and encouragement. She was relieved to hear the rest of the choir join in with her as they moved to the second verse. Everyone faced forward to follow Liam's timing and the whole excruciating moment passed. Kate squeezed her knee. 'You did it.'

It hadn't been her best performance, but it certainly hadn't been her worst either, and everyone else seemed to be worried about their own singing now, anyway. She smiled to herself, pleased and dare she say a little proud to have pulled it off. Liam caught her eye as she glanced up, and he smiled across the room at her. A nod of approval. Sadness at what had happened between them twisted in her stomach.

Now she was primed, it came as no surprise that Liam later

asked her to perform the main solo to the group. She knew why he was doing it – he knew too well that she needed a confidence boost with her singing. He'd probably planned it before everything had gone wrong. Still, the element of surprise wasn't ideal, and Sophie felt a little hurt that he hadn't warned her.

She did her best, which was OK for today. Albert from the rotary club gave a standing ovation, and Greg probably would have joined him too if not for his gammy knee playing up again. Instead, he kind of wobbled up and down on his chair and bent down to rub his knee when he got a bit too excited.

'We're a week and a bit away from show day!' Sophie announced at the end of rehearsal. Her voice might have sounded excited, but the truth was she felt a little nauseous at the thought of it being so soon. 'Everything sounds wonderful. I have no doubt that we'll put on a fantastic Christmas concert.' Everyone applauded, and Albert let out a whoop. 'Remember to sell as many tickets as you can to family and friends. You all deserve to be heard and we need to make as much money as possible for this year's charity. Thanks, everyone!' Another round of applause punctuated the end of her pep talk.

Sophie made her way back through the crowd and helped Kate put on her coat. She was acutely aware of Liam, who tidied up the music stand and then rolled the piano back into the music cupboard. Half of her wanted to run away and never speak to him again, bruised by embarrassment; the other half of her knew he deserved an apology, even if she couldn't give him anything else. Most of her wanted to get out of there. Before she could decide what to do – or be given orders by Kate – Liam made his way over to them and interrupted their exit.

'Have you got a minute, Soph?' He reached for Sophie's arm. She flinched at his touch like it had passed on a burn. Not that she found it unpleasant, just unexpected.

'Kate and I were going to pop to the pub for a drink, actually.' Sophie surprised herself at the assertive tone her voice took. Even Kate looked a little shocked.

'It's OK, Sophie,' Kate said.

Sophie turned back to her friend and widened her eyes, pleading with her to understand what she was saying. She couldn't talk to Liam alone yet. She wasn't ready. Her body was still recovering from the wave of adrenaline that singing the solo had caused. That Liam had caused.

But Kate didn't take the hint, or rather chose to ignore it. 'I'm pretty tired, anyway. I'm sure you two need a little more time to rehearse the solo. Not that it wasn't great.' She winked.

Sophie protested immediately. 'Actually—'

But Liam cut her off. 'Thanks, Kate,' he said, and Kate turned to leave, turning back to smile at Sophie.

Sophie watched her go, imaginary daggers flying through the air into Kate's back. She would most definitely be having words in the morning. Big fat serious ones.

Sophie followed Liam back over towards the piano as everyone else began to disappear, and at last they were alone. She could feel the heat creeping up her neck, flushing her face, and she inhaled a sharp intake of breath.

'Was everything OK with the songs tonight?' she asked, desperate to fill the silence. She wanted to know she'd done an all right job.

'You were great,' Liam said, sitting at the piano. 'Can we just do that ending again?'

She leant on the top of the piano. 'I know I messed up.' She wasn't entirely sure that she was talking about the solo. She clarified, 'You didn't warn me about singing in front of everyone. I was nervous.' She frowned.

'I'm not sorry. You need to see how good you are and I don't think you realise it just yet.'

'I'm not sure tonight was the way to go about it. It felt like a bit of an ambush.' She surprised herself with her honesty.

Liam had the decency to look guilty. He shuffled the sheet music on the piano more than he probably needed to. 'I'm sorry.' He sounded like he meant it.

Sophie regarded him silently for a moment. He looked up from underneath his curls, that lopsided smile that was so attractive to her making her chest flutter.

'I know why you did it. I just wasn't prepared, that's all.'

'No.' Liam stood and came around the side of the piano, leaning on the opposite edge. 'I mean I'm sorry about what happened . . . at the weekend.' He picked at the corner of his music book where the page had become dog-eared.

'You did nothing wrong.' Sophie looked down at her own music and pulled her jumper sleeves down over her hands. 'I panicked.'

'I'm sorry that I behaved in a way that made you panic.' He reached across for her hand, took it briefly in his own and then let go. 'It was never my intention.'

'It wasn't anything you did,' Sophie said. She forgot about the solo and the fact that Liam had made her sing in front of everyone. She was back in his house, back by the Christmas tree, back in the kiss. 'It was just . . . I wasn't expecting things to happen, and I got scared.'

'We should have talked.'

'What do you mean?'

'I mean we should have talked. Afterwards. It was wrong of me to pack you off home like that. I felt awful once you were inside the flat.' He looked down at his hands as he said it, before raising his eyebrows to peep out from under them, checking Sophie's reaction. His hopeful smile was endearing. 'I'm sorry.'

'Why do you keep apologising? You didn't do anything wrong.'

'Sorry,' he said, and they both laughed.

'Stop it.' She nudged his arm playfully. He grabbed her hand to stop her and held it in his own for a moment.

'We should lock up,' Liam said.

'All right.' She was afraid to move or breathe.

Liam reached out and brushed a piece of Sophie's hair back off her face and behind her ear. She felt her cheeks blush afresh as he did. 'Come on, then.' His hand cupped her face momentarily. He cleared his throat again before he said, 'Come on.'

# Chapter Twenty-Four

Wednesday was a glittery explosion of nativity practice, with the end of term in a week – and the nativity performance itself – speeding towards Sophie like a horrible date she couldn't get out of. She didn't see Kate for most of the day, but she knew Kate would have questions, having left her in Liam's capable hands the night before.

'Hi, Kate,' Sophie said as Kate sidled into her classroom.

'Hello.'

Sophie didn't turn around. She continued to tidy up the children's books and returned pencils to the pots in the centre of the tables where children had forgotten – or been too lazy – to do it themselves. When she'd finished, she turned around to Kate, who was still loitering by the door.

'I wonder why you could have possibly made the journey all the way down to my classroom,' Sophie said sarcastically, tapping her chin thoughtfully with one of the black and yellow striped pencils.

Kate at least had the decency to look a little sheepish for a moment. Sophie didn't give in, though. And for once, it was Kate who cracked first. This pregnancy was throwing her decorum right off and Sophie intended to enjoy it while she could, before Kate had the baby, her hormones levelled out and she was back on top form again.

'Ugh! Don't leave me in suspense!' Kate said, flopping down into the reading corner.

Sophie continued to tidy.

'Why haven't you been to the staffroom all day? You know I need you to satiate my innate need for gossip!' She looked at Sophie and smiled a wide, expectant smile. 'How was last night?' she asked finally, when it became clear that Sophie was going to make her beg.

'Lovely, thank you,' Sophie said, collecting up the books from the floor and arranging them on the shelf.

'Oh, come on, Sophie! Was he nice to you this time? You didn't run away again, did you?' Kate knew it was OK to ask, because a grin had spread across Sophie's face.

Sophie came over to where Kate was sitting and joined her on the beanbags.

'He was nice. We talked and then we went home. That was all,' Sophie said, playing with a corner of her cardigan.

'Talked?' Kate asked, disappointed. 'Was that all?'

Sophie rolled her eyes. 'All right, there was sort of a moment but that's all.'

Kate clapped. 'Hurrah! I'm so pleased. Are you going to see him again? Like for a date?'

'No date.'

'But there's something there,' Kate said. 'And you didn't panic this time.'

'No, I didn't panic.' Sophie looked shyly down at her hands.

'Aw! My girl's all grown up. So, am I forgiven for bailing on you?' Kate asked with a grimace.

'Maybe,' Sophie said, tight-lipped and half joking. 'Anyway, I'm off on duty.' She was thankful she could get away from the conversation. Her nails were a state after the past few days. She hoisted herself out of the beanbag and put on her coat. 'I'll let you digest that little lot and I look forward to seeing you at the staff Christmas drinks tonight for the next instalment,' Sophie teased, spinning on her heel and leaving the classroom.

She could hear Kate's excited screams as she walked down the corridor.

Outside, the wind was up and across the playground it looked as though both leaves and children were being thrown about in a tornado. A crisp packet scuttled past Sophie's feet, so she bent down to pick it up and wandered over to the litter bin. She shivered and pulled her bobble hat down a little firmer on her head.

Sophie began her usual figure of eight around the grounds, giving her the perfect view of the playground, but keeping her moving and warm in the process. The children were running in all directions, presumably doing the same. She missed the heady days of summer where children collected in groups and sat on the field to eat their picnic lunches. At this time of year, the games they played became much more boisterous, and duty was a terrifying gauntlet.

As Sophie rounded the corner, three children ran towards her, just missing her in their frolics. She turned to scold them, but changed her mind. They were just having fun and one of them had shouted 'Sorry' as they'd passed. She turned back and noticed a figure sitting on the ground, leaning against the school building. It was Cassie. Her hands were in her pockets, and her hood was up to fend off the icy wind. What little of her cheeks Sophie could see were red and her nose looked runny. If Sophie didn't know any better, she would guess that Cassie had been crying.

'Hello, Cassie,' Sophie said, ignoring the obvious tear tracks down her cheeks. 'How was your lunch?'

Cassie looked up at her and then looked back down at the ground. 'OK,' came the reply, along with a shrug.

'Are you all right?'

'Fine.'

Sophie let the silence hang for a moment. 'You can tell me if something's up, you know.'

'I know.' Cassie still sounded sullen, but relented slightly.

'So . . .' Sophie left the word dangling in the hope Cassie would finish the sentence with what was bothering her.

'I just want to be by myself.'

'Shall I go?' Sophie asked.

'No. I didn't mean that. You don't have to go.'

Sophie sat on the floor next to her, pulling her skirt and coat underneath her bum to try to protect herself from the frozen ground.

'Where are your friends?' Sophie said.

'I haven't got any.'

'What do you mean?'

'Everyone's on Lily's side. No one wants to be my friend.'

Sophie hated 'sides'. They caused all kinds of trouble and were really hard to break down once they'd been created. She pressed on. 'I don't think that's true. Plenty of children would be lucky to have you as their friend.'

Cassie stayed quiet, scuffing her feet on the ground. 'I hate this stupid place. I wish we'd never come back.'

'Come on,' Sophie said, jumping up and offering Cassie her hand. Cassie took it and she pulled her to her feet. 'Let's sit over here.' Sophie walked her over to the friendship bench, and they both sat down. 'I'll bet in no time at all someone will come over and ask you to play – plus, it's warmer and dryer than the ground. And in the meantime, you get to tell me all about your plans for Christmas.'

Cassie looked at Sophie for a long moment, as if wondering whether or not to trust her. Sophie willed her to engage in the conversation. It would be a genuine breakthrough, and she was keen to see Cassie happy.

Cassie didn't say anything, but tucked some of her long hair behind her ears. 'Well, it'll just be me and Dad in the morning,' she began after a stretch of silence. 'It always has been since Mum, but I like it that way.'

Sophie smiled, thinking of the bond between Liam and his daughter. It was endearing to see that despite such tragedy, Cassie and her father had such a lovely relationship.

'Don't you visit any other family?' Sophie asked.

'Grandma and Grandpa come over and help us cook Christmas dinner,' Cassie said, her body visibly relaxing, 'except we always have it in the evening.'

'That's lovely. I bet they enjoy coming over to help, and seeing you both,' Sophie said, imagining Liam's kitchen full of Christmas fare and excited chatter.

Cassie nodded, but before she had even begun her next sentence, Jocelyn, a little girl from the other Year Six class, came bounding over and enthusiastically squashed them up on the bench so she could sit down too.

'Hi, Cassie,' she said.

'Hi,' Cassie replied shyly. Sophie recognised herself in Cassie as she became physically smaller and folded her arms. She knew what it felt like to feel anxious in social situations and wondered whether that too might be something Cassie was having to deal with.

'I heard you talking about Christmas. You're lucky you've got your nan and grandad coming over. One of my nans lives in Australia and the other one died last year. I can't wait for Christmas, though. It's only a few days away now. I can't wait for school to finish. But I don't want the nativity to end. I love playing a shepherd and after Christmas we have to do boring SATS practice.' The girl barely drew a breath. 'What have you asked Father Christmas for?' She paused only briefly before proceeding to list her own requests while Cassie listened. It reminded Sophie of her mother's telephone conversations, and she made a mental note to call her again. They'd not spoken since she'd bumped into her at Fortnum & Mason. She surprised herself at feeling the pull to do so.

Cassie pulled down her hood and turned to face her new little friend as she told Jocelyn what she'd asked for from Father Christmas. It warmed Sophie to see her talking to another child and looking happy about it. Jocelyn was a lovely little thing, too.

While they spoke, the drizzle had developed into snowflakes

and they began to fall at an alarming rate to a chorus of squeals from the children in the playground.

'Come on,' Jocelyn said after watching for a moment as the heavens opened and the deluge began. It was already heavy enough that the school building was almost obscured from sight across the playground. 'Let's have a snowball fight!' Jocelyn jumped up and ran off into the centre of the playground, where children were already gathered, scraping the snow from the climbing frame and picnic benches quicker than it could land. After glancing at Sophie briefly and Sophie giving her a nod of approval, Cassie joined her, less self-conscious than Sophie had seen her in a long time, if ever.

She let them play for a minute until she was forced to blow the indoor whistle to get the children out of the snow; it was fast turning to icy sleet. With ten minutes left of lunch, at least Cassie and Jocelyn would be allowed to mingle in the wet rooms before the bell went for afternoon lessons. Sophie didn't want to cut their conversation short. She had a good feeling about Jocelyn.

With the festively themed art-come-D&T lesson opened up to both Year Six classes, Sophie watched as Jocelyn and Cassie pulled out their projects and found a table to work at together. Today they would be putting the finishing touches to their Christmas decorations. Let the festive glitter extravaganza commence.

Jocelyn beetled around the classroom, collecting supplies. At the table, Cassie pulled back her long hair and tied it up so she could get down to the very important business of gluing a glittery pipe cleaner halo onto her Angel Gabriel toilet roll. It was the first time Sophie had ever seen Cassie with her hair up and she was beautiful – the same big hazel eyes as Liam looking out from under her messy fringe. It made such a difference to her face and to her mood. For once, Cassie seemed much less introverted and chatted happily to Jocelyn while they stuck silver and gold sequins onto their angel decorations. Across the room, Cassie caught Sophie's eye and gave her a smile, which she returned, pleased to see her content for once.

At the end of the day, after some quite serious cleaning up of glitter and glue, Sophie walked to the school gate with both Year Six classes. Cassie and Jocelyn were still chattering away, and another child, a little boy called David, had joined them. At the gate, Cassie waved to Jocelyn and David, and ran into Liam's arms as he waited for her. She squeezed him tightly, and he returned it, looking up to see Sophie across the playground. He smiled and looked down at Cassie, running his fingers through her tied-up hair. His eyes were asking Sophie how she'd done it. She shrugged, but smiled and waved before walking back into the school building.

# Chapter Twenty-Five

'You don't look very pleased to be here, Kate.'

'You'd be right there, Sophie.' Kate didn't bother disguising her irritation. She shifted from side to side on her seat and folded her arms high on her chest, poking out her bottom lip like a caricature.

'Are you unhappy because the pub's busy or because you're sober?'

'Both. And I'm fat.' A small smile broke from behind her arms. 'And it doesn't help that Tom seems to have consumed enough drinks for us all.'

Sophie turned to see their TA, Tom, standing on a table and bending into a deep bow, having just shared some kind of performance with his adoring fans – all two of them. He already had his tie around his head and it was only 6.30 p.m. She was glad when someone grabbed him by his waistband from behind as he went to crowd surf on top of the two dinner ladies who were clinging on to each other as well as Tom's every word.

'I think they do a mulled apple juice cocktail at the bar. Shall I get you one? I might get Tom a pint of water too.'

'Go on then.' Kate smiled and uncrossed her arms.

'I'll be right back.'

Sophie pushed her way through the festive crowds towards the bar. She had to step onto the gold bar that ran along the bottom of it to see over the taps. She leant on the edge of the bar, which was covered in a prickly green garland, to keep her balance. Huge bows hung down along the front of the wooden panels and behind, merry little workers were dressed as elves.

She ordered and pulled her purse out of her pocket to find the money while the barman poured her drinks.

'Hi.' A man sidled up next to her, squeezing his way through the crowds and queues. He was tall and wearing far too much aftershave. Supermarket own brand at best, Sophie guessed. His plaid shirt, jeans and sheer size gave him the air of a lumberjack. He wasn't unattractive.

'Hello,' Sophie replied.

'Did you manage to get served? It's mad in here, ain't it?'

Sophie glanced sideways at him, but kept her head forward. She nodded. 'It seems everyone's out for office Christmas drinks.'

'Yeah, I'm here with the boys.' He nodded towards a group of similarly dressed men perching around one of the standing tables. Sophie couldn't work out whether they were in fancy dress or perhaps real-life tree surgeons.

'We work over at the builders' yard,' he added, as if reading her mind.

'My lot are over there.' Sophie indicated the group of school staff, skewing her direction slightly to pretend Tom didn't belong with them now that he was doing a very enthusiastic Macarena with the dinner ladies, despite the jukebox playing 'Rockin' Around the Christmas Tree'.

'I don't think I've seen you around before,' he said, and then put his order in for another round of beers when the barman came his way.

Sophie felt her cheeks colour. Kate's specialist alcohol-free drink was taking for ever and she could really do with it arriving just about now to get her out of what she assumed was about to become an uncomfortable situation. 'No, I've not been here in a while.'

Sophie recalled the last time she'd come to the pub and remembered the balloons bobbing about as she tried to keep them contained. Her thoughts flickered to Liam. He was such a different person to her now compared to the man who'd taken her on that awful date.

'Maybe I could tempt you out for a drink sometime.'

There it was. The suggestion that Sophie had dreaded since the man had pushed himself through the crowds to settle at the bar next to her.

'Perhaps.' She didn't want to sound impolite.

The barman returned with the man's beers on a circular tray. He paid up and pulled a card out of his wallet. 'I'm Mike. Give me a call if you fancy it.'

He winked at her and then carried the tray over to his mates, who cheered when he offered them round. Sophie didn't know if they were pleased their drinks had arrived or if they were being lads about the scene that had just unfolded in front of them.

She went up onto her tiptoes and looked along the bar to see her barman still playing around with apple slices and fancy straws. She twizzled Mike's card between her fingers. It was flattering to be asked, of course, but she wasn't used to having a total stranger ask her for a date out of the blue. The internet had been her dating tech of choice – not that it had worked overly well in the past year.

'Who was that?'

Sophie looked up to see Liam, and she smiled, surprised.

'I don't know. Just someone who was buying drinks next to me at the bar.' Her cheeks coloured again, and she felt the warmth rising on her face. 'What are you doing here?' she asked, attempting to divert Liam's attention away from the man who had just asked her out on a date. It wasn't exactly the kind of thing she wanted to share with him.

'Christmas drinks with the boys from the farm.'

He nodded over to where he'd been sitting, but Sophie couldn't really see beyond the crowd of people at the bar.

'I didn't realise a Wednesday night would be so popular.' Liam looked around at the throng of people jostling to be served.

'Most of them are with me. Teachers very much enjoy a Christmas night out.'

'Is that one of your lot?' Liam looked over to where Tom was resting his head on the headteacher's shoulder, his tie now wrapped around his head but covering his eyes. Miss Davies didn't look best pleased.

'Afraid so.'

'Well, he looks like he's had a great night.'

'I don't think he'll agree when he has to survive thirty seven-year-olds at eight thirty tomorrow morning.'

Liam laughed as the barman finally put Sophie's drinks down in front of her. She passed him a ten-pound note.

'Not drinking?'

'God, yes! It's the only way to survive this thing. Mine's the wine, that's for my pregnant friend and the water's for Tom.'

She looked up at him and smiled. A moment passed where neither of them spoke. Sophie didn't know what to say.

She was about to pick up the tray and turn to go when Liam said, 'The last time I came here was with you . . . and an enormous bouquet of balloons.' He smiled but bit his bottom lip with the embarrassment of the memory.

'That was the last time I was here, too. I couldn't bear to return after the humiliation.'

'Hey!' Liam frowned with mock hurt.

Sophie laughed.

'I'm sorry about that,' he said. 'It was a pretty awful date and I'm sure that was almost entirely my fault.'

'It probably was,' Sophie agreed.

'Oi!'

She laughed again.

'I wasn't at my best either,' she said. 'Balloons terrify me and I had to contend with far too many of them for my liking.'

'I didn't know you were actually scared of them. I thought you were just embarrassed.'

'Well, that too.' Her smile mirrored his. She tucked her hair behind her ear and looked down at the floor and back up to him. 'I should get back to my friends.'

'Sophie.'

'Liam.' She smiled.

But Liam looked serious, his eyes locked onto hers. 'I don't think I can be friends with you.'

She put the tray back down on the bar. She felt a knot in her stomach and a pain in her chest. 'What?' She frowned.

'Wait. I didn't mean . . . Let me start again.' He was playing with his hands and looked down at them before looking back at Sophie and pushing his curls back off his face. 'I don't think I can *just* be friends with you.'

The butterflies in Sophie's stomach woke up like an unexpected alarm had just gone off and she was suddenly very aware of the beating of her own heart. Words eluded her despite a part of her wanting to reach out and hold him and tell him she felt the same way. She might be scared, terrified in fact, to allow herself to feel something, to put herself at risk of losing something again. But it didn't stop her from wanting him.

Liam leant forward and ran his thumb across her cheek.

'I just want you to know that I'll wait until you're ready.' He bit at his bottom lip again. 'As long as it takes.'

Sophie's heart lurched. It wasn't over. Despite everything, Liam was telling her things were salvageable, that he'd wait until she was ready.

She reached up on her tiptoes and rested her hands on Liam's shoulders before kissing him on the side of his mouth. She pulled back until Liam was in focus, trying to read his expression. Outside the two of them, Sophie could no longer hear the Christmas music or the raucous laughter of her friends and colleagues. The barman putting Liam's drink down in front of him made Sophie fall back into the moment.

'You're not going to call him, are you?' Liam looked down at the card that lay on the bar between them.

'I have to get back to my friends.' Sophie picked up her tray of drinks, smiled at Liam and turned to go, leaving Mike's card on the bar behind her.

# Chapter Twenty-Six

Sophie spent the next twenty-four hours basking in the glory of having judged a romantic social situation perfectly at the exact moment it had actually happened. She was pretty sure it had never happened to her before.

After her conversation with Liam at the bar, she had spent a pleasant evening chatting to her colleagues, who she quite liked, it turned out, and catching Liam's eye across the room. Every time their eyes met, one of them would look away. It was an odd game, but Sophie enjoyed it. By the time she left the bar to go home, she was fairly sure she was in love.

At the end of the school day on Thursday, Sophie was still in a Liam-based daydream.

'What is up with you?' Kate asked. 'You've been in an odd mood all day.'

'Nothing,' Sophie said. 'I'm fine.' This time, she didn't want to share what had happened. She and Liam had a little secret of their own, and Sophie was enjoying keeping it that way.

'Ooh, twelve o'clock,' Kate said, jabbing Sophie in the arm and pointing across the playground. Sophie turned to see Liam walking across the yard.

'Hi, Soph,' he said. His lovely voice saying her name made her happy. She felt Kate move away as she turned to greet him.

'Liam, hello.'

'Cassie's been telling me all about her new friend Jocelyn,' he said, barely able to conceal his joy at this new revelation. Cassie ran up behind him, smiling.

'Yes, well, Jocelyn's a lovely girl and they seemed to be the best of friends by the end of yesterday,' Sophie said, smiling at Cassie.

'You helped me,' Cassie said. She still looked timid and shy but with her hair tied back again there was something a little braver about her today; she seemed more open somehow.

'Well, thank you. This is the happiest I've seen her in a long time.' Liam looked down at his daughter. She returned his look with a smile. It was such a different reaction to the one Sophie had received only a few weeks earlier.

'I didn't do anything. Like I said to Cassie yesterday – Jocelyn is lucky to be friends with her.' She added a conspiratorial wink in Cassie's direction, and she giggled.

'Cassie and I were just talking, and we wondered whether you might want to come over for dinner tomorrow. It's nothing special, just spaghetti bolognese.'

'It's my favourite!' added Cassie, looking at Sophie expectantly.

'Mine too,' Sophie said, surprised into not knowing what else to say.

'Oh, well, I hope it lives up to your expectations then.' He pulled a worried face. 'Would you like to join us?'

Cassie turned away to talk to Jocelyn, whose mum was

huddled close by, together with several others attempting to arrange a playdate. They weren't alone, but suddenly the conversation felt a little intense.

Sophie swallowed. She didn't know what to say. The part that wanted to run away was still tugging at her – *just say no and nothing can go wrong. You won't get hurt*, she thought. But Liam's expectant eyes held Sophie's gaze, and she knew she wanted to say yes, even if it was just dinner. There was nothing she wanted more at that moment than to spend more time with Liam Hawthorn.

'That sounds lovely,' Sophie said eventually.

'I can pick you up at—'

Sophie interrupted him. 'I can drive, it's fine. Besides, how will I get home once Cassie's in bed? You can't leave her.'

Liam thought for a moment. 'Good point.'

'I'll be careful, I promise.'

Liam seemed to consider this for a moment. 'All right. As long as you promise.'

'Should I bring anything?'

Liam shook his head. 'Just yourself. I'll cook and Cassie said something about a slumber party.'

Like a sleepover? 'Um . . .' Of course, words escaped her. Of course, she was about to make herself look foolish. At these key moments in life, Sophie always fluffed it up.

'Nothing funny.' He smiled. 'Just a fort made of sofa cushions and probably far too much ice cream. That's what ten-year-old girls love, I'm told.'

'That actually sounds lovely,' Sophie said, feeling herself relax.

'So, it's a date?' he asked, raising his eyebrows above his beautiful eyes. His expression faltered, only momentarily, having realised he'd used the D word.

Sophie's stomach did a somersault and landed on the floor; the butterflies inside catapulted from one side to the other. She considered her response for a second and then went for it. 'It's a date.'


'It's funny that spaghetti bolognese is Miss Lawson's favourite too, isn't it?' Cassie said, as Liam made sure she was belted safely in the Land Rover.

'It is, isn't it?' he agreed.

'Are you worried she might not like yours?'

Liam jumped in the other side of the vehicle. Well, he was worried now. He suddenly felt like a teenager again, worrying that he might not be good enough. That he might do something that Sophie didn't like. That she'd run away again. He was so pleased that she'd agreed to come over for dinner. He wanted everything to go perfectly so that he didn't scare her off this time.

'No, not at all,' he lied.

'It's yummy, so you'll probably be OK,' Cassie said, looking out the window.

'Thanks, sweetheart. Are you sure it's all right for Sophie to come over tomorrow night?' he asked.

'Sure.' She shrugged, sounding more and more grown-up to Liam every time they talked. 'Do you think Jocelyn could come too?' Cassie said, changing the subject, much to Liam's frustration. More than anything, he needed Cassie's approval, or blessing at least, now that he found himself in the position of wanting to invite a woman over that wasn't Cassie's mother.

'Maybe not tomorrow but Jocelyn can definitely come over for tea one day in the Christmas holidays if it's all right with her mum,' said Liam. 'Or you can go over to hers.'

Cassie smiled to herself, but Liam saw it and felt relieved. He was pleased that Cassie seemed to have made a friend. Her hair was still tied back, and it was lovely to see her face. It was so like Emily's that his stomach twisted in yearning. He didn't feel like that as often these days, but sometimes Cassie would pull a particular expression or her hair would fall just so and he'd feel like he'd taken a punch to the gut.

So often she'd sit sullenly looking out of the window as they drove across town and out to the farm, but here they were almost having a conversation, and he could actually see his daughter's eyes. Liam couldn't help but think this had something to do with Sophie, and he found himself feeling grateful that she had found a way into their lives.

# Chapter Twenty-Seven

That afternoon, Sophie escaped from the classroom a little earlier. She wanted to visit Lulu and see how she was getting on. It had been a week or so since her fall and Sophie hadn't seen her out and about in town, which was unusual, albeit understandable. She went armed with flowers and a bottle of sherry – Lulu's favourite tipple.

Lulu's house was on the edge of town. It had to be because it was vast and there was simply not enough space for it anywhere else. At first glance, it exuded chic glamour. But as Sophie neared it for the first time, she could see that the apparently ornate gate posts, spherical stone balls balanced on the top, were actually looking a little worse for wear. And as she made her way through the garden to the front door, she could see that the planting was wild and overgrown. Its façade had slipped only slightly, just like its owner.

She rang the Gothic bell and waited, wondering whether it was taking Lulu so long to answer because of her injuries or because of the sheer size of the house. If she was at the far side, it would surely take an age to get to the front door.

'Just a moment.' Lulu's voice was muffled.

She could hear rummaging inside as Lulu undid the locks and chains.

'Sophie, honey!' Lulu opened the door wide and beckoned her into the house. 'Come in!'

'Hello, Lulu,' Sophie said, giving her a hug and passing her the gifts she'd brought with her.

The inside of the house took Sophie's breath away. It was a time capsule from the golden age of Hollywood and would have been impressive ordinarily, but decked out for Christmas, it was magical. The foyer spanned the entire height of the building and there was a Christmas tree, maybe eight feet tall, reaching up into the space. It was decorated with oversized baubles and twinkling fairy lights. Evergreen garlands covered every available surface, winding up the staircase and framing each window. Through an archway, Sophie could see that the festive decorations continued, with more fairy lights and garlands hanging from every possible place.

'Christmassy, huh?' Lulu said in her American twang.

Sophie nodded, stepping further into the house and looking around in awe. It was only then that she looked at Lulu properly, wrapped in a dark red silk house coat and wearing a turban, a large crystal embellishing the front and a long feather sticking up from the centre.

'It looks magical,' Sophie said, feeling like a child again.

'Come on in, won't you?'

Lulu showed her through into a large sitting room and Sophie followed, continuing to look around her and notice the details of the Christmas decorations. It was only when they'd travelled a significant distance to get to the sitting room that she noticed Lulu seemed to be walking perfectly unaided. There wasn't a stick or a Zimmer frame in sight. She tilted her head in an attempt to appraise her walk as she followed her through into the large living room. But there was nothing odd – and definitely nothing ailing – about it.

'How are you feeling?' Sophie asked, as she settled into a large armchair, the back of which rose up like something out of the Mad Hatter's tea party.

'Horrendous!' Lulu spoke with a dramatic flourish and lowered herself into a similar chair opposite. 'The fall was such a shock but I'm mostly upset that I can't sing at your wonderful concert.'

'Oh, Lulu, it's fine, really. I just hope you're not doing too much and giving yourself time to recover.' She looked around at the festive decorations and hoped she'd hired help. She must have done.

'I am, I am,' she said, waving her hand madly.

Sophie narrowed her eyes. To be honest, she didn't look like she needed to recover from anything.

'Who have you got to do the solo now?' Lulu asked. 'I can't tell you how distraught I am not to be singing.'

'Well . . .' Sophie paused, knowing that once she said it out loud to Lulu, there would be no going back. 'Me, actually.'

'Bravo!' she said, clasping her hands together in excitement – almost too quickly, as if it was the answer she expected. 'You'll be wonderful. I really can't think of anyone who could do it better.'

'I don't know—' Sophie protested, but Lulu interrupted.

'No, no, no,' she said, gesticulating madly again. 'We'll have none of that self-deprecating rubbish! You'll be fabulous.'

Sophie smiled.

'Can I offer you a cup of tea?' Lulu said.

Sophie nodded, half expecting Lulu to ring a little bell and for a servant to appear. They didn't. Instead, Lulu stood – unaided and pain-free – and walked into the kitchen. Sophie followed her through the archway and into a kitchen that Sophie guessed hadn't been refurbished in fifty years or so. She liked it, though. It reminded her of the Hollywood musicals she was so fond of – all Bakelite and melamine.

Lulu made the tea while they engaged in small talk. Afterwards, they brought the drinks back into the sitting room and Sophie set Lulu's down on a dark mahogany side table.

'So, what about that Liam fellow?' Lulu asked.

Her out-of-the-blue question threw Sophie, and she spilt a little tea onto the saucer. She put her cup down on the side and shuffled in the chair.

'What about him?' she asked, blushing.

'He seems nice.' Lulu raised an eyebrow that disappeared up into her turban.

'He can be,' Sophie said, 'when he's not being difficult.' She hoped her disregard would get Lulu to move on to a different topic.

'You're blushing,' Lulu said wickedly, pointing a finger at her. 'You like him, don't you?'

'It's a little more complicated than that,' Sophie said, wondering how Lulu was so in tune with these things.

'I'll bet he's been wonderful helping you with the solo,' she said. 'You must have got to spend lots of time getting to know each other a little better.'

Surely Lulu hadn't . . . ? Sophie shook the thought out of her head. She wouldn't have dropped out of the concert on purpose. It wasn't in Lulu's nature. Was it?

'He's been very helpful,' Sophie said. Now she came to think of it, she doubted she'd be anywhere close to agreeing to step in if Nigel had still been in charge.

'He's a good 'un, that Liam,' Lulu said, picking up her cup and taking a sip of her tea. 'And how's Greg and Albert and the others?' She surprised Sophie with her sudden change of topic.

'They're fine. Everyone is missing you, though. Do you think you'll be back for the concert?' Part of her hoped Lulu might sweep in and take her solo back just in the nick of time.

Lulu shook her head. 'I'm afraid I'm out, this time. I can't stand for too long right now and the doctor wants me to rest. And you know me, I couldn't do anything half-heartedly.'

Sophie smiled, but it didn't reach her eyes. The longer she spent in Lulu's company, the more she suspected she was up to something. She decided not to press it. 'But you'll be back for the Easter concert?' she asked hopefully.

'You just try and stop me, kid,' she said, her eyes sparkling. 'Have you got any flyers so I can pass some on to my friends at bridge club?'

Sophie shook her head. 'Not quite yet. They're still being printed.' She ignored the tightness in her chest, which now appeared without warning whenever she thought about the flyers. She would never trust Albert again after this mess.

'When they're done, be a love and bring some over, won't you?'

'No problem, Lulu.'

'Would you like to stop for a spot of dinner?' Lulu asked. 'You're looking awful wiry.'

'No, thank you. I'm fine. It's a school night and I've got lots to do before the end of term so I should really get home and do some work.'

'Sure thing.' They both rose from their chairs.

'Don't get up,' Sophie said. 'I can let myself out.'

'I ain't dead yet, kid,' Lulu said, lifting herself from the chair. Her eyes met Sophie's across the room, and she wobbled dramatically and reached out for a stick that had been resting against the wall during Sophie's entire visit. 'Can't get anywhere without this these days,' she said quickly, before leading the way back to the front door.

She was up to something. Sophie chewed the inside of her cheek thoughtfully as she walked to the front door, Lulu taking tiny steps and occasionally making a noise to suggest she was in pain.

'It was so lovely to see you, honey,' Lulu said, bringing Sophie in for another hug when they'd reached the entrance hall.

'And you. I'm glad you're managing to get about a bit.'

'Nothing can stop me, Sophie, you know that.' She smiled, her red lipstick cracking in places. 'Thank you for the flowers and the tipple,' she added, winking. 'I'll enjoy a glass later.'

'You're welcome, Lulu. We can't wait to see you back at choir.'

'Just you try and stop me,' she said. 'I'll be back as soon as

I can be. Goodbye!' She waved flamboyantly as Sophie walked back out along the garden path.

It was good to see Lulu, and she seemed happy about Sophie taking over her solo – a little bit too happy. She thought Lulu might have been disappointed to know the solo had gone to someone else. As it was, she seemed pleased that it was Sophie and oddly chuffed that it had led to her spending more time with Liam. She thought again about how spritely Lulu had seemed despite her fall, and wondered if she'd made more of it than she needed to. The thought was replaced with a wave of nausea linked to the concert being so close now and the fact that the solo was only a few days away – and just a little bit of excitement that her date with Liam was in only twenty-four hours' time.

# Chapter Twenty-Eight

As predicted, Friday rushed past in a torrent of festive giddiness. The nearer the end of term, the faster time passed. The positivity of the staff looking forward to a well-deserved break; the children starting to get excited about Father Christmas; the festive nativity play and Christmas dinner in the canteen all came together for a lovely few days. For Sophie, there were other exciting things happening too, and she floated around in happy daydreams all day.

'You are far too happy,' Kate said, who in the very latter stages of pregnancy was getting particularly grouchy and was never happy unless in receipt of juicy new gossip or a comfortable chair.

Sophie carried their two drinks over from the counter as Kate settled at their table in the corner of Greg's coffee shop. 'Here you go,' Sophie said, putting the After Eight hot chocolates down on the table. They'd escaped school on time for a change and got their usual seat next to the window, where Greg and his team had used snow spray to give the tiny panes of glass a Dickensian feel. A wall of small white fairy lights adorned the window.

'I'm not sure about this one,' Kate said, picking it up and giving it a suspicious sniff.

'I am.' Sophie took a sip. 'Greg said it had been a big seller this week.' Foam fizzled under her nose. She wiped it away and licked her lips.

'Ugh, you're even happy about your hot chocolate.' Kate shuffled in the seat, trying to get comfortable and failing.

'When are you due again?' Sophie laughed.

'A week and a half to go!' Kate said, even though they both knew the answer to Sophie's question was Christmas Day.

'A week and a half too much, if you ask me,' Sophie said.

'Oi!' Kate threw a sugar sachet at her across the table.

'Sorry.' She held up her hands in defence. 'I'm sorry for being too happy. It's just that things are actually coming together. Rumour has it the flyers are finally finished. Albert should have been over to collect them this afternoon. I've not had a panicked phone call yet so I've got my fingers crossed they're all right this time.' She crossed her fingers in the air.

'I'm not sure that no news is good news when it comes to Albert and flyers.'

'Good point. I'll not hold my breath until I see them.' Sophie took a spoon to her hot chocolate and scooped some of the powder off the top.

'Are you excited about tonight?' Kate asked.

Sophie nodded. 'I am but I feel sick too.'

'You wouldn't be you if you weren't totally freaking out about it, though, would you?'

Sophie shook her head. 'Nope.'

'I'm surprised you agreed to come for a drink,' Kate said, taking a tiny sip of her hot chocolate and pulling a face. 'I thought you'd be rushing home to get ready. I assume you're going to shave your legs?' She wiggled her eyebrows and the sugar sachet came hurling back towards Kate.

'We're just friends,' Sophie said. 'And besides, Cassie will be there, so there'll be no funny business.'

'Cassie will be there?' Kate said, her expression registering the information. 'That's almost more serious than sex.'

'What do you mean?'

'Well, if he's bringing his child into it, then you must be something special. It's too high-stakes otherwise.'

'I suppose,' Sophie said. She let Kate's comment wash over her and, once processed, came to the same worrying conclusion. 'Although that terrifies me even more!'

'Of course it does.' Kate rolled her eyes.

'Any last-minute advice?' Sophie asked as she slurped the last of her drink and began to put all the layers she'd shed back on again. She grabbed Kate's hands and used all of her body weight to winch her out of the sofa.

'Just be yourself,' Kate said, placing her hands on Sophie's shoulders, partly for balance – they were supporting each other here – and looking her straight in the eye. 'Also, don't mess it up. And make sure you're safe.'

It was Sophie's turn to roll her eyes. 'Enlightening advice, as always. Thank you.'

'You're welcome.'

'Sophie! I'm so glad you're here!' Albert bounced through the door with a large cardboard box and two carrier bags. 'The flyers! They're here!'

He dumped the box and bags onto the coffee table and bent over to catch his breath. His cheeks were red with exertion and his comb-over flopped in the wrong direction.

'Well? Do they look OK?' Sophie asked.

'I've not looked,' Albert said through deep breaths. 'I was too scared.'

'Let's see.' Kate took charge and used a key to cut through the tape on the cardboard box.

Sophie pulled open the flaps and lifted out the flyers. She looked at Albert, who was grimacing while he waited for Sophie's verdict.

'These are great, Albert. You've done a fantastic job,' Sophie said finally, passing the flyers around for Kate and Albert to see.

They were the right festive colours, contained the correct information and dates, and included the name of June's charity at the bottom. Perfect. Sophie breathed a sigh of relief.

'Greg,' Sophie shouted over the increasing bustle of the coffee shop.

He looked up from where he was frothing milk behind the counter.

'Can I put a couple of these up?' she asked, waving the newly printed flyers in the air.

'Of course, love.'

Sophie pinned a couple to the notice board and left a little pile for people to take – a few patrons moving over to see what the fuss was about even before she was finished.

'Christmas Eve concert,' Sophie said, thrusting a flyer into their hands. 'It's going to be very festive.'

'And this one's got a solo,' Kate added, much to Sophie's embarrassment.

'We're supposed to be making people want to come,' Sophie said as they left the coffee shop.

'They will. And you'll be wonderful.'

Sophie wasn't so sure, and the familiar tightness appeared momentarily in her throat.

'You will,' Kate said, reacting to Sophie's silence. 'Now get home and get ready, please. I need you to go to Liam's tonight and create some gossip for me.'

'I'll try my best,' Sophie said. She laughed but couldn't help feeling incredibly nervous inside.

Sophie spent an hour getting ready, and the time raced past. For some reason, she didn't feel nervous any more. She knew where she stood after Liam's revelation in the pub on Wednesday, and for some reason, removing the uncertainty helped her feel less anxious and more confident. It wasn't familiar to Sophie, but she liked it. She spent the drive over to Liam's running through conversations, scenarios, how she'd greet him when she got there. OK, so maybe a little anxiety was creeping in, but she was also smiling and excited.

She pulled into the courtyard outside the farmhouse and got out of the car, pleased to have chosen more appropriate footwear this time around. She knocked on the front door.

Liam opened it. He was in well-worn jeans and a grey jumper, his hair tightly curled and still damp where he'd not long been in the shower. He smelt of soap and aftershave.

'Hi,' he said.

'Hi.' Sophie knew she was grinning like a crazy person, but she couldn't stop herself.

'Come on in.' He stepped back to let her pass. 'How was the drive?'

She turned back to speak to him. 'It was fine. You're right, it was a bit icy, but I took it slow and I'm here in one piece.'

'Glad to hear it.' He smiled. 'Tea?'

'Please.' She was relieved that the initial greeting was over and that she'd survived the small talk. In the kitchen, Liam made them a cup of tea and they sat at the dining table. They talked some more, still guarded, still shy.

'Where's Cassie?' Sophie said.

'Playdate with Jocelyn.'

Sophie smiled at that. She was happy that Cassie and Jocelyn were building a friendship and pleased that Liam was nurturing it.

'I need to swing by and pick her up, if that's OK? It wasn't the plan, but she asked to stay a little later as she was having so much fun.' He did air quotes with his fingers.

'Of course,' she said. 'What time?'

Liam looked at his watch. 'Oh crap. About now, actually. Can we go? I'll make more tea when we get back.'

'Let's go.' Sophie stood up and shrugged her coat back on. When she turned, she came face to face with Liam's jumper. 'Sorry.'

Liam looked down at her with those hazel eyes and she didn't break the eye contact. Liam's breathing deepened, as did her own, and she sensed the butterflies in her own stomach stirring. If they didn't go now . . .

'Come on,' she said, stepping away and doing up her coat. 'We need to pick up Cassie.'

'We do,' Liam said, clearing his throat and waiting another beat before he moved.

Outside, they climbed into the Land Rover, Liam giving Sophie a leg up so she could get in safely.

'It's not far, this side of town,' Liam said as he pulled out of the farm and onto the single-track road that would take them back to civilisation.

They pulled into a cul-de-sac just before the edge of town, not far from the road that led to the farm. Liam jumped out.

'Won't be a minute,' he said, jogging towards a house on the corner. He knocked on the door and waited.

Jocelyn's family was one of those that had gone slightly overboard with the lights and decorations. Sophie looked around to try and work out where the projector was that was displaying 'snowfall' on the house. She suspected they'd hidden it behind one of the five light-up reindeer that were grazing on the front lawn.

Cassie came bounding out of the house, straight past her dad and jumped up into the back seat of the Land Rover. 'Hi, Miss Lawson.'

Liam followed her up the path and checked Cassie's seatbelt was on properly before he hopped back into the driver's seat.

'When we're not at school, I think it's all right for you to call me Sophie.' She looked round at Cassie, who smiled.

'Is everybody in?' Liam said.

Sophie and Cassie chorused, 'Yes,' and Liam pulled away.

The car journey was spent with Cassie chattering away about her afternoon with Jocelyn. It appeared the two of them were getting on very well.

'I hope you've not ruined your appetite,' Liam said after Cassie had told them about the popcorn they'd eaten while watching *Nativity*.

'Nope,' she replied with a vigorous shake of the head that Sophie could see in the rear-view mirror. 'Never. I've always got room for spag bol!'

'I'm looking forward to this famous spag bol,' Sophie said.

'Don't get your hopes up.' Liam grimaced and glanced sideways at her.

They pulled into the courtyard by the farmhouse and one by one they got out of the Land Rover, Liam coming around to help each of them make the leap from the vehicle to the ground.

When they got inside, Cassie turned on the Christmas lights. Since Sophie had been there last time, Liam and Cassie had added more decorations to the room and so now, under the Christmas tree, there were three two-foot-tall wicker reindeer. The mantelpiece above the log burner was adorned with greenery and littered with tiny fairy lights, and on the coffee table in the centre of the room, there was a poinsettia and bowls of chocolates and nuts. The room oozed Christmas and the only difference between her own flat and the decorations here was the lack of chocolates and nuts on the coffee table back at Sophie's – for the simple reason that she couldn't trust herself not to eat all of them in one sitting. That, and Liam's living room was about ten times the size of Sophie's entire flat.

'Shall we try another cup of tea?' Liam asked, heading for the kitchen.

'Yes, please.'

Both Cassie and Sophie followed him into the other room.

Cassie sat down at the table and pulled her knees up underneath her chin. Liam busied himself with mugs and tea bags.

'Can we decorate the Christmas cookies for Grandma?' asked Cassie.

'We?' Sophie said, pointing at herself as Cassie addressed the question to both of them.

'Can you help?' Cassie asked hopefully.

'I can try.'

'Dad, can we?'

'If Sophie's sure she doesn't mind,' Liam said, lighting the hob and turning around to check.

Sophie shook her head and smiled. 'I don't mind. But *you* might mind when you see what my cookie-decorating skills look like.'

'Yay!' Cassie said.

Liam passed her a Tupperware full of cookies that they must have made the previous evening. Sophie liked that they did things like that together.

'Here, you have this one,' Cassie said, passing her a bauble-shaped biscuit with a hole in the top. Tubes of icing and pots of glitter and silver balls were already spread out on the table – almost as if Cassie had planned it.

Liam poured out two mugs of tea and set one down in front of Sophie, who was already smearing a bright red base layer of icing onto her biscuit.

'Thank you,' she said, without looking up, her tongue poking out from between her lips in concentration. Cassie looked across at Sophie and mirrored her actions, choosing white icing as a sensible starting point for her snowman biscuit.

While they worked, Liam made his way around the kitchen, concocting his famous spag bol. At one point, Sophie looked up to see him emptying a tin of baked beans into the pan. But she guessed that suddenly finding yourself as a single parent to a young child probably led to its culinary challenges – and experiments.

'Right, here we go!' Liam said, lifting the pan off the hob and bringing it over to the table. He had attempted to lay out the mats and cutlery around the mess that Sophie and Cassie had made with their biscuits.

Sophie quickly shuffled things around and put the decorating paraphernalia to one side. 'Maybe your dad will let us try one afterwards,' she said, with a conspiratorial wink towards Cassie.

'Can we, Dad?' Cassie wriggled in the chair to get in a suitable position for eating.

'Only if you eat all your veggies,' he said, placing a well-timed bowl of steamed vegetables on the table. Cassie went straight for the serving spoon, clearly wanting to make sure one of the cookies came her way for dessert.

Sophie scooped up a spoonful of the spaghetti bolognese and popped it into her mouth. 'It's actually very good.'

'You sound surprised,' Liam said.

'Well, you did put baked beans in it,' Sophie said, a little uncertainly. Cassie laughed from across the table.

'Ok, you have sort of got a point there,' agreed Liam.

Dinner didn't last very long. The spaghetti bolognese turned out to be delicious and although Sophie thought she'd probably be too nervous to eat, in fact, Liam and Cassie made her feel at home and for the first time she could remember in a long time, she felt relaxed. They devoured the meal in no time.

Sophie didn't relax for long, though. Only an hour or so later, it was Cassie's bedtime. And she knew that once Liam had put Cassie to bed, they'd be alone.

'Say good night to Sophie.'

'Good night, Sophie,' Cassie said, skipping over to Sophie and giving her a hug. Sophie was surprised and bent over to hug her back. She kissed Cassie on the head.

'Thank you for inviting me to dinner,' she said. 'Good night, Cassie.'

Cassie went upstairs and Liam followed her. 'Back in a minute,' he said before disappearing up the stairs behind her.

Sophie brought their two mugs of mulled wine over to the sofa and sat down. It was softer than she'd expected, and she sank suddenly into it, holding her wine up in the air to avoid it spilling everywhere.

Liam had already filled the room with candles and lit the wood burner so that the space was flooded with a pool of ambient light. The Christmas tree lights twinkled in the corner, glinting off the ornaments they'd hung together the previous weekend.

'She's already closing her eyes,' Liam whispered as he re-entered the room and shut the door to the hallway softly behind him.

'She's a lovely girl,' Sophie said. 'You've done such a good job with her.'

'Her mum had her on the right track before she died,' Liam said, sitting next to Sophie on the sofa and reaching over for his wine.

'What happened?' Sophie asked. She couldn't help herself. If anything was going to happen with this man, she needed to know what he had dealt with in the past, before they'd met.

Liam looked thoughtful, and his eyes glazed over as if his mind were travelling to a different place. He ran his finger along the edge of his wine glass. 'She skidded on some black ice just before Christmas five years ago. Her car went across the middle of the road. The lorry coming from the other direction just didn't have time to stop.'

Sophie watched him as he spoke. His voice was even; he seemed so calm. Sophie felt her breathing deepen and her chest tighten as she empathised with what he must have been through.

'That's tragic,' she said. Her voice caught in her throat as she said it, suddenly overcome with emotion.

'It was an awful time, especially for Cassie. That's why we moved away for a while. She just didn't understand where her mum had disappeared to. It's tough explaining that to a young child.' Liam looked into his wine as he spoke, perhaps reliving a conversation or a moment between him and Cassie.

'I'll bet,' Sophie said, placing a hand on his arm to comfort him. He reached for it with his own and stroked a thumb across the back of her hand. His reciprocation didn't go unnoticed, except this time, Sophie didn't feel the need to get out of there and run away.

'Cassie was great, though. I don't think I could have done it without her.'

'Is that why you insist on driving me and everyone else everywhere?'

'I don't normally explain it, but yes. Emily skidded on ice

she couldn't even see. I hate to think of anyone I love driving unnecessarily.' A loaded moment hung between them as Sophie realised what he had said, and she wondered whether he meant it. Was she someone that he loved?

'But it was a long time ago now,' Liam said, a little louder. He sat himself more upright to symbolise the change in mood. 'I'm moving on, we've moved back here, I'm dating again. It's what Emily would have wanted.'

Sophie smiled at him over her mug of wine.

'And what about you?' Liam said.

'What about me?'

'What about your past? Any hidden ghosts? You mentioned an ex before.'

Sophie hid her face behind a cushion and groaned.

'Are you ready to move on?' Liam said.

She put the cushion down and stared into her mulled wine. 'It's complicated,' she said eventually. 'I may never be ready to move on.'

Liam's face turned serious. 'That doesn't sound too promising. Do you want to talk about it?' he asked.

She regarded him for a moment while she considered what she did or didn't want to share with this man. She didn't know why, but she trusted him entirely and, for once, felt like she could share her story with him.

'You may recall I'm not a fan of balloons,' Sophie said.

'Don't remind me.' Liam shook his head, embarrassed.

'My ex, Jordan, brought balloons as a gift the very last time I saw him. We were planning to celebrate. I'd been for a scan that day and found out that I was having a little girl. We'd been excited before, of course. But knowing the sex had made things so much more real.' Her voice grew shaky, and she paused to collect herself. Liam remained silent and listened to Sophie's story.

'I'd texted him to let him know the news, and he'd been out in his lunch hour to buy them. When I called an hour later, I told him he needed to get to the hospital. I was in pain and there was . . . I don't need to go into all that.' She paused and wiped a tear from her nose. 'By the time he got to the hospital, it was all over. I'd lost her.'

A silence descended over the pair of them.

Sophie could still see Jordan turning up in the hospital suite, his face falling when he saw the state that Sophie was in and that the clear plastic cot alongside the bed was empty. They'd talked and cried, and when he'd left later that day, she'd never seen him properly again. She'd never found out whether it was the excuse he'd been looking for to get out of the relationship, or because he couldn't stand the sight of her for failing so appallingly at being a mother.

Tears ran freely down Sophie's face. Liam passed her a tissue, and she wiped them away.

'I can't believe he did that, that he'd leave you when . . .'

'I'm glad he did now. If he couldn't support me through a miscarriage, then he wouldn't have been there for me for anything else. It was a lucky escape, I suppose,' she said, sniffing.

'God, Soph. I'm so sorry that happened to you,' Liam said, shifting closer on the sofa to wrap his arms around her.

'It was a long time ago,' she said into his jumper.

'That doesn't mean anything.' He released Sophie from his

embrace. 'Awful things happen and they affect us for ever. It doesn't mean we can't move forward, but it does mean that we're changed by the past.'

She smiled and finished the last of her mulled wine, setting it down on the table and getting comfortable on the sofa again. 'I guess you know why I was so pushy with the concert raising money for Mum's charity now.'

'What do they do exactly?' Liam asked.

'They support mothers like me, you know, after it happens.' Sophie picked at a nail.

'That sounds like a very worthy cause. I'm glad we can raise money for it.'

'I just hope that we do,' Sophie said, still nervous that the concert might not bring in the sizable donation that her mother was expecting.

'With your solo, I've no doubt that we will.' Liam smiled.

Sophie had forgotten about the solo with the excitement of everything, and a fresh wave of nausea swept over her. 'Fingers crossed.'

'We will,' Liam repeated. 'Can I get you another drink? A hot chocolate perhaps? A tea?'

Sophie was enjoying Liam's company and wasn't ready to go home just yet. 'Yes please, just a tea, though. I'm driving.'

They went into the kitchen and Liam made them cups of tea.

'Thank you,' she said, as he passed her the mug.

'You've got mascara,' Liam said. 'Everywhere,' he added with a smile.

Sophie was mortified and tried to look at herself in the

window's reflection, with little success. Liam moved closer and wiped some away with his thumb, his touch sending warmth through Sophie's body. She swallowed and put her mug down on the table before standing on her tiptoes and reaching up to brush his lips lightly with hers. They both looked at each other, waiting for some kind of blessing from the other to know it was OK to continue, that nothing in their complicated pasts was still there to stop them. Sophie still had a lot to work through, but kissing Liam made all of it feel ever so slightly better.

'How's your war wound?' Liam asked, moving his thumb to where the bruising was beginning to subside on Sophie's cheek.

'I'm healing,' she said, reaching her hand up to brush back the curls that had fallen over his face.

It was all the invitation he needed, leaning down to kiss Sophie properly on the lips. His hands left her face and circled her waist, holding her as close as he possibly could. After a second, he pulled away. 'Are you OK?' he asked, his brow furrowed.

'I'm not going to run away this time, if that's what you mean,' Sophie said. She smiled and then looked down, embarrassed about the last time they'd been in this position.

'And you're not going to chase after that lumberjack from the pub either, are you?' His expression looked like he meant the question seriously.

'Definitely not.'

'Good.' Liam lifted Sophie's face by the chin so that she was looking right at him. 'There's just something about you, Sophie

Lawson,' he said, and kissed her again.

Even though it wasn't their first kiss, the intensity surprised her. Sophie's stomach flipped like it always did when Liam was near, her skin sensitive to his touch as he put an arm around her waist to bring her closer to him again. He kissed her cheeks and eyelids and nose softly before kissing her mouth. Sophie's breathing hitched as the kiss deepened. All thoughts about why kissing Liam would be a bad idea melted away to be replaced with a focus on the fact that Liam was kissing her and that it was perfect.

Liam pulled away again and looked her in the eye. She smiled, breathless from the kiss and from the stirrings it made her feel in the pit of her stomach and lower.

'I'm not going to run away,' she said, 'but I don't think I should stay.'

Liam looked hurt, one eyebrow slightly raised.

'Cassie's got enough going on without waking up to find me here. Imagine if you'd woken up one day to find your teacher at your house.'

Liam laughed. 'My Year Six teacher was a very short, very old and beardy man.'

'Exactly. It would have been weird.' Sophie smiled.

Liam ran a hand through his hair, clearly wrestling with what he wanted to do and what he should do. Sophie smiled at his indecision. It was nice to think she had that effect on him.

Eventually he let out a groan. 'Ugh! It's just like you to put everyone else's feelings before your own.' He pulled her into a hug, his arms high on her back, and kissed her forehead.

She pulled back so that she could reach up and kiss him

lightly on the lips. Something about having Liam with her made her feel safe and more confident, even.

'You know it's the right decision,' she said softly.

'I do. But you know I would have you stay for ever if I could.'

Sophie smiled. 'I know.'

'Will you come back for breakfast tomorrow? I'm making my speciality pancakes.'

'Not another culinary experiment.' Sophie groaned, hiding her head dramatically in her hand.

'I'll have you know,' he said, tilting her chin up, 'that my pancakes are particularly good and you'll eat your words once you've tasted them!' He kissed her again and thoughts of why Liam's pancakes were a bad idea disappeared.

'OK, I'll come back in the morning for breakfast,' she agreed.

Liam took her hand and Sophie smiled.

'I'd better get home.'

# Chapter Twenty-Nine

One week until Christmas

Term was finally coming to an end. Sophie only had to make it through three more days until the end of Wednesday, but there was a lot to fit in within that short amount of time, not least the final concert rehearsal on Tuesday night, which Sophie was beginning to fret about.

'It's not that I'm worried about the concert,' she said to Kate as they sat writing Christmas cards to the children in their classes. 'Oh God! It is, actually. Ugh!' She groaned. 'What have I got myself into?'

Outside, children were racing around as they burnt off energy after their lunch. The screams and giggles filtered through the cracks in the windows. Kate looked over to see what was going on, but Tom was out there on duty again and all looked to be in order.

'You had to do it, though. Once Lulu was out of the picture, it was the only way to save the concert,' Kate said. She slipped the top of the envelope inside itself to avoid licking it closed.

'I know,' Sophie replied, doing the same to one of hers and putting it in the pile that had built up on the table. 'But I don't have to like it,' she added.

Kate smiled at her across the table.

'Have you seen Lulu recently?' Sophie asked.

'No, why? Is she OK?'

'She really is,' Sophie said, thinking back to how agile she'd appeared when she'd visited last week. 'I went to see her the other day, and she's not using sticks or anything. She seemed fine.'

'That's odd,' Kate said, finishing another card and adding it to the pile.

'Mmm.' Sophie stopped what she was doing for a moment and regarded Kate.

Kate put down her pen and looked at Sophie. 'What? Do you really think Lulu would pretend to have a fall and give up a solo just so you could do it?' She laughed.

Kate was right. That didn't sound very much like Lulu at all. She would never give up the opportunity to perform. But still . . .

'I suppose not.' Sophie went back to writing her cards.

'I think, secretly, you're quite enjoying it,' Kate said.

Sophie thought about it and realised Kate was right. Somewhere deep inside her she really did want to do the concert and was pleased that Liam had asked her, even if it was sort of by default because of Lulu's absence. The thought that anyone believed in her singing ability – especially Liam – was an incentive.

'All right. You've got a point. But I'm still feeling anxious and until it's over, I fully intend to blame you and Lulu! Liam would never have known what my singing was like if you and Lulu hadn't forced me into auditioning,' she said, sliding another card over to write.

'You didn't have to,' Kate said.

Sophie was about to protest when a crescendo of noise from outside made them both look up.

'Do you think we should . . . ?' Kate asked.

'I'll go,' Sophie said, standing up. 'If we wait for you, it'll all be over.'

Kate scowled and then laughed. 'Good point.'

Sophie grabbed her coat from the hook and went outside, using her classroom fire door for a quick exit. A group of children were squabbling and jeering, and in the middle, she could just see Tom's hi-vis jacket. The teaching world's most hideous fashion accessory had finally paid off.

'Excuse me,' Sophie shouted above the furore. 'Move out of the way.' And a few of the children did, wandering off in twos and threes but looking back to bear witness to the action.

In the centre of the circle, she found Tom holding two girls away from each other. Sophie instantly recognised one of them as Cassie.

'Can you deal with one of these, please?' Tom said, breathless and angry. His cheeks were red and his jacket and hair dishevelled from the ruckus.

'Of course,' Sophie said.

'Lily, you go with Miss Lawson.' He gently manoeuvred Lily, and the sullen-looking girl walked towards Sophie.

Sophie considered asking for Cassie instead, then decided against it, thinking that it might be a conflict of interest having to deal so directly with Cassie's behaviour, especially when it wasn't even in her classroom.

'Come on, Lily,' she said, and Lily followed her back into the building. Kate had already vacated the room to allow for the conversation to take place.

'Are you hurt?' Sophie asked. Lily slumped herself down

into one of the chairs and shook her head. 'What happened?'

'Nothing,' Lily said, looking down at her feet.

'It didn't look like nothing.' Sophie looked at Lily, whose hair was sticking out all over the place. She had marks on her face where Cassie had apparently clawed at her.

'Cassie was being annoying,' Lily said. 'And she stole my pencil case.' She held up the offending item. 'I was just getting it back.' She sniffed and wiped her nose with a muddy and wet sleeve. Sophie passed her a tissue.

'Well, Lily, you know there are other ways of resolving an argument like that. Fighting with someone is never OK. We've been through this.'

'She stole my stuff,' came the angry reply.

Sophie could see she wouldn't get anywhere with Lily while she was this wound up. It was always difficult dealing with the students who habitually flouted the rules. Sophie concentrated on her breathing and composed herself.

'Why don't you go and sit outside Miss Davies's office? I'm sure she'll want to speak to you this afternoon,' Sophie said once she was happy Lily wasn't injured.

As a frequent visitor to the head's office, Lily groaned and took herself off in the direction of the corridor in which visitors to the head sat and waited. The children called it the corridor of shame and it was the fifth time Lily had spoken to the headteacher in the past fortnight. It obviously wasn't working. Sophie made a mental note to speak to someone about Lily and what else they might be able to do to address her behaviour, or whatever was behind it.

Sophie rubbed a hand over her face and brushed her hair back – part exhaustion and part frustration. She would have to speak to Cassie now, and then she'd have to speak to Liam too after school. This was not the next conversation she'd envisaged having with the man she had spent such a wonderful evening with only a few days ago.

'Miss Lawson?' Tom poked his head around the door frame with Cassie loitering in his shadow. 'Can you look after Cassie? I'm happy to have the talk with her but she needs a first aider before that.'

'Of course. Come in, Cassie.' Sophie indicated a seat for her to sit in.

While Cassie sat down, Sophie went and found the first aid box from the craft cupboard. Tom mouthed a thank you to her before closing her classroom door and calming down the children that were congregating outside.

Cassie's hair was as messed up as Lily's. She'd worn it up again today, but now bits of it hung out of the hair bobble and she already had a bruise forming on her chin.

'Let me look at you,' Sophie said, waiting for Cassie to give her permission to tend to her injury. Above where her chin had clearly been walloped, Cassie's eyebrow had a cut that was dripping blood down onto her top. Sophie knew it was likely to appear worse than it was, but it didn't stop her from recoiling as she took a closer look. Cassie's blood-splattered top didn't help the situation, either.

'Sir said I should come and tell you what happened,' Cassie said, sitting on her hands.

'I'm listening.' Sophie cleaned the wound with an antibacterial wipe. It was quite deep, and Sophie was in two minds as to whether or not this was the kind of first aid that was slightly beyond her. It looked clean despite its continued bleeding. She held a gauze to it for a minute or two to assess just how much blood Cassie was losing and to decide what her next move would be.

'I took something of Lily's,' Cassie said, playing nervously with the ribbed edging of her school jumper.

'I know. She told me.'

Tears started to roll down Cassie's face, mingling with the blood and dirt that was already there.

'Do you want to tell me why you did it?' Sophie pulled the gauze away briefly to see if the bleeding had stopped. It hadn't. Concerned, she pressed it back down again.

'She was being mean to me again, and I wanted her to stop. I thought if I took her pencil case she'd think it was someone else and be mean to them instead.' She wiped a sleeve across her face, snot smearing across her jawbone and onto the jumper itself.

Sophie handed her a tissue, and she blew her nose loudly.

There was a slightly strange logic behind Cassie's plan, thought Sophie, but then reminded herself that despite Lily's misdemeanours, Cassie was also in the wrong here. She couldn't let her feelings for Liam cloud her judgement.

'So, what was happening outside a moment ago?' Sophie asked.

'Someone told Lily they'd seen me take her pencil case, and she wanted to fight me. I was trying to get away.'

'Cassie, you know better than to do any of the things you did today. It's wrong to steal, and it's wrong to get into fights,' Sophie said, keeping eye contact to try to relay the seriousness of it all.

'I know,' she said, sniffling and crossing and uncrossing her legs over and over. 'Will you tell my dad?'

'I'll need to speak to him, yes.'

A fresh wave of tears shook Cassie's body. 'But it's not my fault,' Cassie said through her snorts.

'I know it doesn't feel like that, but it's important to talk about these things with your dad so he and I can try to help you. Stealing and fighting are wrong, but that's not what this is about. This is about you being unhappy because Lily is unkind to you. That's why I need to talk to him. Lily's teacher will talk to her parents too.'

Cassie looked up and steadied her breath.

Sophie pulled the gauze away again. It had grown warm under her hand and when she looked at it, she could see the whole thing was bright red. She was going to have to go to A&E.

'Cassie, I think we're going to have to pop down to the hospital and get someone to have a look at this. It's a bit stubborn and won't stop bleeding. It might just need a bigger plaster than the ones we've got here,' she said, trying to allay any panic that Cassie might have felt at the mention of the hospital. 'Come on.'

Cassie sniffed loudly. 'Will you come with me?' she asked quietly.

Sophie looked at Cassie's red eyes. She looked so small. Someone else would have to cover her afternoon lesson. 'Of course I can. You stay there a minute. I just need to find Miss Davies.'

Liam growled. 'Soph, why can't you just answer the damn phone?' Since she'd left the message about Cassie half an hour earlier, he'd called five times and still not managed to get through. He pulled to a stop by the traffic lights and tapped at the steering wheel for something to do with his hands. Reaching over for his phone, while stationary, he tapped to listen to the message Sophie had left once again.

*'Liam, I'm sorry to have to leave a message. There's been a bit of an incident with Cassie.'*

The message sounded tinny, like she was calling from a car – hands free, he hoped. He shivered at the thought of it and swallowed, finding it hard to breathe with the heater blowing directly into his face. He fiddled with the dials in the front of the Land Rover and looked up to see the traffic had moved.

*'She's fine,'* the message continued. *'There's just been a bit of an accident and I need to take her down to A&E. There was another fight. I'm just on my way to the hospital with her, no ambulance or anything,'* she'd added, as if that would make things better.

He felt a fresh wave of annoyance as she withheld the damage and focused on the scenario. It was just like Sophie to think about the bad behaviour and not the consequences.

*'Apparently, Cassie took something belonging to another child and when that other child found out, they got into a fight. Anyway, you don't need to know all of that. I'm driving and I'm getting into the busy bit of town. Call me when you get this, or meet us down there.'*

As the message finished, Liam could hear Sophie react to something on the road, exclaiming something inaudible before the phone clicked off. Even having listened to the message several times over, his breath caught in his chest. Emily.

Just the journey to the hospital was bringing back horrible memories. On that day five years ago, he'd rushed to A&E as soon as he'd heard of Emily's accident, driving recklessly himself to get there as fast as possible. The most vivid part of the memory, though, was rushing through the automatic doors of the hospital and being hit with the acidic smell of antiseptic and antibacterial cleaner. When he thought about that day for too long, the sting in the back of his nose and throat was palpable. When he smelt those things for real, he would almost black out at the memory, his brain unable to think back and process the hideousness of it all.

And now he was going back. And Cassie was hurt. And he was being forced to drive recklessly across town, to the one place he'd vowed never to step foot inside again. And it was all Sophie's fault.

'Where is she?'

Sophie stepped back to avoid Liam as he stormed past her to the empty reception window in the hospital foyer.

'She's just finishing up with the doctor.' Sophie clasped her hands together in front of her and took a step towards Liam. When he turned and she saw the rage and worry in his eyes, she took a step back again. 'She's going to be fine. It was just a cut across her eyebrow. Apparently the skin is fragile there. I wanted to be sure it was all OK.'

'She's going to be fine? That's really not the point. Once again, Cassie has been attacked by another pupil at school and this time it's even worse than the times before.' Liam held out his arms to the waiting room. 'We're in hospital.'

'Yes, I know that, Liam. And I'm sorry.'

He tutted, sucking his cheeks in. Without responding, he began to pace.

'The doctor said she'll only be a few minutes. She didn't need stitches, but they have glued it together to make sure it heals well without too much of a scar.'

Liam huffed at the mention of a scar, shaking his head.

When he didn't say anything, Sophie said, 'I'm sorry.' Her voice was smaller than she'd hoped.

Sophie hated the metres between them. She thought about going to him; she wanted to comfort him, but could see the anger in his eyes. She'd blown it this time.

'Daddy!' Cassie ran out of the doctor's room, half joyful, half tears of relief at seeing her father after the ordeal.

The doctor followed her out, pushing a biro into the top pocket of her white coat. She tucked a wisp of greying hair behind her ear. 'She's going to be fine, Miss Lawson. Luckily, the cut is in a good place to heal nicely.'

'I'm her father.' Liam held Cassie in his arms, stroking her hair down her back. 'Let me look at you.' He held her head in his hands. He had a physical reaction to seeing his daughter in pain, wincing when he saw her wound.

'Sorry, Mr . . .'

'Mr Hawthorn.'

'Well, Mr Hawthorn. I'm sure Miss Lawson has filled you in.'

Liam glanced over at her, his look cold.

'But do you want me to talk through things with you briefly before you take Cassie home?'

Liam nodded and followed the doctor back into her office.

'Come here, Cassie,' he added, so that she had to follow her father into the room.

Sophie flopped down onto a plastic chair in the waiting room, utterly exhausted. This was awful. After everything she'd overcome – they'd overcome – to have got together, now she'd gone and ruined it. Liam would never forgive her for this. The pain and loss she'd feared had happened, except this time it was entirely her fault.

She picked at the corner of a nail, chipping her nail varnish off at the same time.

She stood when the door of the doctor's office opened.

'We're going home.' Liam's voice was low as he passed her, dragging Cassie behind him.

Sophie followed him a few steps. 'Liam.'

He turned suddenly. 'Don't! Just don't!' She could see tears in his eyes, and his body shook as he stood there. Then, his voice even and low: 'I can't believe you made us come here.'

Then he turned sharply and strode out of the building.

Sophie heard the doctor clear her throat and then retreat back into her office. In Liam's absence, the waiting room grew silent. Sophie took a deep breath and sat down on the chair again. She hadn't thought about it, not really. Bringing Cassie here, bringing Liam back to the hospital. It probably wasn't just an A&E to them. It was a place haunted with memories and she'd brought them all back.

'What the hell were you thinking, Cassie?' Liam instantly regretted his curse as he watched Cassie cry harder out of the corner of his eye. She didn't answer, her whole body convulsing with sobs.

They drove the rest of the way back to the farm in silence. Liam's thoughts switched between rage at Cassie's behaviour, anger at the way the school had dealt with it, and frustration that whatever he'd started with Sophie was ruined. Cassie was snivelling and crying quietly the whole time. For a second, he thought he might shed some tears of his own, but he was too angry.

When they pulled into the courtyard, Cassie undid her seatbelt and allowed her father to help her out of the car. In silence, Liam opened the door and Cassie followed him in, both removing their shoes. It was like the fight had gone from them both, but Liam couldn't let it go. If they went to bed without resolving things, he wouldn't sleep and they would probably never talk about it.

'What happened today?' Liam said. He attempted to sound less angry, but was only marginally successful.

'Nothing,' Cassie said, making her way towards the stairs.

'Don't walk away from me, Cassie. What happened? I thought things were getting better at school.'

At his tone, Cassie turned and stood awkwardly in the hallway.

'What happened?' he asked again.

'I don't want to talk about it.'

'Well, you don't have a choice. We're going to talk about it now.' Liam knew his voice was coming across harsher than he intended it to, but Cassie was being so difficult today.

'I've already told Miss Lawson. She told you. Why do I need to say it all again?'

'I want to hear your side of things.'

'No, you don't. You never listen to me anyway.' Cassie finally plucked up the courage to walk away from her dad. She slammed the door, and he heard her race up the stairs into her bedroom.

He was left standing in the hallway, his fists clenched and his arms shaking. He blinked back a stray tear. How had he got this so wrong? He looked up as if to ask Emily for an answer. But, of course, she wasn't there to help him. So often, he felt like he needed her help, but she was never there.

He walked into the kitchen and sat down, his head resting on the cool table. He replayed the afternoon in his mind – from the moment he'd received Sophie's phone call to now. He'd not handled a single thing successfully, but then, neither had Sophie nor Cassie. He thumped the table with his fist and let out a groan.

He cursed himself for letting Sophie and the concert get in the way of what he truly wanted to do, which was being there for his daughter. His daughter, who at just five years old had lost her mother. An enormous cloak of guilt came over him that he had even considered other aspects of his life to be so important when Cassie, the single most important thing in his life, was going so horribly wrong.

# Chapter Thirty

Mortified, and far too exhausted to do any more work, Sophie packed up her things and went home. It was only 5 p.m. when she walked from her car to the flat but it was pitch black outside and, through the entrance to the car park, she could see the street was lit with Christmas lights. Employees were leaving the shops, while the windows remained festive, brightly lit and decorated. Ordinarily, Sophie would have felt warmed by such things, but tonight she just felt sorry for herself and the only thing she noticed about the outside was how cold it was. She sniffed and pulled her scarf up to cover her mouth and nose, hurrying to her flat to get away from the Christmas cheer.

Inside, she didn't bother with the Christmas lights. Instead, she opened the fridge to find something to eat. There wasn't much. She reached for a yoghurt. One of the ones with fruit in the corner. It was a couple of days out of date but it would have to do and besides, she'd lost her appetite. How had things changed so suddenly from the bliss she'd found herself in on Friday night? She'd ruined everything with Liam, and now she worried he was so angry with her that he might not turn up to the final rehearsal or the concert at all. He wouldn't be that petty, would he? She swallowed down a knot of anxiety.

Muffled steel drums came from her bag. She ignored them and finished her yoghurt. When they rang again a minute later, she took her time to put the empty yoghurt pot in the bin and answered. 'Hi, Mum.'

'Hi, love. How are things?'

Sophie opened her mouth to answer, but was interrupted before she could begin talking.

'Just wanted to see how you'd got on with your flyers?'

'Good actually,' Sophie said, relieved that in amongst all the hideousness, she finally had some positive news for June. She ignored the tugging at her brain that reminded her getting the flyers sorted might have been a complete waste of time after all, considering that the concert might not even take place now. 'They've been reprinted and I've put them up all over town. We should get a good crowd.'

'That's great news, love.'

Sophie toyed with telling her mother that she had taken on the solo given Lulu's fall, but with the nagging worry that Liam might pull out of the concert completely, she decided against it. The less they spoke about the concert at this point, the better. That way, when it didn't happen . . . who was she kidding? Fundraising was far too important to June and her charity. Maybe she should sow the seed just in case . . .

'Yes, hopefully,' Sophie said.

'Hopefully?' June took the bait.

'You see, there's been a bit of a problem with the musical director, and Lulu, our soloist, took a fall.' Sophie stood up and paced back and forth between the living room and the kitchen – all four steps of it. She couldn't keep still.

'Sophie, this concert *is* going to happen, isn't it?' June's tone was clipped and already sounding worried.

'Yes. Yes, I think so.'

'You don't sound very certain.'

'Well, I just want you to be prepared in case things don't go as planned. I'll make sure that I raise the money for the charity, though, whatever happens. I promise.'

'And how exactly will you do that?'

'I'm not sure yet, but I'll figure something out. Maybe I'll do a sponsored run or something.' That would never happen, but Sophie was desperate to placate her mother.

'Couldn't someone else do the solo?' asked June.

Sophie let out a strained laugh. Yes, they could if they'd not fallen in love with the MD and then let his child get injured in a fight.

'Couldn't you do it?' June pressed her.

'It's not that simple, Mum. Things are complicated here.'

'Typical,' June said unkindly.

'What's that supposed to mean?'

'This is what you do, Sophie. Things don't go to plan and you run away or bury your head in the sand. You need to follow through with your commitments.'

'Things haven't just got tough, Mum. I'm potentially missing a conductor and a soloist. A concert can't take place without those things.' Sophie sat down on the sofa, her nerves bristling.

'You have to overcome problems like this, come up with solutions.'

Sophie shook her head. 'I don't know what the solution is yet. I'm working on it.'

'This is just like you.'

'What?'

'You ran away to the countryside last time things got tough.'

'This is hardly the same.'

Her mother scoffed.

'I didn't run away to Cranswell,' Sophie said. 'I left for my job.'

'That's what you keep telling yourself, love. You should have stayed here, faced the music.'

'There is no music to face when you lose a child.'

There was silence on the other end of the phone. Sophie focused on her breathing and tried to see past the red mist that had descended. Her mother was infuriating. Why couldn't she see how hard it was? It was the first time Sophie had mentioned what had happened to June in a long time.

'Why can't you see it, Sophie? Why can't you see that staying here would have helped you to heal?' June said. Her tone was gentle, but Sophie was past caring.

'Why can't you understand, Mum? I will never heal.'

'Sophie, I—'

'No! Why can't you accept that I had to get away? Losing my baby girl was the single most appalling thing that has ever happened to me, or is ever likely to happen to me. I lost my child, my home and my partner in the space of forty-eight hours and after a week everyone thought I should be getting better, getting over it, as if it wasn't the same as losing a parent or a best friend. She was twenty-two weeks old. I gave birth to her. She was alive in my eyes before I lost her. You insisted on

going on, acting as if nothing had happened, willing me to get out there again and restart my life.'

Sophie's mother breathed in as if to respond, but Sophie continued.

'I will never get over it. Ever. Losing my little girl has changed me for ever. Why can't you accept that and support me instead of trying to paper over everything as if it needs forgetting?'

'Sophie, love . . .'

Sophie didn't wait to hear what her mother had to say next. She threw her phone down onto the sofa and sat as far away from it as she could before bursting into tears.

# Chapter Thirty-One

Inevitably, Tuesday came around again like a depressingly predictable bus journey in the rain. Sophie missed the days where she felt excited about going to rehearsal. These days, she always seemed to be a bag of nerves. And this week was no different, except to add to her anxiety, she felt desperately low after the previous day's events. She met Kate, and they walked over to the town hall together, Sophie having filled her in about everything over the phone the night before, including what had brought her to Cranswell in the first place. They'd both cried, and Kate had stayed on the phone while Sophie stared into space, mourning her loss. Kate had been patient and understanding – a far cry from the way her mother had behaved. Only after a long time had they spoken again until Sophie had fallen asleep and Kate had hung up, sending a message to let her know if she woke and needed her, just to call.

'You'll be fine,' Kate said as they crossed the threshold into the hall.

They arrived as several other members of the choir did. Sophie wrestled her way to the front of the group and opened the door, letting them all in. Inside, she set about putting out the chairs while Kate made herself comfortable. Greg and Albert waved when they entered and Sophie waved back, a slight smile on her face – just to keep up appearances. Nobody else needed to know her fears for the concert, or how awful things had got over the past couple of days. She just hoped Liam turned up – for the sake of the villagers and their concert.

It was only once the chairs were set out and people had taken their seats, looking around to see where their musical director was, that Liam finally made his entrance. He apologised as he hurried to the front of the room and busied himself rolling out the piano and setting up the music stand. 'I'll be five minutes,' he said.

Sophie was both relieved and on edge. It was exhausting. Liam looked fraught with something on his mind, too. His hair was slightly dishevelled and his music books more disorganised than usual. He was red from his walk to rehearsal, and Sophie could tell he was hot and bothered. She felt numb when her stomach didn't do the usual flip it did when she saw him.

Liam popped his head up from where he had been unpacking things from his bag on the floor. He put the music on the piano and stood to signal he was waiting for quiet. The choir settled down. Sophie was pretty sure the entire hall could sense his slightly fractious demeanour this evening. She definitely could from where she was sitting. It was coming off him in waves.

'Right, let's get going,' Liam said brusquely. 'I'd like to start with the group numbers. Let's stand up.' He certainly was frosty this evening. Everyone stood up, looking at each other to try to work out why their MD was angry. He played the introduction a little faster than normal, and they sang through each of the songs.

'That sounds good,' he said robotically when they'd finished their repertoire. 'Sophie.' He used her full name, she noticed. 'Can you come out front so that we can do "White Christmas"?' he asked, without looking at her.

She had sort of expected this, but took a moment or two to stand up and make her way forward, a half-smile plastered on her face for the benefit of the choir.

'Don't mess it up, Sophie,' whispered Albert, grimacing. 'He might throw his baton at you.'

Sophie smiled weakly. She made her way out of the middle of the group of chairs and stood next to Liam and the piano.

'Not here,' Liam said.

Greg looked up at the sharpness of his comment.

'You can stand over there.' He pointed to what would be centre stage. 'You should know the words by now.'

Sophie's eyes bristled with the feeling of impending tears, but they were of anger and embarrassment rather than sadness. Liam was being an idiot. And he looked it in front of the assembled choir, who were whispering and fidgeting nervously in their seats.

As Liam played the introduction, for once, she didn't feel too nervous. Her preoccupation with Liam's mood helped her to forget what she was about to do, and she sang her verse through perfectly. The room was silent. She suddenly felt very powerful and after the whole choir joined in to finish, she glanced over at Liam, who was looking at her in such a way that her stomach finally did the flip she'd been expecting from it earlier.

Afterwards, of course, he made her sing the solo too, which she nailed and the room erupted into applause when she'd finished. She only hoped that she could carry it off on the evening of the concert. There was so much riding on it.

'Drink?' Kate asked, as they put their coats back on at the end of the rehearsal.

'God, yes!' Sophie said. She glanced in Liam's direction, caught him looking over at her, and continued to gather her belongings.

She had almost managed to sweep out the door before he had time to come over and say something, but not quite.

'Soph?'

She stopped and turned to speak to him, her whole body stiff with anger. Kate waited by the door.

'What is it, Liam?' She hugged her arms around her body, her body language not quite matching up to her assertive tone.

'We need to talk about the end of the solo,' he said, surprising her.

'I don't want to talk about the end of the solo,' Sophie said. 'It was fine.'

'I just think if we changed the note slightly, there'd be less pressure on you to hit it. I know it's been worrying you.'

Sophie shook her head. 'Don't pretend like you're doing me a favour. You don't get to be nice to me any more.'

'Look.' Liam put his hands on his hips and looked down at the ground for a moment. 'Maybe one of us should take a step back from the concert.'

'What?' That wasn't what she was expecting.

'After what happened, I just don't know if we can work together.'

Sophie couldn't believe what she was hearing. She'd been

cold because she wanted him to realise he'd made a mistake with her; she hadn't wanted him to step away from the concert completely. It was too important. Her mother was counting on her.

'I'm not giving up this concert. I've worked too hard, and it means too much.' Sophie heard herself speak and was surprised at how serious she sounded. 'You should know that.'

'Fine,' he said dejectedly. 'Then I guess I'll have to be the one who pulls out.' He turned away, and Sophie watched as he pushed the piano back into the music cupboard and gathered his belongings. 'Bye,' he said, when he passed her to leave the hall.

Kate held her hand up in a small wave as he left. 'Did that just happen?'

Sophie nodded. 'I think it did.' She scrunched her face up and held the back of her neck with her hands. 'What am I going to do?'

'We could ask Danielle from school. If she can conduct a bunch of five-to-ten-year-olds through a musical version of the nativity, I'm pretty sure she could whip us lot into shape,' Kate said.

'That might work.' Sophie bit her bottom lip as she ran through all the people she knew with any amount of musical ability and desperately tried to ignore the ache that Liam's desertion had caused to settle in her heart.

'You sounded great, at least,' Kate said.

'I couldn't let Liam win. He was being a grump and making me do the solos without warning again was unreasonable. Besides, I wanted to give him something to think about.'

'That's so not like you,' Kate said, sounding impressed. 'I like this new version.'

Sophie smiled sadly. 'I wish I didn't have to be like this, though. I'd sooner have Liam conducting the concert and . . .' She sighed. 'Well, I guess all that's over now.'

Liam dealt with some real-life pathetic fallacy on the walk home. The wind was getting stronger and large drops of rain blew into his face. He was seriously annoyed. Not with anybody else but himself, though. When he'd arrived at the hospital the previous day, he'd been so angry and he'd taken all of that anger out on Sophie. Only now did he realise that none of it was her fault. It was a difficult situation, sure, but he'd handled it with zero aplomb. In fact, he had been an outright idiot, and he knew it. Tonight should have been a chance to make amends, but he'd blown it. And now he'd stepped away from the concert – the one thing he could have done to make things OK again. He cursed his ego.

The mud and puddles were getting deeper as he walked down the lane towards the farm. He held his phone out as a torch and trudged through the sludge in a funk. Could he ever hope that Sophie would forgive him? He was only trying to protect Cassie – surely that was obvious. And his crappy mood this evening? He could only chalk that up to a bizarre self-preservation strategy. And look where it had got him. It had backfired so spectacularly. Sophie had reacted with such anger, and he couldn't blame her.

By the time he reached the farmhouse, Liam was freezing and seething.

'You don't look so good, love,' said his mother, as he pushed through the door with his stand and bag of sheet music. He dropped it to the floor and rubbed his shoulder where the bag had cut into his muscles.

'It's not been the best night, no,' Liam said, trying and failing not to sound annoyed with Barbara too.

'Well, maybe this will cheer you up,' she said, handing him an envelope in exchange for the other music books he was about to drop. She stepped back and perched on the edge of the sofa.

'What is it?' Liam took off his coat and hung it behind the door.

'Me and Cassie had a long talk this evening, and she decided there were some things she needed to say,' Barbara said, wiping her hands on the apron she wore, before untying it and walking through to the kitchen to hang it up. 'You should read that,' she said, putting her coat on, ready to leave. 'She's going to be OK, you know.'

Barbara reached up and touched her son's face before pulling him in for a cuddle and an air kiss. 'I'll see you tomorrow, love,' she said, leaving Liam in the kitchen, holding on to the envelope she'd given him.

His hands were cold. He could barely feel his fingers. So, he put the kettle on and poured himself a cup of tea. Opening the envelope, he sat at the kitchen table to read:

*To Dad,*

*I'm really sorry that I've been grumpy these last few weeks. I didn't like moving here at first. Sorry I got into a fight and stole Lily's pencil case. I know it was wrong. I've been feeling a bit sad and I don't know why. Please don't be mad with Miss Lawson. She's just doing her teacher job and I would like her to come over for tea again one day. It was nice because she made you smile. She's one of the good things about being back here – as well as Nanny and Grandad.*

*Sorry, Dad.*

*Love from Cassie XXXXX*

The page was decorated with smiley faces and Christmas pictures and she'd found glitter somewhere, which now dusted Liam's knees. He smiled and felt the prick of tears at the corner of his eyes. Cassie's advice was just the sort of thing Emily would have said to him.

Without a second thought, he made his way upstairs to where Cassie was sleeping and perched on the edge of her bed, brushing her hair back from her face. He kissed her head.

'You still awake, sweetheart?' Liam whispered.

Cassie made a noise that sort of sounded like she was.

'I got your letter.'

That made her roll over and shuffle up her pillow so that she was a little more upright.

'I'm sorry I've been angry with you these past few weeks,' he said.

'I'm sorry too.'

'I'm just trying to do my best for you and I know you probably won't understand that until you're older but I just wanted you to know that.'

Cassie stretched and yawned. 'I already know that, Dad. It's hard without Mum, isn't it?'

Liam swallowed, his throat tight. He nodded. 'It really is. But you and me, I think we're doing an OK job.'

Cassie reached over and wrapped her arms around Liam's neck. 'Me too.'

'Love you, Cass.'

'Love you too, Dad.' Cassie snuggled back underneath the duvet and rolled over. In seconds she was sleeping again, breathing faintly.

Liam stood and went to leave the room, turning to look back at his daughter as she rested peacefully. He had a lot of making up to do.

# Chapter Thirty-Two

## Christmas Eve

Sophie stared into the dressing room mirror (or the office-come-dressing room that had been set up at the back of the town hall). She put the finishing touches to her make-up, unaware of the chaos that was going on around her.

She rifled through her bag for the red lipstick, which seemed to have gone missing from her make-up bag. At the bottom of her holdall, she found the bauble she'd bought in London, ready to give to Liam on the night of the concert – but he wasn't going to be there. She picked it up and turned it upside down to watch the tiny flakes of snow drift down over the treble clef and musical note. It would have been the perfect gift to say thank you for the concert – well, to say thank you for everything – if everything hadn't gone so spectacularly wrong. She placed it carefully back in the bag, making sure she wrapped it in her spare jumper so that it wouldn't break. Maybe she'd put it on her own tree when she got home as a reminder of how not to pursue a relationship.

With only a few minutes to go before the concert began, Sophie ran the bright red lipstick across her mouth in an attempt to give herself a little more confidence and to cheer herself up – red lipstick had a way of doing that. She admired the way it matched the red dress she had picked out to wear. The dress code was festive, so she'd gone stylish rather than cheesy (despite how much she loved a Christmas jumper) and settled for a knee-length red dress with black tights and ballet pumps. Her earrings were tiny little snowflakes and her black cardigan was woven with the odd strand of silver thread so that it shimmered in the light.

The buzz of an impending performance continued on around her, with everyone doing a last check of their outfits and hair. Some of them were applying a little make-up to take the shine of the lights off them. Sophie was obtusely aware of a conversation taking place next to her about harmonies. She could have joined in, but instead she tried to focus and concentrate on her breathing, which was becoming more and more irregular with every minute that passed.

As it was Christmas Eve, Greg had come prepared with some fairy lights and a tiny tree that he'd taken from the coffee shop to brighten up the dressing room. Everywhere Sophie looked there were twinkling lights, or vibrant jumpers, or sparkly festive jewellery.

She wasn't feeling quite so sparkly inside, though. Her initial defiance in the face of Liam's stubbornness had melted away as the evening of the concert had drawn near. Even Kate couldn't cheer her up despite rocking a Christmas jumper that had a generous Christmas pudding on it in the place of her colossal bump.

There was a knock, and Nigel popped his head around the door. 'We're on in five,' he said, flashing a smile.

Luckily, Sophie had persuaded Nigel to come back and lead the concert. His mother had had a good week, and he'd even brought her along to enjoy the show and stay with the rest of his family for Christmas. Sophie was pleased that in one way, at least, things had worked themselves out.

'Thanks, Nigel,' Sophie said. 'Right, folks, it's time.' She stood to address the choir. They settled down, and the chaos of the room dissolved into silence. 'We've worked so hard for tonight. I can't wait for us to all get out there and show the audience the true meaning of Christmas.' There was a ripple of giggles, Albert's laugh heard above everyone else's.

Sophie looked at the choir – her choir – and felt a lump in her throat. She wanted nothing more than to see Liam's face out in the crowd. She swallowed.

'You guys are amazing. Thank you for being so wonderful.' She paused a moment, desperate for the tightness in her throat not to turn into tears.

'And congratulations to Sophie too. Thank you for everything you've done,' Greg said, and the room erupted into applause.

Sophie was pleased with his distraction and relaxed, the threat of tears subsiding. 'Let's do this, everyone!'

Kate let out a cheer and led the group out of the room; they chatted excitedly as they went. Sophie looked at herself in the mirror again as they filtered out of the dressing room and into the wings. Although she couldn't see any tears, they felt spectacularly close to the surface. The rest of the choir would be in the hall warming up shortly, but Sophie didn't feel like joining them. Besides, she'd sung sad show tunes in the car all the way to the venue. 'On My Own' had been on repeat for the vast majority of her journey. Her vocal cords were well and truly ready for action.

Through a crack in the door, Sophie could hear the audience gathering and beginning to settle. The flyers had done the trick – thank goodness, after all that fuss – and whether or not her mother was speaking to her, and vice versa, she was pleased to think that she'd probably done a good job of fundraising, after all. She realised her thoughts were simply a way of putting off the inevitable. She'd have to go out there, eventually. She applied another coat of lipstick and blotted it on a tissue, took a couple of deep breaths and got ready to go.

'Right,' she said to herself, smoothing down her dress and running her fingers through her hair. When she joined the rest of the group in the wings, Kate squeezed her hand in the darkness. She squeezed back.

They had made use of the hall's staggered seating, so once they were on the stage they would look out to something akin to what it must feel like to be on the stage of a real theatre. Sophie loved the heat and the lights. There was a particular smell that the hall had – probably a cocktail of wet rot, damp and dust – but still, to Sophie it was the comforting smell of performance day and home. She particularly loved the fact that often the bright lights masked her view of the audience, so it was like she was singing with the choir in rehearsal, which was just how she liked it.

The group shuffled onto the stage and stood in their prearranged lines as the audience applauded their entrance. Nigel walked on last and stood with his back to them to bow to the audience. Then he turned around and lifted his arms, a baton in one hand.

Sophie felt an overwhelming sense of sadness that it wasn't Liam's hazel eyes staring back at her, but instead Nigel's watery blue ones. In his suit and under the lights, Liam would have looked ridiculously good. She let out a heavy sigh of disappointment that she and Liam wouldn't be sharing the successes of the evening together after all their hard work.

The first half of the concert comprised several group numbers – a couple of performances from the choir, one or two musical pieces and a carol for the audience to join in with. Sophie found herself enjoying moments of the festivities but then remembering that Liam wasn't there, her heart deflating.

The interval consisted of two cups of water and three nervous wees. Sophie's solo was in the second half of the concert and the gravity of the situation was making her lungs hurt. She clutched at her chest as she downed a third cup of water.

'Will you please just relax?' Kate said. 'You're making me nervous and *I* can't go for a nervous wee because once these tights come off, they're not going back on again until after this baby is born!'

Sophie smiled at her joke and apologised, excusing herself for a final nervous wee before the second part of the concert began. She looked in the mirror to see purple bags under her eyes. She was weary. It had been an exceptionally odd and chaotic few weeks. But in some ways, she'd done OK; she'd survived at least, even if neither Liam nor her mother were talking to her. At the end of the day, she'd set out to put on a fundraising concert and she'd done just that. She put on a bonus layer of red lipstick and a little extra concealer under her eyes before making her way back to the auditorium.

The choir piled back onto the stage, and this time Sophie wasn't able to disappear within the crowd. Instead, her position was forward and centre. The second half of the concert started with one ensemble song, followed by Sophie's solo.

Nigel returned to the stage to rapturous applause and signalled for them to begin their singing. Sophie was vaguely aware of her harmonies and the glorious noise that the choir was making around her, but the fact that the solo was imminent left her distracted and startled at the stage lights shining in her eyes.

The song ended as she knew it must and the audience applauded until the cheers died down in anticipation of the next song – Sophie's song.

Nigel shuffled the sheet music on the piano stand. Was he going to play? Nigel normally only conducted, but Sophie supposed someone would have to play the music. She wished Liam was there to play for her. He was the only one who knew how she truly felt about singing and the only one she really trusted to make everything OK.

Nigel began the introduction. Sophie swallowed again and again as he played the first few bars, but her mouth went dry, her throat constricted and she felt sick. She couldn't do this. Her ears were ringing, and she was only vaguely aware of the room around her; her head a little fuzzy. The music paused before Nigel moved into the main accompaniment. It was fight or flight. Sophie froze, her mouth open, but no sound came out. Nigel looked up at her, confusion across his face. He raised his eyebrows and nodded, as if to signal she should sing.

Sophie saw a flash of leopard print as someone shuffled in their seat on the front row and wondered for a moment whether it was Lulu. Had she made it? Did she even want Lulu there to watch her take her beloved solo? She squinted into the audience and made out Lulu's wizened face and beehive. She held up two enthusiastic thumbs. She could do this. Everyone was there to support her and, besides, she'd promised a Christmas concert and she needed to give them one. She'd come this far . . .

She glanced nervously back at Nigel, swallowed and nodded, inviting him to play the introduction again. As he paused in the same place, Sophie sucked in a huge breath of air and opened her mouth to sing.

'Wait!' There was a commotion at the back of the hall. Whoever had shouted had also knocked over a display board and run into the back row of seats. They raced forward, but Sophie couldn't make out who it was – the stage lights were in her eyes. It was only when the suited figure jumped up onto the stage, she realised it was Liam.

He turned to the audience. 'Sorry, everyone.' He was breathing heavily, like he'd run to get there. 'I just needed to . . . I had to . . . Look, it's not my big moment, it's Sophie's. Let's begin the song again.' He walked over to the piano. 'Sorry,' he said again before turning to sit on the piano stool Nigel had just vacated.

Liam scanned the stage for Sophie and smiled at her. It was a smile of regret. In his suit, he was as beautiful as she'd imagined. It was black and tailored in all the right places. He'd done something to his hair, but it had slipped back into its unruly ways in his rush to get there. He made himself comfortable and then looked up again at Sophie. She smiled at him, trying to convey just how grateful she felt that he'd come to play for her solo. Perhaps everything would be OK.

He lifted his arms and started to play. It sounded different somehow when he turned his hands to the keys. It felt like home. She began to sing. And despite the fear and the tightness in her throat, and the fact that one of her knees refused to stop wobbling for the entire performance, it was the best she had ever sung it. She hit every note and every nuance that she had gone over with Liam in their rehearsals. It was perfect. And when she reached the huge note at the end to finish and left the auditorium silent when it ended, the audience burst into applause, and so did Liam.

Sophie bowed and scurried back to her place in the middle of the choir to pats on the back and congratulations from her fellow singers.

'What's he doing here?' Kate asked as Sophie returned to her spot. They watched as Liam stood, gave way to Nigel again, and hovered in the shadows of the wings.

'I've no idea. I'm just glad he showed up,' Sophie said.

'You were ridiculously good.' Kate squeezed her hand.

'Thanks. I'm just glad I can relax and enjoy the rest of the concert now.' Which she did.

When it came to 'White Christmas' at the end, she knew she could do it and it was received wonderfully by the audience, who joined in enthusiastically for the last verse. And to her surprise, when the lighting changed during the final applause, she could see her parents – front row and centre. They'd come to see her. David and June stood to clap, beaming smiles across their faces.

'That was great!' Greg said as Sophie helped him off the stage and into the dressing room.

'It really was fun, and very Christmassy!' Albert said.

'Sophie, honey!' Lulu's familiar voice echoed through the crowd.

Sophie turned around. 'Lulu!' She was pleased to see her. And while it wasn't fancy dress, Lulu had chosen to wear a flapper dress, complete with a long leopard-print coat and a feather in her hair. The overall look was eccentric, 1920s Hollywood glamour merged with her signature 60s beehive. Sophie expected nothing less from Lulu, who was making her way comfortably across the hall. Sophie met her halfway and went in for an embrace. Cuddles from Lulu, especially when she was wearing so many layers, were particularly delicious.

'You look . . .' Sophie grasped for the right word. 'Recovered.' She narrowed her eyes.

'Oh, it was just a little fall, kid. You were wonderful.' She stood back to take a look at Sophie. 'Really wonderful.'

'I hope so,' Sophie said. 'Yours were pretty big shoes to fill.'

'But you did it so beautifully. Maybe it was a good thing that I took a fall after all, eh?' she said, winking conspiratorially. 'And it got you spending so much more time with that lovely Liam. I couldn't have planned it better myself!'

Sophie found herself once again wondering how likely it was that the fall had been a fabrication to get Sophie singing . . . or dating?

'Anyway, now that everything's sorted and I'm back to my

old self, I'm raring to return to choir practice so we can get ready for our next concert. Maybe Liam will let us do a duet?' she said, clasping her hands together excitedly.

'I'm not sure that Liam will be sticking around.'

'Oh? Why not?'

Sophie didn't get a chance to reply as a hand tapped her on the shoulder. She turned as Lulu found someone else to hug.

'Hi, Sophie love.' Her father pulled her in for a hug.

'Hi, Dad,' she said, pulling away. 'Mum.' Sophie realised her mouth was hanging open.

June shuffled her feet on the spot and wrung her hands together. 'Hello, Sophie. I owe you an apology.'

'I didn't think you would come,' Sophie said.

'I didn't know if you'd want me to, to be honest,' June said. 'Not after—'

Sophie interrupted her. 'Of course I wanted you here. This whole fundraiser has been for you, for the charity.'

'I know,' June said. 'I realise that now. I can see that raising money for the charity, helping other mothers like you – it was really important to you and it was how you were dealing with things.'

It was the first time she had acknowledged the fact that Sophie was a mother, and it meant everything to her.

June reached over and took Sophie's hand. 'I do understand how you were, how you *are* feeling. After what you said, I can see that now. I'm sorry I ever pressured you to move on and to forget. I should have known better. I should have realised that it was far more complicated than that.'

Sophie smiled. 'Thank you, Mum. That means a lot to me.

I'm sorry I lost it with you on the phone.'

'It was understandable,' June said, lifting her aged eyes to meet Sophie's. 'You were wonderful, by the way.' She pulled Sophie towards her and squeezed her tightly as her cheeks flushed red. Sophie buried her face in her mother's hair and inhaled. It was such a familiar scent. She wished they could be like this more often.

'You really were fantastic,' David said, who until now had allowed them to make their apologies and stood silently by. His face was all smile, and proud tears threatened to fall from his eyes.

Sophie hugged him too. 'I didn't think you were coming,' she said again.

'Neither did I,' said her father, 'But your mother insisted that she wanted to come and make amends – and find out just how much you've raised for the charity, of course.' He chuckled.

Sophie and her father shared a look. 'Well, I'm glad you came,' she said. 'And at the moment, I think we've raised about £700 but by the time we add up the last-minute tickets and programmes and bar money, I think we'll get that up to over a thousand.'

'Goodness!' June clapped her hands together. 'That's fantastic news! We can help so many people with that money. People who are going through what you went through.'

Sophie smiled at her mother's happiness. She might even go as far as to suggest that June looked proud.

Sophie held back the tears of relief that were pooling behind her eyes. 'Are you staying for Christmas?'

'We've booked into a hotel, so we're not in your way,' June

said. 'But yes, we're here for a few days. It would be lovely to spend some quality time with you. Maybe we could see that flat of yours?'

'I was going to make Christmas dinner, and there's definitely enough for all three of us. I can make it stretch. Will you come over for lunch and spend the afternoon with me?'

'We'd love to,' David said, before June could answer in any other way. 'We're so proud of you,' he added, nodding his head towards the stage.

'Thanks, Dad. It means so much that you got to see it.'

'I wouldn't have missed it for the world.'

Sophie swallowed the feeling of tears and bit her bottom lip to curb her emotions. 'A few of us are going across the road for a Christmas drink, I think,' she said, 'if you'd like to join us?'

'Oh, I don't know if your father . . .'

'We'd love to,' said David, obviously squeezing June's hand.

'Great,' Sophie said. 'I just need to go and collect my stuff from the dressing room and I'll be over in a minute.'

'I'll get you a drink,' David said.

Sophie could hear her mother raise concerns about drinking and socialising this late as they left.

'We'll be fine, June,' David said as they tottered through the door and followed the crowd to the pub.

'Pub?' Lulu asked.

'Definitely,' Sophie said, joining the throng of choristers as they shuffled out of the auditorium.

'What fun that was,' Greg said.

'It really was,' said Kate.

'I'm so glad I got better enough in time to see the performance,' Lulu said, linking arms with Greg.

'I think you were well enough weeks ago,' Albert said under his breath.

'On to preparations for the next one?' said Sophie.

Kate let out a groan, stopping the conversation dead. 'I think I might be in labour,' she said.

They all laughed, familiar with Kate's sense of humour.

'No, really.' She rubbed her bump. 'It's been coming on since "Santa Baby", ironically.'

'Oh God, Kate. Let's get you to the hospital,' Sophie said, going into practical friend mode.

'No, no, no.' Kate shook her head. 'Baby won't come for at least twenty-four hours. Let's get a festive drink first. To the pub.' She pointed her finger over their heads in the general direction of the pub.

Everyone cheered despite the potential severity of the situation.

'Are you sure?' Sophie said, raising her eyebrows, uncertain. 'I really think that perhaps we should go to the hospital. Maybe I could call Gav?'

'Sophie, it's not every day my girl faces her fears and smashes her performance. I want to take you for a quick drink. I won't be free for a catch-up for another eighteen years after tonight, so you'd best make the most of it.'

Sophie smiled. 'As long as you're sure. I'll text Gav to let him know. I just need to pop and grab my stuff. I'll be over in a minute.'

She was mildly concerned about Kate, but she seemed to be

in the capable hands of Greg and Lulu, who, despite enjoying a bit of drama, looked to be taking good care of her.

Sophie went back to the dressing room and gathered up her things. She caught herself in the mirror and smoothed down her dress again. Rifling through the make-up bag, she pulled out her mascara and added another layer, then brushed her hair. She was just checking out the back of her dress when she noticed the door opening slightly. It was followed by a knock.

'Hello?' Sophie said.

'Hi, Soph.' Liam opened the door further and loitered on the threshold of the dressing room. 'Can I come in?'

Sophie suddenly couldn't swallow, her mouth going instantly dry and her breath catching in her throat. She didn't answer him but waved a hand, gesturing that he could come in and sit down. She turned away and stuffed her belongings into her bag. In the mirror, she watched him come into the room and stand awkwardly while she fussed with her clothes and make-up bag.

'You came back,' Sophie said. Her tone was a little cooler than she'd meant it to be.

'You were amazing tonight,' Liam said.

'Thank you.' She paused briefly and then continued to fuss with the things on the dressing table. She needed to be doing something to make this less awkward than it felt. She didn't know why Liam was here, but she felt terrified that if she let her guard down, even for a second, she would get hurt.

'Soph, please, can you stop?' Liam said. He sounded fed up. 'I'd really like to talk to you properly.'

Sophie stopped, jumper in hand. She sighed and sat down

on the make-up chair, running a hand over her face and through her hair. 'What made you come back?'

'I couldn't bear thinking about you doing the solo by yourself. I knew how nervous you'd be feeling, and I wanted you to feel as confident as possible. You deserved it to go really well. I wanted that for you.'

'Well,' Sophie said, softening. 'Thank you. You're right. You being there did help me.'

'I also wanted to apologise.'

'Oh?' She wasn't expecting that. She waited silently for him to continue.

'I had a long conversation with Cassie last night and it was her who made me see sense, really.'

'What did she say?'

'She wrote me a letter when I was out at rehearsal the other night. She said she was in the wrong when she stole from Lily. She had to convince me of that, really. She explained how hard she found moving back. Even though she was young when . . . it happened, this place means something to her and she had trouble processing that. I couldn't see it myself when I was trying to be a parent.' He sat down on the chair opposite Sophie's, passed her Cassie's letter and brushed his curls behind his ear.

'You weren't trying to be a parent, Liam. You *were* being one. And I totally understand why you would feel let down by what happened, by me.' She looked down at her knees, reflecting on how she could have dealt with the situation better. She opened Cassie's letter and smoothed it out on her lap.

'I should never have doubted you would do everything you

could to look after her. I was just angry, and I dealt with it in a really stupid way.'

'Yes, well,' Sophie said, nodding. A smile played at her lips. 'I've had better conversations with parents.' She looked over Cassie's festive doodles and smiley faces and read the lovely sentiments in her letter. Sophie really had made a difference.

'Well, anyway, Cassie told me that actually you've been a real comfort to her over the past few weeks. She told me how she'd been feeling about Emily. I'd not even realised she'd been carrying all that around with her for such a long time. We talked and we're going to look into some professional counselling for her. She had been speaking to a doctor but I think it's time to find someone who she can really talk to about things so she can start to heal.'

'That sounds like a good idea.'

'But whatever you've been doing in the meantime, I really appreciate it. And so does Cassie,' he added.

Sophie looked over at Liam as he spoke. He seemed a little shy, playing with his hands as he explained. He brushed some of his curls back off his face. His hazel eyes met hers, and they held each other's gaze for a few delicious moments.

'You and Cassie are very welcome,' Sophie said eventually, breaking the moment. 'I was just doing my job,' she added with a friendly smile, and stood to carry on packing her things away.

Liam stood too and made to leave. He hesitated at the door and turned back. 'You really were unbelievable tonight,' he said.

'Thanks, Liam.' She took a deep breath, suddenly feeling very sad about the whole situation, about how it could have turned out so differently. She realised she didn't want him to leave. 'Thanks for helping me to get there.'

Liam smiled and turned to leave. As Sophie placed her jumper into the bag, her hand brushed the carefully wrapped bauble she'd been carrying with her hopefully for the past few days. She'd only bought it a couple of weeks ago; so much had happened since then.

She lifted it out of the bag and said, 'I bought this for you.' Her cheeks instantly coloured as she said it, feeling foolish for offering him a present when he'd made it clear they were nothing more than friends at the very most.

Liam paused and turned to take the object from her hand, his fingertips brushing her palm and making her stomach flip like she knew it would when he was near. He unwrapped it and held the ornament up to the light. 'It's beautiful, Soph.'

'I saw it when I went to London and it reminded me of you, even if things were all a bit horrible at that point.'

'I love it,' he said, smiling at her. 'And I can't wait to add it to the tree.'

Sophie smiled sadly. She was pleased and relieved that Liam and Cassie would finally get to enjoy a Christmas tree, but disappointed at the thought of the ornament not being Sophie and Liam's first ornament together on the tree. For a while there, she thought she was about to get what she'd wanted all those weeks ago when she was first putting up her Christmas tree: the boyfriend and the ornament from their first Christmas together. But it wasn't to be.

As the silence hung between them, Sophie turned to gather her belongings from the dressing table. If she lingered any longer, she was worried that she might shed a tear. Putting everything back into her make-up bag, she sensed Liam turn to leave. Sophie sighed a heavy sigh of disappointment.

'Soph.'

She looked up to see Liam taking several steps back across the room. He reached out to hold one of her hands, his sudden but welcome touch radiating through her body. 'I really am sorry.'

She looked down at where he held her hand in his and for a moment thought about taking it away. It was the sensible, safe thing to do. But she really didn't want to. She liked the feel of his rough palm on hers.

'I'm sorry too.' Her breath responded to his touch.

'Come here,' he said, using his grip on her hand to pull her closer. The make-up bag she held fell to the floor, and she let out a yelp, falling against his chest. Liam tilted her chin up towards his and kissed her, brushing her hair back from her face and running his fingers down her neck, along her collarbone. His touch was exquisite, and Sophie realised she had wanted this more than she knew. Before she had time to think about why she shouldn't be doing it, they were kissing like teenagers. Their hands were everywhere, and the kiss became something more, very quickly. Sophie pulled away, breathless.

'Liam, my parents . . .' She searched for what she wanted to say, but was overwhelmed and distracted by her pounding heart and fluttering butterflies.

'Are not who I want to talk about right now,' Liam said with a laugh. He pulled her to him again, brushing her hair away from her face. 'I think I might be falling in love with you, Miss Lawson.'

'I think I might be falling in love with you too,' Sophie said, as Liam leant down to kiss her once again.

# Epilogue

One year later

Christmas Day

Sophie opened her eyes one at a time and she looked at her surroundings – Liam's surroundings – the memory of their delicious anniversary dinner coming back to her, delicious in more ways than one. Not their proper anniversary, of course. It had only been a year. But the memory of the Christmas concert and the glorious turn of events that evening was something they'd both wanted to celebrate.

Rolling towards the window, she pulled the curtain to one side and let out a scream. Liam sat bolt upright and looked around.

'What? What is it?' he gasped, grappling for any part of the duvet that might cover up his suddenly naked body.

'It's snowing!' squeaked Sophie.

Liam flopped back down onto the bed.

'I thought we were being attacked,' he said sleepily, rolling away from Sophie and pulling the duvet back up to cover his torso.

Sophie snuggled back underneath it too. 'But it's Christmas Day, and it's snowing. It's going to be a white Christmas!'

Liam rolled over to face her. 'Merry Christmas,' he said, kissing her softly on the lips.

'Merry Christmas.' A smile played at the corner of her lips.

They kissed again before Liam pulled away from her. 'I'm sorry. As much as I would love to lie here with you all day – and I really would,' he said, his voice low, 'there is an eleven-year-old girl in the next room – who you've probably just woken with your screams, I might add – and as such, Christmas will begin at any moment.'

Sophie looked over at the clock. It was 5.45 a.m. 'Really?' She knew Cassie was an early riser, but before six o'clock was a little extreme.

'I'm afraid so. Why don't we shower and then we can go downstairs for breakfast? We can open presents with Cassie before your parents arrive for dinner.'

'That sounds great. I especially like the bit about us showering,' Sophie added mischievously.

'Come on, then.' Liam jumped out of bed in all his naked glory and held out a hand for Sophie to take.

Afterwards, Liam went downstairs to boil eggs and toast soldiers, which was a Christmas tradition in the Hawthorn household. Sophie was attempting to do something useful to her hair without having her straighteners with her when her phone vibrated off the bedside table. She reached for it and swiped to see a text message, letting out a little scream. Liam bounded up the stairs two at a time and rushed into the room.

'Are you all right?'

'Look!' screamed Sophie, waving her phone in front of Liam's face. On the screen was a picture of Noah, Kate's perfect one-year-old, holding a grainy black-and-white scan image of baby number two. It was accompanied by a message from Kate to say:

'Isn't it wonderful news? And Noah is just gorgeous in his little Christmas elf outfit.'

'Yes,' Liam agreed and passed the phone back. 'But you really need to stop yelping. Every time you do I think something terrible has happened.'

'What is it?' Cassie asked, joining them in the bedroom. Sophie pulled the towel up more tightly around her, tucking it in so she wouldn't lose it. 'It's Mrs Donovan's son dressed as an elf,' she said, showing Cassie the picture.

'Aww!' Cassie said, completely missing the image of the baby scan and changing the focus of her attention almost immediately to the task at hand. 'Can we open presents now?'

'You know the rule, missy. Breakfast and showers first,' Liam said.

'That's so mean,' groaned Cassie.

'It really is,' agreed Sophie.

'Come on, you two. Eggs and soldiers are ready to go, and if we don't have breakfast soon, Sophie's parents and Grandma and Grandpa will be here and dinner won't be ready!' Liam said, guiding Cassie out of the bedroom. 'See you in a moment,' he added in Sophie's direction with a smile.

'I'll just be a minute.'

Sophie drew back the curtains and looked outside to see the courtyard and the fields covered in a blanket of snow. It was Christmas-card perfect and this year, Sophie thought, with her parents and Cassie and Liam all together, Christmas may well end up being perfect too.

# Acknowledgements

This book is the product of the hard work and unwavering support of so many people. Firstly, thank you to 'I Am In Print', whose romance novel competition got my manuscript in front of my wonderful agent Saskia Leach – and thank you to Saskia and everyone at Kate Nash Literary Agency for believing in me and my story. Thank you, too, to everyone at Allison & Busby for guiding me through the publishing process and helping me to make *A Concert for Christmas* the best book it can be.

Thank you to all my writer friends who I've met over the years: the wonderful Christmas Collective for helping me to dip my toes into publishing, the CBC discord gang for helping me shape my manuscript in the first place and for supporting me ever since. And to the wonderful RNA, without whose support I'd never be where I am today. Special shouts out to Jennifer Page for your friendship and guidance and to Milly Johnson for responding to a tweet that ignited my passion for writing and gave me hope for finishing my story in the first place.

Huge thanks to my friend Yolly for reading lots of early drafts of everything I've ever written and for not laughing when I told you that I wanted to be a writer (and thank you for having such a hideous date in the first place, which was where the story of

Sophie and Liam began). And to Sarah and Emma for being my cheerleaders throughout.

To Mum and Dad who have been there to support me through everything. I'm so incredibly grateful and glad you're finally going to get to read a finished story. Thank you.

And finally, to Matt and Audrey who are my whole world. This is for you.

HELEN HAWKINS is a writer, editor and English teacher. *A Concert for Christmas* is her first novel and was shortlisted for Penguin's Christmas Love Story Competition and highly commended in the I Am In Print Romance Competition in 2022. When she's not writing, Helen can be found editing, singing and dancing with her local operatic society in Oxfordshire.

*@helenwritesit*
*helenhawkins-author.com*